The Jedi

C000296461

Also published by Arktos:

Archeofuturism
by Guillaume Faye

A Handbook of Traditional Living

Tradition & Revolution
by Troy Southgate

Can Life Prevail?
A Revolutionary Approach to the Environmental Crisis
by Pentti Linkola

The Initiate: Journal of Traditional Studies

Metaphysics of War:
Battle, Victory & Death in the World of Tradition
by Julius Evola

The Path of Cinnabar:
An Intellectual Autobiography
by Julius Evola

THE JEDI IN THE LOTUS:
STAR WARS AND THE HINDU TRADITION

Steven J. Rosen

ARKTOS MEDIA
MMX

First edition published in 2010 by Arktos Media Ltd.
© 2011 Steven J. Rosen

Neither this book nor its contents are endorsed or approved by or
affiliated in any way with George Lucas or Lucasfilms Ltd. The opinions
contained herein are those of the author only. *Jedi*™ and *Star Wars*™ are
all trademarks of Lucasfilms Ltd. All rights reserved.

No part of this book may be reproduced or utilised in any form or by
any means (whether electronic or mechanical), including photocopying,
recording or by any information storage and retrieval system, without
permission in writing from the publisher.

All of the quotes from the *Bhagavad-gita* in this work are either taken
directly from His Divine Grace A. C. Bhaktivedanta Swami Prabhupada's
Bhagavad-gita As It Is (Culver City, California: Bhaktivedanta Book
Trust,1973), or adapted by the author's translation of the text.

Printed in the United Kingdom

ISBN **978-1-907166-11-2**

BIC classification: Hindu sacred texts (HRGS);
Space opera (FLS)

Editor: John B. Morgan
Cover Design: Andreas Nilsson
Layout: Daniel Friberg

ARKTOS MEDIA LTD

www.arktos.com

TABLE OF CONTENTS

Dedication:

To the loving memory of my noble teacher, His Divine Grace A. C. Bhaktivedanta Swami Prabhupada, who embodies all the finer characteristics of a true Jedi Master, and so much more.

ABOUT THE AUTHOR

Steven J. Rosen (Satyaraja Dasa) is an initiated disciple of His Divine Grace A. C. Bhaktivedanta Swami Prabhupada. He is also founding editor of the *Journal of Vaishnava Studies* and associate editor for *Back to Godhead*. He has published twenty-one books in numerous languages, including the recent *Essential Hinduism* (Rowman & Littlefield, 2008); *The Yoga of Kirtan: Conversations on the Sacred Art of Chanting* (FOLK Books, 2008); and *Krishna's Other Song: A New Look at the Uddhava Gita* (Praeger, 2010).

FOREWORD
by Jonathan Young, Ph.D.

The *Jedi in the Lotus* reveals how the wisdom of India permeates the *Star Wars* films. Mostly, this ancient lore is conveyed indirectly, but its presence is what gives the space epics their profound appeal. Steven J. Rosen takes us inside the tales of the Jedi to document the profound Eastern teachings that George Lucas conveys in the series – to make explicit what is generally implicit in the films.

To begin, Rosen shows how Lucas was influenced by Joseph Campbell's popular writings on initiatory patterns. Campbell's affection for the myths of India saturates his extensive writings and clearly seized Lucas.

My work with Campbell and later as the founding curator of the Joseph Campbell Archives and Library gave me access to the details of how he came to be so attracted to the wisdom of the East. It is through Joseph Campbell's prodigious scholarship that symbolism from India migrated into the *Star Wars* films. This history is not the main focus of Rosen's work, but a crucial background note, so I want to recount the essential events.

There is a poetic kinship with the title of this book in the fact that Campbell's romance with India began on a ship called the S.S. Lotus. It was on a crossing of the North Atlantic for a visit to Europe in 1924 that 20-year-old Joseph Campbell became a good friend of Jiddu Krishnamurti, as Rosen points out in the introduction. At the time, Krishnamurti was only 29 himself, but he was already famous. He introduced the young American to the traditions of India. They had many long philosophical discussions over the decades.

It was some years later that another encounter with Eastern ideas deepened Campbell's study of the lore of India. In 1939, one of his students at Sarah Lawrence College said his Schopenhauer lectures had sounded a familiar note. She gave him a copy of the *Mandukya Upanishad.* Campbell said it was a most important event for him. The student's mother was active in a Vedanta centre. She introduced Professor Campbell to the translator, Swami Nikhilananda, the group's leader.

In 1941, Nikhilananda introduced Campbell to Indologist Heinrich Zimmer, who had just arrived from Europe and was about to give a series of lectures at Columbia University Library on the myths of India. Zimmer was a longtime friend of Carl Jung. He had played a major role in the Eranos conferences, with which Jung was closely associated. Zimmer's lectures filled out Campbell's understanding of how depth psychology builds on a mythic perspective.

In 1942, Swami Nikhilananda enlisted Campbell to help on a new translation of the *Gospel of Sri Ramakrishna.* As the project advanced, the lion's share of the work fell to Campbell. He found working in Sanskrit both exhilarating and exhausting. His enormous contribution to the book is acknowledged in the introduction. He went on to edit a new edition of the *Upanishads* for Nikhilananda. Both books are central to the awareness of the Hindu traditions in English. In all, Campbell did three years of comprehensive work on these great sacred texts. The impact on his thinking was to last a lifetime.

During this same period, Heinrich Zimmer died suddenly of pneumonia. His widow asked Campbell to edit Zimmer's posthumous writings. The project took twelve years to complete and resulted in four books of scholarship on the wisdom of India. Campbell wrote the books from lecture outlines and other notes left by Zimmer.

Campbell took a break in the middle of the Zimmer project to write his own groundbreaking book *The Hero with a Thousand Faces,* published in 1949. By this time, Campbell was steeped in Indian mythology. Throughout the book, the main examples of the stages of initiation are from the tales of India.

As Rosen observes, *The Hero with a Thousand Faces* provided the template for George Lucas to shape the *Star Wars* adventures. Campbell was an effective conduit for the great ideas of the East. He did not invent the theories of initiation that were so influential for Lucas, but did provide a compelling distillation of the ideas. Campbell acknowledged several thinkers as the sources of his theoretical framework.

A central reference was Adolf Bastian (1826–1905), who argued that myths from all cultures seem to be formulated from the same 'elementary ideas'. This monomyth, as it were, is what Campbell called The Hero's Journey - the great initiatory tale told all over the world. The term *monomyth* itself came from James Joyce (1882–1941). Rosen gives further details in this book. The idea that there is a pattern of initiatory stages builds on the work of Arnold van Gennep (1873–1957). Campbell's contribution was to elaborate on van Gennep's outline of the rites of passage.

The details of the different initiatory stages as described by Campbell serve as the direct inspiration for many of the scenes in the *Star Wars* episodes. Rosen documents how the rich examples from Indian culture and scriptural tradition plainly inspired Lucas, which he carried into the monomythic schema.

Lucas maintains that *The Hero with a Thousand Faces* was the first book that began to focus what he had been doing intuitively. 'It was all right there and had been there for thousands of years.' Lucas went on to read other books by Campbell, including *The Flight of the Wild Gander*, and *The Masks of God*. He also studied tapes of Campbell's lectures.

When Joseph Campbell was awarded the New York Arts Club National Gold Medal for Literature, Lucas acknowledged the important contribution that Campbell had made to his scripts. 'It's possible that if I had not run across him I would still be writing *Star Wars* today. He is really a wonderful man and he has become my Yoda.'

George Lucas and Joseph Campbell socialised on several occasions. Lucas invited Campbell and his wife, Jean Erdman, to Skywalker Ranch Studios in the San Francisco Bay area to view the first three *Star Wars* films, all in one day. As Rosen notes, a few years later, Lucas loaned his formal library to producers at PBS for their TV series, *The Power of Myth*. I have visited that elegant facility. It is all elaborate cabinet work, balconies, and stairways in the hand-carved redwood style of Victorian era San Francisco.

Campbell thought that Lucas presented the elements of initiation clearly and accurately. He had high praise for how well Lucas understood myth and metaphor. 'I saw things from my books being rendered in modern terms. I admire what he's done immensely. He opened a vista, knew how to follow it and it was totally fresh. It seems to me that he carried the thing through very well.'

It should be mentioned that George Lucas has been a generous supporter of Campbell's legacy. He serves on the advisory board of the Joseph Campbell Archives and Library. He attended the launching of the Joseph Campbell Foundation, held at the Smithsonian, in Washington, D.C. One of our archival challenges was to build a library of the many recordings of Campbell's lectures that existed in various collections. Once assembled, we made the sad discovery that the quality of many of the tapes was poor or uneven. Lucas arranged for digital audio experts to re-master the tapes. As a result, much of Joseph Campbell's teaching is now available – teachings that would have been lost.

My own associations with George Lucas have all been very positive. I sense that his quiet style conceals the depth and intensity of a seeker. He has always been gracious to me – and encouraging of the efforts to continue Campbell's work.

One of the gifts of *The Jedi in the Lotus* is to reveal, in careful detail, the wealth of ideas that Lucas brought to the screen from the work of Joseph Campbell. Steven J. Rosen shows us, in vivid examples, how the radiant ideas of the East shine through the powerful *Star Wars* dramas. He does a great service to those who love the films and would appreciate a deeper knowledge of primary sources. The book is also a substantial contribution to scholars of myth and ritual. It reveals how the wisdom of the ancients can be alluringly presented in contemporary form.

The Jedi in the Lotus is a thoughtful work with many facets. As one example, Rosen's chapter on the Force is a marvelous exploration of this mysterious theme and how Lucas drew from many religious traditions. He raises many important questions:

> In *Star Wars,* the Force sometimes seems synonymous with instincts, with listening to one's own inner voice. Of course, some people are more in touch with that voice than others. Where does this voice come from? Is it our conditional responses to the external world? Or is it something from another dimension? Is it material or Divine? Jedis are supposedly a race of beings who hear it in their heart of hearts; they are guided by the Force, who communicates with them in no uncertain terms.

As a psychologist, I am drawn to the implications of the Force as a form of internal guidance. The idea of the Force certainly speaks to those seeking a link with the divine. This theme is also of interest for those whose inner journey is framed as psychological maturation. These two perspectives share some common ground.

In a 1999 *Time* magazine article, Bill Moyers refers to my work: 'The psychologist Jonathan Young says that whether we say, "I'm trusting my inner voice", or use more traditional language – "I'm trusting the Holy Spirit", as we do in the Christian tradition – somehow we're acknowledging that we're not alone in the universe.'

Moyers then goes on to ask Lucas, 'Is this what Ben Kenobi urges upon Luke Skywalker when he says, "Trust your feelings"?' Lucas responds, 'Ultimately the Force is the larger mystery of the universe. And to trust your feelings is your way into that.'

This comment supports a natural collaboration between the inner psychological journey and the yearning for connection to the transcendent. Carl Jung asserted that the unconscious held some of our most beautiful, radiant, and powerful qualities. Developing ways to be receptive to the treasures of the unconscious is a central task in what he called the journey of individuation.

The Force could be an awareness that there are powers greater than our conscious personalities that can aid us in difficult situations. Unlike Freud, who tended to be wary of the energies of the unconscious, Jung was convinced that gifts awaited us in this mysterious inner realm.

The topic of the unconscious is, essentially, speculation. It is, after all, shrouded in mystery. It is beyond our ability to consciously map or define. In that sense, encounters with the unconscious are experienced much like spiritual stirrings. This is not to equate the two, only to say that both are forms of contact with mysterious energies. The Force could be the most noble qualities a culture has to offer. These would wait in our hidden places until a need for deeper wisdom arises. The Force might, simultaneously, be whatever divine inspirations are honored by the world's religions.

The posture of earnest seekers is similar in both situations. We try to find ways to be receptive to that which is beyond our full understanding. There is an essential loss of control. A strong need for clarity or certainty is a handicap. Both forms of revelation are inherently humbling.

In the films, the Jedi are the high priests of the Force. The order began in earlier times as a theological and philosophical study group. Only after long consideration of the Force did they take up the idea of fighting for high principles. They are, first of all, seekers. They are also aristocrats. As knights, they are part of the nobility. Lucas seems to have taken this detail from medieval tales where the protagonists are often of noble birth.

Steven J. Rosen offers a masterful explanation of the nature of the Jedi in chapter five, but here I want to underscore the aspect of their aristocratic status as a psychological symbol. Fascination with the nobility is a staple in science fiction and fantasy. It does not necessarily mean that the audience longs to live under the rule of royalty. The symbolism may be deeper still. It could be a yearning for the larger meanings of all those grand roles.

The traditions of highborn titles included devotion to great causes. These were lives with meaning and dedication to service. The psychological significance might be that we long for our inner nobility. The qualities of character and purpose associated with such positions may be what is missing in our endlessly practical age. Bottom line: seeking one's truly noble qualities is a worthy endeavour.

The lineage of Luke Skywalker is also royal. He grows up unaware of his true beginnings. Finding that we have a legacy of significance is a universal theme. Whether it is royal blood, divine origins, or a destiny worthy of great efforts, there is something to claim. It is the dignity of our lives, the calling that simultaneously meets our deepest yearnings and makes a contribution to others.

At some point, the individual's actions must become synchronised with universal Forces. This shift eases life's basic loneliness. You are enmeshed in a larger purpose. You are meant to be in a certain place and fill a particular role. You are being yourself, truly and entirely for the first time. You have energies that you never knew about before.

Our core choices and values must be informed from sources beyond the collective, whether personal or spiritual. Then, ultimately, it all turns around, and one must find a place in the world. A mythic story shows how we must find our own footing as individuals, and also how we can return from separation to find belonging with others. If the story only showed how to rebel against conventionality, it would leave us as hermits or lost souls. The greater challenge is to rejoin the community, but in a way that honours our individuality.

As Rosen demonstrates, George Lucas is a serious student of myth. The *Star Wars* sequence takes the most compelling aspects of the patterns Campbell described and presents them back to us in gripping dramas.

Some have noticed that the *Star Wars* episodes are similar to each other. Yet, Lucas is not making the same movie over and over again. He is aware that one must go through many initiatory cycles to claim the many lessons. Each time out, the initiate is able to accomplish something new that seemed impossible. Each effort is successful because it is in the service of a calling. When one is motivated by higher causes, you can sometimes do amazing things.

The releases of this series of films now span generations. Many who saw the first *Star Wars* movie as a teenager brought their own children to see the series of prequels. Each member of the audience faces challenges and lessons appropriate to his or her age group. There is a character on the screen at the right stage in the long, unfolding story for each person to follow.

The intense followers of the *Star Wars* sagas are an amazing phenomenon. When each new film was released, fans camped out well in advance to attend the first screenings. In an Australian census, more than 70,000 people declared themselves to be followers of the Jedi faith. The impact on popular culture is enormous around the globe.

The success of the *Star Wars* films mirrors the growth of a fascination with all things mythic. There has been what some call a mythic revival in the last thirty years, which can be traced mainly to the work of Joseph Campbell.

The *Power of Myth* television series has been broadcast repeatedly. Many viewers then begin reading Campbell and other well-known writers on myth. An enormous number go on to study world mythology in depth. When I was organising a department of Mythological Studies at the Pacifica Graduate Institute in Santa Barbara, the administration had no sense of how strong the interest would be. After all, earning a humanities doctorate is no longer a guaranteed path to employment. The response was overwhelming.

Campbell's influence continues to rise. When the religious and intellectual history of this era is written, the impact of Joseph Campbell's work will surely be a major event in our collective evolution. For many, their first glimpse of Eastern wisdom was the lore depicted in the *Star Wars* films. George Lucas has made an enormous contribution to the growing awareness of the treasures to be found on the initiatory journey.

In conclusion, I can only say that *The Jedi in the Lotus* is a breakthrough book when it comes to understanding the mythic depth of the *Star Wars* epics. Steven J. Rosen uses his masterful grasp of the Eastern traditions to explain the secrets of the most successful film series ever. This book also shows us why Joseph Campbell loved the wisdom tales from India, and, for those who found the *Star Wars* adventures memorable, this is a truly illuminating book.

Jonathan Young, Ph.D. is a psychologist and is the Founding Curator of the Joseph Campbell Archives. He is also the Director of the Centre for Story and Symbol in Santa Barbara, California.

INTRODUCTION

At first glance, it might seem that *Star Wars* and Hinduism have little in common. *Star Wars* is a modern science fiction classic, produced for entertainment purposes. It makes use of futuristic spaceships and imaginative weapons that the real world has not yet seen. Hinduism, for its part, is an ancient religious tradition, meant for spiritual enhancement and personal fulfillment. What, if anything, does the film have to do with the religion? True, *Star Wars* has been interpreted as having an underlying spiritual message. There have been books about the Christian dimension of the film;[1] others that explore it from a Buddhist point of view;[2] and even a volume dedicated to studying *Star Wars* in terms of general philosophical principles.[3] This latter book includes an essay on how *Star Wars* relates to Eastern wisdom.[4] But even here, it goes too far East, looking at the science fiction/fantasy more from a Taoist perspective than from anything else. No Hinduism.

The question is, 'Why?' Why the great silence in terms of the Hindu religious tradition? There have been a few articles on the subject over the years, but too few to fill the gap, especially since full-length books have appeared in relation to the world's other great religions. It would be one thing if there were no connection, no overlap, in the themes

1   See, for example, Dick Staub, *Christian Wisdom of the Jedi Masters* (San Francisco, California: John Wiley & Sons, 2005).

2   Matthew Bortolin, *The Dharma of Star Wars* (Boston: Wisdom Publications, 2005).

3   Kevin S. Decker and Jason T. Eberl, eds., *Star Wars and Philosophy* (Peru, Illinois: Open Court Publishing, 2005).

4   Walter (Ritoku) Robinson, 'The Far East of Star Wars', in *Star Wars and Philosophy*, ibid.

and ideas conveyed in the epic film series and in the Hindu religion. But, as this book will show, there are multiple connections and overlap, so much so that one could conceivably argue that Hinduism was a major influence – either directly or indirectly – in the making of *Star Wars*. And so, again, we must ask, 'Why?' The book you hold in your hands seeks to fill this curious lacuna.

To begin, this Introduction will serve basically two purposes. First, it will introduce readers to *Star Wars*, giving an uninterrupted summary of each of the major films, from the first official release to the last of the prequels. As a result, even if one has not seen the movies, the book will still be intelligible and accessible. Second, we then offer a brief explanation of what Hinduism actually is, especially for outsiders who might have basic misconceptions about the religion. Subsequently, the bulk of the book will explore the connections and parallels between *Star Wars* and the ancient Hindu religion.

The *Star Wars* Epic

We should say from the outset that our analysis will rarely take into account the massive peripheral literature or the 'apocryphal texts' that have grown up around the central *Star Wars* movies. In fact, we only draw on this literature to provide background for the story, or, later on, to bring out certain parallels that might otherwise remain obscure. Nor will we emphasise the corpus of comics, graphic novels, and popular media paraphernalia that have glutted the *Star Wars* cosmos. This 'Expanded Universe' (EU), as ancillary *Star Wars* projects are called, remains in the background for the duration of this work.

Rather, our focus in this book is on the primary trilogy (which interestingly begins with Episode IV, *A New Hope*) and also on the three official 'prequels' – Episodes I, II and III – which give the essential background of the initial trilogy. Though a bit confusing in terms of sequence, *Star Wars* does have a beginning and an end, though neither was apparent to audiences when the first movie was released in 1977. George Lucas, the writer/producer/filmmaker behind the *Star Wars* franchise, initially provided audiences with a seemingly self-sufficient adventure story, but it soon became clear that a continuing saga was not far from his mind. In fact, at least two components of the first film indicated that, just perhaps, Lucas was interested in sequels, at least if the movie should prove successful. First, though we are informed of the sinister Emperor through the film's dialogue, we never see him face to face – and he is not 'defeated' by the end of the film. Where does he go? What does he do? Second, even though the Rebel Alliance destroyed the Death Star, they did not do away with the entire Empire. Was this a portent of things to come?

And so even though we enter the *Star Wars* universe in the middle of a story, Lucas proceeds to conclude this story with Parts V and VI, which were called *The Empire Strikes Back* (1980) and *Return of the Jedi* (1983), respectively. After these movies had achieved monumental success – after the Empire struck it rich – Lucas released *The Phantom Menace* (1999), the first prequel, sixteen years after his last *Star Wars* movie. It has been said that *Menace* was the most anticipated motion picture of all time. In 2002, the second prequel (*Attack of the Clones*), also greatly anticipated, appeared in theatres around the world, but neither of these prequels were as successful as their forebears. The final episode, Part III (*Revenge of the Sith*), was eventually released, too, and its reception has been unprecedented. Many say that this is the best *Star Wars* film of all.

As for Part IV, the first of the films, we enter in the middle of an intergalactic civil war.[5] The events leading up to this war are as follows: it begins with the Sith, an ancient people who live in peace. As the centuries pass, however, they are forced into war and conquered by evil warlords. The initial conflict is instigated by a renegade Jedi Knight who tries to use 'the Force' – the mystical energy at the core of the universe – to gain control over the Sith. Jedis have the unique ability to commune with the Force and to use it for good purposes. They also train as righteous warriors for the purpose of protecting the innocent. Thus, they quickly reject the errant knight – a rejection that leads, just as quickly, to the Sith War, a terrible battle taking millions of lives.

For eons, Jedi Knights battle with evil troops who embody the 'dark side of the Force'. As the misguided Jedi conquerors gain the upper

---

5   Excellent summaries of the initial *Star Wars* movies can be found in David Wilkinson, *The Power of the Force* (Oxford: Lion Publishing Company, 2000) and in Steven A. Galipeau, *The Journey of Luke Skywalker* (Chicago: Open Court, 2001). In addition, the 'At the Movies' reviews by Alfred Collins in *The San Francisco Jung Institute Library Journal*, Volume 4, Number 3, 1983, were helpful in constructing my own summaries. Also useful were the on-line reviews by Roger Ebert. All of these and others, along with my own viewing of the films, were used to construct the synopses of the *Star Wars* films found in this chapter.

hand, they adopt the 'Sith' name as their own, symbolising their victory over the prominent people of the day. Thus, the dark Jedi become known as the Sith, while those who embrace the positive side of the Force continue to be called 'Jedi'. This takes place 4,000 years before the galactic civil war raging at the commencement of the *Star Wars* movies (that is, Part IV). Eventually, the Sith are defeated and the few survivors go underground. The Jedi Knights become the protectors of a just democratic government incorporating most planets of the galaxy known as the Republic.

As Part IV begins, the Sith have again re-emerged and they believe that they have destroyed the Jedi forever. Emperor Palpatine, himself a Sith Lord, had seized control of the Republic, which he has gradually been turning into a ruthless, totalitarian Empire. The only force which resists the Empire is a ragtag band of believers in the original Republic, who are known as the Rebel Alliance. The Empire uses its massive, heartless military force to enforce their unquenchable thirst for power on all the planets of the galaxy and to hunt the Rebels. It has been building an ultimate weapon, known as the Death Star, which is a massive, moon-sized space station which has the power to destroy entire planets in the blink of an eye. They plan to use it to intimidate all the worlds of the galaxy into submitting to their will and to extinguish the Rebels, and the last vestiges of the Old Republic, once and for all. The Death Star has just been completed as Part IV opens, and the Rebel Alliance, an extremely weak force compared to the Imperial military, realises that they are doomed unless it is destroyed. Princess Leia, an aristocratic adherent to the Rebels' cause, steals a set of plans which reveal a fatal weakness in the Death Star's design, which she tries to smuggle back to the Rebels' secret headquarters. She is discovered and pursued, however, by the sinister Darth Vader, a power-mad warlord and Sith Lord who betrayed his original position as a Jedi Knight for the dark side of the Force. Although human, Vader sustained severe injuries in his past, and is only kept alive by always wearing an armoured life-support suit. He kidnaps Leia and imprisons her aboard the Death Star.

Before being captured, Leia hides the plans for the Death Star's destruction inside an android and instructs him to bring it to Obi-Wan Kenobi, one of the last of the Jedi Knights who has been in hiding since Palpatine's coup. This android, R2-D2, and his companion C-3PO land on the desert planet Tatooine, near the simple 'moisture farm' of Luke Skywalker, an idealistic youth who yearns for adventure as a pilot. His uncle forbids him from leaving the farm, however, saying that adventure is bad and that farm work is much more practical. They take in R2-D2 and C-3PO, thinking that they will be useful as workers, not knowing the secret that they carry. Luke discovers their mission and is startled to learn that the droids are in search of Obi-Wan, whom he only knows as a simple hermit by the name of Ben Kenobi, unaware of his Jedi background.

Luke and the droids go to see Kenobi, who is an old man. R2-D2 conveys a message from Princess Leia to him, and he realises that he must deliver the Death Star plans to the Rebels' headquarters and rescue Leia. He tells Luke that he needs his help and must come as well, revealing that Luke is actually the son of a Jedi Knight, Anakin Skywalker, who was once friends with Kenobi until he was betrayed and murdered by Darth Vader. Kenobi believes that now Luke must take up the ways of the Jedi Knights and the mysterious 'Force' that grants Jedis their mystical powers. Kenobi also gives Luke his father's 'lightsabre', a type of sword which was preferred by the Jedi, the blade of which is made from pure energy. While Luke is tempted, he at first refuses, believing that his proper place is back on the farm. When he returns home, however, he discovers that Imperial stormtroopers have destroyed the farm and killed his aunt and uncle, believing that they were hiding R2-D2 and the plans. He returns to Kenobi and agrees to go with him on his mission.

To get off Tatooine, they hire a spacecraft, the *Millennium Falcon*, which is piloted by a renegade and smuggler named Han Solo and his co-pilot, an alien creature ('Wookie') with human-like abilities named Chewbacca. At first believing that he is simply carrying two criminals and their droids out of a local law enforcement situation, they are pursued by Imperial forces as soon as they take off from Tatooine. In searching for the Rebel headquarters, they stumble across the Death Star and are captured by it. Fighting their way through the station, they manage to free Princess Leia and get back to the *Falcon*. Luke is clearly attracted to Leia. Obi-Wan confronts Darth Vader and has a lightsabre duel with him as part of a ploy to distract Vader and the stormtroopers while the others escape. Obi-Wan is killed by Vader, sacrificing himself for the sake of the mission. Leia guides the *Falcon* back to the Rebel base, pursued by the Death Star. The Rebels manage to use the plans carried by R2-D2 to launch a counterattack in a group of fighter craft. At first, the mission seems impossible when the Rebels' computers fail, but Luke switches off the computer in his fighter and surrenders to the Force instead, and delivers the blow which destroys the Death Star moments before it attacks the Rebel headquarters. He is even assisted by Han and Chewbacca who, despite originally only being interested in money, have come to see the worthiness of the Rebels' cause. Vader manages to escape unnoticed. The film ends with a heroes' welcome for Luke, Han and Chewbacca, even though they all realise that the war is far from over.

The Empire Strikes Back[6]

The second film (Part V) was released three years after the initial *Star Wars* movie. For this project, Lucas worked with Director Irvin Kershner, a vegetarian and a student of Zen Buddhism. As a result, the characters are imbued with greater spirituality, and Eastern themes underlie or even monopolise the story.

As the movie opens, the Rebels – including our heroes from the previous movie – are hiding out on a remote, arctic planet known as Hoth; Luke has still only begun to explore his Jedi proclivities. Vader and his Imperial Starfleet, under the direction of Emperor Palpatine, are still searching for them. Shortly after the film begins, Vader discovers the Rebel base and attacks, scattering the Rebels across the galaxy. Leia and Solo, for their part, escape in the *Millennium Falcon,* but even in doing so, they get caught in a dense asteroid field. Solo, with his considerable experience, manages to evade the Imperial fleet by landing in what at first he believes is a deep cave on an asteroid which turns out to be 'the belly of the beast', or the stomach of a giant space slug. Once again, Solo and Leia barely escape with their lives, flying out through the slug's mouth. Forced together by contingency, the gruff Solo and aristocractic Leia, initially hostile, begin to develop affection towards each other.

Luke, who escapes separately, has a mystical vision of Obi-Wan Kenobi in which he is instructed to search out the 800-year-old Jedi Master named Yoda, the Master who had trained Kenobi himself, on the planet Dagobah. Luke travels to Dagobah and soon finds Yoda, a small, gremlin-looking being, alluring and impish at the same time who at first hides his actual identity. During their initial exchange, the

6   Ibid.

stranger talks in riddles, playing thought-provoking word-games with Luke, games that help the young hero look at himself more closely. As a result, Luke is able to see his own flaws – his impatience, his selfishness, his superficiality, and so on. He also sees the value of honesty, non-aggression, and other such qualities in a way he never had. The mysterious newcomer's pithy words of wisdom teach Luke the value of truth and righteousness, the foolishness of anger and greed. It soon becomes clear that the diminutive, odd-looking fellow is Yoda himself, and that Luke has just undergone his first initiation and basic training in the ways of the Force. Luke then begins the intense and difficult Jedi training. The training seems to come to a climax when Yoda instructs Luke to enter a dark cave where he is confronted by an image of Vader. They fight a lightsabre duel and Luke cuts off Vader's head; when his mask is removed, however, it is revealed to be the face of Luke himself.

Meanwhile, Vader receives a message from his Master, Emperor Palpatine, commanding him to either destroy the young Skywalker or to turn him to the dark side of the Force to serve the Empire, fearing the resurrection of the Jedi Knights through him. Thus, Vader sets a trap for him. The *Falcon* lands in nearby Cloud City, a small town that floats in the sky of the planet Bespin and is ruled by Solo's old friend, the gambler Lando Calrissian. Unbeknownst to Han and Leia, Vader had known that they would come there and blackmailed Lando into luring them in. They are soon captured by Vader, who has Han frozen into a block of carbonite to be returned to the infamous Tatooine gangster Jabba the Hutt, who has placed a bounty on Solo's head. They are then used as bait to bring Luke to Cloud City.

Sure enough, through his newly-developed ability using the Force, Luke senses that Leia and Solo are in danger. Though Yoda insists that Luke's training is incomplete and that it is dangerous for him to leave the training so soon, telling him that Vader will try to tempt him to the dark side of the Force. Luke, overconfident in his own abilities, ignores his warning and rushes off to rescue his friends. When he arrives at Cloud City, he soon finds himself in an actual lightsabre duel with Vader, who cuts Luke's right hand. After cornering Luke, he reveals the long-hidden truth: he is Luke's father. He tells the boy that the dark side of the Force is inconceivably powerful, and that, together, they could use it to take over the Empire and establish a new dynasty to rule the galaxy.

Luke chooses to destroy the temptation by destroying himself – he jumps, in what some have called a symbolic fall from innocence, to an almost certain death. But the Force has different plans, and Luke is rescued from his final demise by grabbing onto an exhaust pipe on the exterior of Cloud City before falling to certain death into the atmosphere of Bespin, hanging on for dear life. In the meantime, Lando has had second thoughts about his betrayal. Although there is nothing he can do for Han, he rescues Leia and flies her to safety aboard the Falcon. Leia hears Luke's cries for help through the Force and they manage to rescue Luke before escaping back to the Rebel fleet. Luke's severed hand is replaced by a mechanical one and the film ends as he is pondering his relationship to Vader. Luke represents organic reality and earthly realism, a sort of goodness that comes from innocence and purity; Vader, on the other hand, is half-machine, only kept alive by his suit, the illusion of power and the need for galactic conquest. By the removal of Luke's hand and its replacement with a mechanised prosthesis, the viewer is reminded that Vader is Luke's father, and that the boy, if he is not careful, could be overcome by the same unnatural forces that defiled his father.

Return of the Jedi[7]

Originally titled *Revenge of the Jedi,* the title was changed for obvious reasons – Jedis do not seek revenge; they fight only in self-defence and with the utmost compassion, which they have even for their enemies. As *Return of the Jedi* opens, Lando, Luke and Leia are all on Tatooine to rescue Solo from Jabba the Hutt, a worm-like creature, and his criminal gang, who keeps the frozen Solo like a trophy on his wall. At first, Leia herself is captured by Jabba, who has her parading around him, scantily dressed, as a slave girl. Luke has matured as a Jedi, his former innocence now replaced by certainty and confidence. He is still learning the ways of his renowned Jedi predecessors, but still, the decadent Jabba and his henchmen are no match for Luke. He goes to the rescue of his friends. Han is unfrozen, Leia is rescued, Jabba is killed, and in the end they all leave Tatooine to return to the Rebel Alliance.

Before returning to the fleet, however, Luke goes back to Dagobah to see Yoda again. Yoda has grown old, and is preparing for death.

---

7   Ibid.

Though Yoda briefly reminds Luke about the inevitability of the body's demise, he informs him of something far more pertinent for the future of man: that he must confront Darth Vader, remaining true to the positive side of the Force. Only then would he prove himself as a Jedi and save the galaxy. With that, Yoda's body dies, and then Luke is visited by the ghostly form of Obi-Wan Kenobi. Obi-Wan tells Luke that Yoda's spirit will always be with him, as his Master. Luke wants to know why Obi-Wan had told him that Vader had killed his father many years earlier, when in fact Vader was his father. Obi-Wan explains: Vader is his father's dark side, and when that part of his father took over, the earlier, righteous man had disappeared. In this sense, his father had 'died' and given birth to Darth Vader. Obi-Wan further reveals that Leia is Luke's twin sister. Then Luke leaves to rejoin the Rebels.

Since the events of the last film, we learn that the Empire has been constructing a second, and even more powerful Death Star which is protected by an impenetrable force field emanating from a nearby moon, Endor, which is covered with forests. This time, Emperor Palpatine himself arrives to take command of the Death Star and begins plotting the final destruction of the Alliance and the turning of Luke to the dark side. The Alliance develops a strategy to destroy it which requires the destruction of the shield generator on Endor, followed by an all-out assault on the Death Star itself by the Rebel fleet. Luke, Leia and Han lead the expedition to Endor, where Leia finds help in the form of Ewoks, an aboriginal race of bear-like creatures who also hate the Empire and agree to help the Rebels in their attack on the shield generator. As the attack is being prepared, Luke allows himself to be captured by Vader, who brings him aboard the Death Star to confront the Emperor.

The Emperor attempts to anger Luke by insulting his friends and his loyalty to them, for anger is how the dark side overtakes a person. He further tempts Luke with visions of power, hoping to evoke lust and greed, the twin sisters of degradation. Luke, however, tells his father that he can sense some remaining goodness in him, and his conflicted view of what he has become. Vader angrily denies this, saying that if Luke does not turn to the dark side, they will simply kill him and seduce Leia instead. Luke becomes furious and he and Vader have a violent lightsabre duel, and Luke soon overpowers his father, cutting off Vader's mechanical right hand, and ends up with his blade at Vader's throat. The Emperor is actually pleased by this and invites Luke to kill Vader, telling him that he can take his father's place at his side. Luke, realising what he is at risk of becoming, puts down his lightsabre and refuses, causing the Emperor to try to kill him by shooting bolts of electricity into his body from his hands. Some remnant of goodness stirs in Vader, and he cannot simply sit by and watch his only son being destroyed. He seizes the Emperor and hurls him into a pit and certain death. Mortally wounded, Vader thanks his son for saving him from evil. As one last, loving gesture, Vader asks Luke to help him remove his mask so that he can look upon his son using his own eyes, rather than electronic ones, and Luke complies. The symbolism here is significant, as removal of the mask will cause Vader's death. *Star Wars* is showing us that, in a sense, we all wear masks, and we only reach our true potential when we take them off, whatever the cost.

Luke removes Vader's famous mask. Underneath, he sees his father's war-torn face. It is a face that expresses the misfortune of his fall. Vader then dies, and Luke escapes the Death Star with his father's body. The Rebel attack is a success and the Death Star is destroyed. Leia and Solo can now concentrate on their long-awaited relationship (since she now knows that Luke is her brother), and all is set right in the kingdom of life. Luke places his father's body upon a funeral pyre – the just end for a righteous warrior. An earthy ritual celebrates the passing of Darth Vader and the victory of the Rebel Alliance. During the celebration, Luke sees a vision of the three most important people in his life: Obi-Wan Kenobi, Yoda, and his father, as he had looked before becoming Darth Vader, his soul having been redeemed. They stand before him, obviously pleased with all that has taken place, and also letting Luke know that death is not the end for a Jedi Knight.

The Phantom Menace[8]

Years after the success of these three initial *Star Wars* movies, Lucas released the first of three prequels: *The Phantom Menace*. Here, he hoped to add depth and clarity to the events of the *Star Wars* universe. Set several decades before the events in the original trilogy, it begins with a controversy regarding the taxation of trade routes. Two Jedi Knights are sent in to resolve the conflict. One of them is the renowned master Qui-Gon Jinn – the other, his apprentice, is a youth named Obi-Wan Kenobi.

---

8   Ibid.

The two Jedis are working with an inept Gungan, Jar Jar Binks, from the planet Naboo. Because of their association with the laughable Jar Jar, they come across a young Naboo queen, Amidala, who finds herself in the middle of the conflict. The Jedi Knights seek to rescue her from certain doom, but their spacecraft's hyperdrive breaks down, and they are forced to land on the planet known as Tatooine. Once there, Qui-Gon first encounters the slave boy named Anakin. He senses that the boy is closely attuned to the Force, and observes that he also has amazing technical abilities. Indeed, he is so impressive that Qui-Gon is reminded that the Jedi Knights have long believed that a messiah would soon appear, someone who will bring balance to the positive and negative sides of the Force. Anakin might just be this person. He also learns that Anakin's mother is a virgin. Qui-Gon wins Anakin's freedom in a wager with the boy's master, and convinces his mother to let him take her son away, and thus he takes Anakin away to train him as a Jedi.

Although in this time the Republic is still flourishing and the power of the Jedi is secure, danger still lurks. A Sith Lord, Darth Maul, is the lieutenant of Darth Sidious, whom we eventually find out is none other than Palpatine, who is still only a Senator of the Republic at this time. Palpatine, who seems to his colleagues to be a well-meaning politician, is secretly manipulating the Trade Federation to gain control of the Republic. This is at the root of the taxation problem that the two Jedis had come to investigate. This is the 'phantom menace' in that the simple taxation problem is actually rooted in a complex plan to allow the Sith to take over the Republic.

Neither Palpatine nor the young Anakin yet possess the thoroughly evil characteristics which came to define them in the original trilogy. So what changed them? If the development of evil is a central concern in the *Star Wars* prequels, so is the embodiment of goodness. Qui-Gon sees his meeting with young Anakin as the work of fate, proclaiming that 'nothing happens by accident', a clear allusion to *karma* and divine providence. He says that he met the boy due to 'the will' of the Force, indicating that this otherwise impersonal, abstract divinity is, in some sense, akin to a personal God. We will discuss this more thoroughly in the next chapter. What is important here is Anakin's peculiar relationship with 'the power at the centre of the universe': Qui-Gon's trained eye reveals that the boy has a crude but definite communion with the Force. Further research tells him that Anakin has a high concentration of 'midi-chlorians' in his blood. This is a microscopic element that resides in all living cells, allowing the fortunate few who have it in abundance to benefit from the Force's power. The symbionts known as midi-chlorians also convey the will of the Force to those who develop the art of communicating with it.

A Jedi Council meeting is held, in which Jedi leaders, including a younger Yoda, try to decide if Qui-Gon's intuition about Anakin is correct. Some argue that the boy is already too old to be trained as a Jedi. Some, including Yoda, perceive anger in him, saying that the boy might thus be tempted into the dark side of the Force. Yoda says that Anakin has fear from his past, and that this fear has led to the anger they now see in him. This, in turn, will lead to hate and suffering. These are the qualities associated with the dark side. Obi-Wan concludes that the boy is dangerous, but Qui-Gon will hear nothing of it. He decides to take Anakin under his wing, despite the warnings of his Jedi comrades. Author David Wilkinson sums up these ideas as they appear in *The Phantom Menace*:

> The ground is being prepared for Episodes II and III but already we find ourselves asking, how can Anakin turn to the dark side? The boy will marry Queen Amidala and have two children, Luke and Leia. He will not turn to the dark side until Episode II, but however Lucas is planning to do it, the fundamental question remains. What is it about us that makes us refuse the good? Why are we seduced by power, and can we ever be set free from our bad choices?[9]

Attack of the Clones

This is the second of the prequels, and it takes place about ten years after the events of *The Phantom Menace*. Anakin Skywalker is now a

---

9   See David Wilkinson, *The Power of the Force*, op. cit., p. 50. In an interview with *Time Magazine* (29 April 2002), Lucas is asked about how the innocent Anakin gradually morphs into a futuristic Lucifer. 'He turns into Darth Vader because he gets attached to things', says Lucas. 'He can't let go of his mother; he can't let go of his girlfriend. He can't let go of things. It makes you greedy. And when you're greedy, you are on the path to the dark side, because you fear you're going to lose things, that you're not going to have the power you need.' (p. 64) We see this play out in *Attack of the Clones* – Anakin Skywalker gradually transforms from the most promising of Jedis into the most evil of men. This progression from attachment, pride, and anger into darkness or gross materialism is a central teaching of the *Bhagavad-gita*.

young man and an apprentice to Obi-Wan Kenobi. Anakin's uneasy demeanour and simmering anger is just barely concealed beneath the surface. Kenobi knows that Anakin is trouble waiting to happen, but he is convinced of the boy's uniqueness as well.

The Master and his Padawan apprentice again meet Amidala, who, while formerly a queen, is now a Senator. Anakin has maintained a crush on her since their first meeting many years earlier. Obi-Wan's concerns are more pragmatic – Amidala, it seems, is in mortal danger. She stands in the middle of two political movements in the Senate. One is a loyalist faction, who work to keep the Republic together; another is a pacifistic movement, known as the Separatists, who resent the militarism of the loyalists. Amidala is about to cast a critical vote that could stabilise the Republic, and there are those who would resort to any means to stop her. Anakin is appointed to be her bodyguard.

While protecting the beautiful Amidala, Skywalker decides to reveal his affections for her, despite the fact that this goes against the chastity code of the Jedi. He thinks of himself – and has been told by others – that he has the potential to be the best of the Jedi Knights, yet his weaknesses abound, especially his inability to control his own anger. His clear hatred during battle is contrasted with proper Jedi warfare in a final scene, where the elderly Yoda battles on behalf of righteousness – out of duty and to protect, not out of vengeance and anger. This causes Anakin himself to question his own qualifications to be a Jedi Knight.

When we explore the Hindu epics, we will see that Arjuna, too, had to question whether or not he was a genuine Kshatriya (warrior/ administrator), for in the midst of battle, when so many were depending on him, he gave way to weakness. A true Kshatriya lives for the fight, to protect the innocent, and nothing else. Anakin's future son, Luke, will show more of a Kshatriya spirit by having heart. It is not merely about the battle, but about battling for the right reasons. This is one of *Star Wars'* most enticing themes. It is poignantly brought out when Luke goes through a period of questioning. Like Anakin and Arjuna before him, Luke experiences the classic existential dilemma: who am I? Am I meant to be a Kshatriya, a Jedi? What is life really all about? Only after considering such questions, can one act with any certainty, with any authority. For most of the original trilogy, Luke acts on instinct only.

In one of the final scenes, however, he throws down his sword and makes a conscious decision not to fight. For most Hindus, this decision parallels Arjuna's in the *Bhagavad-gita* (1.32-35), a central Hindu text, when he drops his bow, saying, 'Krishna, I will not fight.' Of course, both Luke and Arjuna eventually find good reason to pick up arms – but not before thinking deeply about it, not before considering the profound need for peace. In mentioning this parallel, we are getting ahead of ourselves. Comparisons with texts like the *Bhagavad-gita* are what this book is all about.

Revenge of the Sith

The story opens with the Jedi-led Republic at war with a droid army created by the Separatist planets to win their independence. Anakin and Obi-Wan are engaged in a mission to rescue Senator Palpatine, who they believe is being held hostage on board a ship in the Separatist fleet. In fact, the situation was created at the instigation of Senator Palpatine himself, who is working with the Separatists to undermine the Republic to his own advantage. The audience soon discovers that Palpatine is the evil Darth Sidious, although Anakin and the Jedi have not yet realised it. The three escape the Separatist fleet alive, although Palpatine's plan was to have Obi-Wan killed in front of Anakin, pushing him further towards the dark side.

We also learn that Padmé Amidala is now Anakin's wife, and that she is pregnant, although this is kept secret so as not to jeopardise Anakin's status as a Jedi. A dream convinces Anakin that Padmé will die in childbirth, and Anakin becomes obsessed with fear for her life. Palpatine uses this to bring Anakin to the dark side, telling him that the Jedi have lied to him about the dark side of the Force, and that only those who master it can conquer death. He suggests that Anakin could save his wife by submitting to his inner ambition and righteous anger. In examining the Jedi code of chastity, the opposition of various monastic orders is brought into question here, even if not explicitly asked. The Hindu stations known as Brahmachari and Sannyasa, celibate novitiate and world renouncer, respectively, are particularly brought to mind, especially for those familiar with Indian tradition.

Palpatine, whose power and popularity in the Senate has been steadily increasing, wants direct control over the Grand Army of the Republic and control of the Jedi as well. Toward this end, he deputes Anakin to be his representative on the Jedi Council, only fueling his existing arrogance and causing him to question the decisions made by his superiors. This does not sit well with the wise Jedi. As Palpatine is increasingly successful in bringing Anakin to the dark side, he reveals his identity as the Sith Lord Darth Sidious. But Anakin doesn't care – now he only craves power and the knowledge to save Padmé's life.

When Anakin reveals to the other Jedi that Palpatine is a Sith Lord, they attempt to arrest him, but he wards off their attempt and tells the Senate that he survived an assassination attempt that was part of a Jedi coup to seize control over the Republic. Alarmed by this news, the other Senators agree to turn over absolute power to Palpatine to see them through the crisis, and declare the birth of the Empire, with Palpatine as its Emperor.

Wasting no time, the Emperor orders his henchmen across the galaxy, who have been assisting the Jedi in their war against the Separatists, to carry out a prearranged plan to wipe out the Jedi altogether. Nearly all of the Jedi are killed in the unexpected attack. The Emperor orders Anakin himself to wipe out all the Jedi in the main Jedi Temple, which Anakin does with zeal, even killing all of the children who were just beginning their training. Then the Emperor dispatches Anakin to kill off the leaders of the separatists, as his use for them is at an end. It is at this time that the Emperor gives Anakin his Sith name: Darth Vader.

Obi-Wan and Yoda both manage to survive the assault, and Obi-Wan confronts Anakin, intending to either save him from the dark side or kill him. Padmé follows them, unable to believe that the Anakin she loves could have done the terrible things he has been accused of doing. When Anakin refuses to listen to reason and states his intention to rule the galaxy, he and Obi-Wan fight a lightsabre duel, and Obi-Wan reluctantly wins, cutting off all of Anakin's limbs and leaving him to burn to death in a fiery pit. Obi-Wan flees with Padmé, who soon gives birth to Anakin's twins – Luke and Leia. As Anakin had foreseen, she dies in childbirth – not for any medical reason, her doctors say, but of a broken heart.

Emperor Palpatine arrives after the battle and rescues Anakin, saving his life by having him encased in the armoured life-support suit that became Darth Vader's trademark. He further tells Anakin, whose memory of the battle is unclear, that he killed Padmé himself in a fit of anger – thus cementing Anakin's crossing to the dark side. Obi-Wan sees to it that the baby Leia is taken to be raised as a princess, while the boy, Luke, is brought to his uncle's farm on Tatooine. On Yoda's instructions, neither of them are to be told the truth about their origins. Obi-Wan and Yoda then go into hiding to preserve the last remnants of the Jedi order – thus setting the stage for Episode IV, the first *Star Wars* film, having come full circle.

What is Hinduism?

What does *Star Wars* have to do with Hinduism? The reader will find in this book a plethora of overlapping themes, correlation in terminology, parallel universes, and, perhaps most importantly, numerous influences connecting George Lucas, the *Star Wars* creator, with India in general and Hinduism in particular.

But before we embark on this journey of comparison, it would be fruitful to offer our readers a few introductory words on what Hinduism actually is.

Interestingly, Hinduism is a family of religions and not a monolithic religious tradition. In other words, unlike the other major world religions, Hinduism is a catch-phrase for a particular group of diverse spiritual traditions, such as Vaishnavism (the monotheistic worship of Vishnu, the 'Oversoul' of the universe), Shaivism (the worship of Shiva, who is the 'supreme Lord' in charge of cosmic destruction), and Shaktism (the worship of the universal Goddess), among others. These traditions see one ultimate supreme Lord who manifests variously for different purposes. Just as Jews, Christians, and Muslims all believe in one God but differ in their conceptions of Him, Hindus all believe in one God but see Him in diverse ways. Ancient sacred texts and specially trained priests, while recognising that God is one, see hierarchical distinctions in the various aspects of the Godhead, but this is technical information beyond the scope of this book.

Nonetheless, each of the Hindu traditions is a very different religion, and do not fit comfortably under one banner. In fact, the words 'Hindu' and 'Hinduism' are misnomers, used only for convenience. The words are not found in any of the classical writings of India. Nor can they be traced to the ancient Indian languages, such as Sanskrit or Tamil. In fact, these words have absolutely no origins within India itself. Their history is eloquently articulated by C. J. Fuller, an Indic historian who underscores the fact that the words initially referred to something geographical, not cultural or religious. In addition, he points out the convenient usage of these terms in separating Muslims from the indigenous peoples in India:

> The Persian word 'Hindu' derives from *Sindhu*, the Sanskrit name of the river Indus (in modern Pakistan). It originally meant a native of India, the land around and beyond the Indus. When 'Hindu' (or 'Hindoo') entered the English language in the Seventeenth century, it was similarly used to denote any native of Hindustan (India), but gradually came to mean someone who retained the indigenous religion and had not converted to Islam. 'Hinduism', as a term for that indigenous religion, became current in English in the early Nineteenth century and was coined to label an 'ism' that was itself partly a product of western Orientalist thought, which (mis)constructed Hinduism on the model of occidental religions, particularly Christianity. Hinduism, in other words, came to be seen as a single system of doctrines, beliefs, and practices properly equivalent to those that make up Christianity, and 'Hindu' now clearly specified an Indian's religious affiliation.[10]

Using the over-arching term 'Hinduism' for the many religions of India, then, is comparable to ignoring the different religious orientations within each of the Western traditions, arbitrarily merging them under a single banner – 'Semitism' (which, like 'Hinduism', merely denotes geographical location). Judaism, Christianity, Islam, and others constitute the diverse religious traditions of the Western world. Just as the term Semitism is too broad and reductionistic to properly represent the unique religious manifestations of the great Western traditions, and just as it would be inappropriate to refer to all these traditions as one religion, the term 'Hinduism' falls short.

'Hinduism', in fact, is more problematic than 'Hindu', since it implies a unified form of Indian religion that can comfortably fit under one umbrella. Considering the varieties of religion that currently exist in India, such as Vaishnavism and Shaivism, a single term is hardly appropriate.

So now that we know what Hinduism is not – it is not a single overarching religious tradition –what exactly is it? Amongst its own adherents it is known as Sanatana Dharma, roughly translated as 'Perennial Religion', or 'the eternal function of the soul'. In other words, 'Hindus' do not see their tradition as one amongst many but, rather,

---

10   C. J. Fuller, *The Camphor Flame: Popular Hinduism and Society in India* (Princeton, New Jersey: Princeton University Press, 1992).

as essential truth, as that core of spirituality that lies at the heart of all revealed religions.

Modern historical methods tell us that the overall tradition originates in the ancient Indo-European Vedic culture, traceable to at least 2000 BCE but with roots that go back much earlier. This culture gave us the Sanskrit *Vedas*, which are perhaps the world's earliest sacred texts. Here we learn that ultimate reality is comprised of both light and dark dimensions. Indeed, the whole Vedic universe, as in *Star Wars,* is separated into light (*prakash*) and dark (*andhakar*) components, culminating in the well known Vedic prayer, 'Lead me from darkness to light' (*tamaso ma jyotir gamaya*).[11] These *Vedas* boast an impressive array of supplementary texts, such as the *Ramayana* and the *Mahabharata*, which are more a part of contemporary Hindu culture than the original *Vedas*. For this reason, our present study will focus more on this secondary 'Vedic' literature.

Today, Hinduism is recognised as the world's third largest religion, after Christianity and Islam, with almost one billion followers worldwide, 96% of whom live in the Indian subcontinent. It also predates most other forms of religious expression. Thus, even in its present form – misconstrued as a single tradition – it is considered one of the largest and oldest of the major world religions. Still, because it is characterised by a diverse montage of belief systems, practices, and scriptures, as in the three major Hindu traditions mentioned above, it is difficult to date. The difficulty is exacerbated by the fact that Hinduism, unlike other religious traditions, cannot be traced to any one founder – again, it is considered eternal truth. Hindu thought is also distinguished by its overwhelming inclusivism, encouraging tolerance for disparate religious ideals.

The earliest strata of Vedic literature views ultimate reality as 'Brahman', an all-pervasive energy, or 'force', that sustains and interpenetrates the entire cosmos.[12] In general, Hindu theological views are quite broad, including notions of monism, dualism, pantheism, panentheism, ani-

---

11 The 'light and dark sides of the Force', so central to the *Star Wars* universe, is a theological notion that originally appears in the Western religious tradition by way of ancient Iranian thought. Early Iranian religion, in turn, draws much of its terminology and its basic concepts from Vedic culture, borrowing names of numerous divinities and theological ideas originating in the East.

12 The connection between the Hindu 'Brahman' and 'the Force' of *Star Wars* will be analysed later.

mism and also polytheism, though a more accurate description would be 'polymorphic monotheism', which means that it acknowledges one Supreme God, or 'Brahman', who exists in multitudinous forms. Traditionally, this diversity is analogised as a single beam of light separated into colours by a prism – implying that the one light is the same, though manifesting variously. In relationship to God, all aspects of this 'light' are suitable for worship, though only under the guidance of one who knows the secrets of such worship, i.e., under a qualified spiritual master (or *guru*).

Still, contemporary Hinduism is best understood in terms of its four major divisions, Vaishnavism, Shaivism, and Shaktism – the three religions mentioned previously – as well as Smartism, which opines that all the 'gods' are distinct but equal, an idea that generally manifests as a form of polytheism. All forms of Hindu religion are characterised by some form of caste hierarchy, belief in reincarnation, the law of cause and effect (*karma*), non-injury, often taken to the point of vegetarianism or total nonviolence (*ahimsa*), and disciplined approaches to the Divine (*yoga*). Many if not all of these motifs, as we shall see, are found in the *Star Wars* story.

Star Wars and Hinduism: My Personal Connection

Early on in my life, as a teenager, I became a 'Hindu' monk. Gradually, I also became something of a *Star Wars* fan, the first of the series' films having been released when I was 22 years of age. In due course, I lost interest in *Star Wars,* and though I continued my passion for Hindu theology, I left the monastery to pursue the academic study of Vaishnava Hinduism. Thus, Vaishnavism is the branch of the religion that will inform most of this book, though we will also draw on other Hindu traditions. My focus on Vaishnavism is not merely personal. Vaishnavas make up nearly 70% of the Hindu world, thus accounting for hundreds of millions of people.[13] More, since the vast majority of

---

13 This statistic was originally discovered by anthropologist Agehananda Bharati and is supported in Gerald James Larsen's classic work, *India's Agony Over Religion* (Albany: State University of New York Press, 1995), p. 20. Eminent scholar of Hinduism, Klaus Klostermaier, concurs. See his work, *A Concise Encyclopedia of Hinduism* (Oxford: Oneworld Publications, 1998), p. 195. It should perhaps be added here that this 'vast majority of Vaishnavas' is probably comprised of not

Hindus are Vaishnavas, looking at the Vaishnava tradition will afford an overall sense of what Hindus in general actually believe.

Regarding my own connection to the tradition, let me be clear: I still consider myself a practitioner, even though I am no longer a monk. And so when Rajiv Malhotra of the Infinity Foundation, a non-profit Hindu organisation, commissioned me to write a book on the parallels between *Star Wars* and the Hindu religion, I quickly became excited about the project.

In the mid-1960s and in the early '70s, when I was approaching adulthood, it was not uncommon for a Western youth to become enamoured by Eastern mysticism and to search out a teacher under whom one might learn the secrets of the cosmos. In many ways, Luke Skywalker, the hero of the *Star Wars* epic series, is not unlike the teenagers of my time, nor is his father, Anakin Skywalker. They are like the proverbial seekers of truth, looking for higher knowledge and an alternative to the humdrum life on their 'home planets'. Luke manages to stay in the light, but Anakin goes to the dark side. Both, however, share the search for something higher. Matthew Bortolin, in relation to Buddhism (though it could easily apply to Hinduism as well), depicts Anakin's quest as follows:

> When we look carefully at Anakin Skywalker . . . we can see that he was dissatisfied with life much like the Buddha was before he awakened. Siddhartha [Buddha] found no solace in the luxuries of his life as a prince; Anakin was unfulfilled by his existence on Tatooine and dreamed of becoming a great Jedi. Both fled the familiar, the easy, the known, in search of something more. Their paths led in different directions, but both demonstrate what it is to be human, how our ignorance and attachments lead to suffering, and how compassion and wisdom lead to freedom.[14]

We, too, the children of the wealthiest region on earth, became dissatisfied with our consumerist culture, with our shallow modernism and our tepid approach to reality. Many found fulfillment in religions closer to home, in Judaism, Christianity, and Islam. Others looked East. Some found fulfillment outside the religious arena. What all have

---

only those who revere Vishnu as 'the Supreme Godhead' but also those who emphasise him as being the best among other divinities.

14 Matthew Bortolin, op. cit., p. xiii.

in common, like Luke and Anakin, is the search for truth, the desire to look beyond the obvious and to reach for something greater. In the best of situations, *Star Wars* fanned that spark. To be sure, it showed the dangers of the quest – the dark side of the Force is always ready to seduce us – but it showed the virtues as well. It gave us 'A New Hope'.

Readers might think that I am overstating *Star Wars'* significance, and perhaps I am. Make no mistake: I am not saying that it had a pivotal place in most seekers' spiritual lives. I am saying that it did for some, perhaps more than we recognise. If one just considers the success of the *Star Wars* franchise – with its millions of fans – one sees its pervasiveness in pop culture, in the consciousness of those reaching maturity in the '70s and the '80s, especially. This culminated in 2001, when more than 70,000 people in Australia, more than 53,000 in New Zealand, and nearly 400,000 in the United Kingdom in their respective censuses declared that they are followers of the Jedi faith, the 'religion' created by the *Star Wars* films![15] We will discuss this faith and its ramifications throughout this book. But what is really being said here? Despite the extremism and absurdity of this statistic – of people adhering to a faith concocted in a fictional film series – experts see in it a pointer to the spiritual dimension of the movies themselves, and how fans tend to pull religious themes out of what is otherwise merely a science fiction epic.[16]

Can people learn spiritual truth from a viewing of *Star Wars?* Most likely not, at least not in any truly substantive way. For that, they'll have to go to established religious texts and the paths traversed by the sages. But the film series definitely offers food for thought, and, in any case, the *Star Wars* universe rages on. Lucas is now re-mastering the entire series – one by one – into special 3-D versions, updated for modern

---

15 The 2001 Australian census found that one in 270 respondents – or 0.37% of the population – listed their religion as 'Jedi', the religious order found in the *Star Wars* films. In New Zealand, 1.5% of the population put down Jedi. Although the national statistics office chose not to count these responses, if they had it would have become the second-largest religion in the country after Christianity (and atheism). Although it is believed that many responders did this as an act of protest against the question or the census itself, or simply to mock the process, there do seem to be many genuine Jedi adherents. See '390,000 Jedi There Are', from the *National Statistics Online* Web site, which can be found at www.statistics.gov.uk/CCI/nugget.asp?ID=297&Pos=&ColRank=2&Rank=1000. Accessed 1 October 2010.

16 Roger Hamly, *The Religious Impact of Star Wars* (Sydney, Australia: Pushpin Publications, 2005).

times. New TV shows based on *Star Wars* are planned for upcoming seasons. And you now hold in your hands a book that will show you parallels between this consequential film epic and one of the earliest religious traditions known to humankind. What's next? Only the Force will know for sure. May Brahman be with you!

1

SETTING THE SCENE

'I'm telling an old myth in a new way.'
—George Lucas, creator of *Star Wars*

A beautiful princess is kidnapped by a powerful but evil warlord. With determined urgency, a mysterious non-human entity delivers a distress call to a budding young hero. The youthful hero, a prince, comes to the princess's rescue, aided by a noble creature that is half-man and half-animal. In the end, after a war that epitomises the perennial battle between good and evil, the beautiful maiden returns home. The valiant efforts of the prince and his comrade, who were assisted by an army of humanlike bears in the fight to return the princess to safety, are duly rewarded, and peace and righteousness once again engulf the kingdom.

In the eastern part of the world, the story evokes memories of the *Ramayana*, an ancient epic from which many of India's myths and religious traditions originate: the princess is Sita, kidnapped by the power-mad Ravana. Her loving husband Rama, the archetypal hero who, as the story goes, is Vishnu (God) in human form, soon becomes aware of her plight and anxiously pursues her. How did he learn of Ravana's nefarious deed? The good-hearted Jatayu, a vulture-like creature with the ability to speak, sworn to protect the princess, sees the demon-king forcibly abduct Sita. He attempts to rescue her on his own, but he is mercilessly cut down by Ravana. Luckily, Rama happens upon the dying Jatayu, who reveals all that has taken place. After a period of intense grieving, Rama engages his devoted half-human/

half-monkey companion, Hanuman, in an elaborate search for the
princess and, after a complex series of events, a massive war breaks
out to get her back. Aided by an army of Vanaras (bears and monkeys
who have humanlike characteristics), Rama rescues Sita from the evil
Ravana. The forces of the underworld defeated, Rama-raja (the kingdom of truth and righteousness) reigns supreme.

In Western countries, the story is more reminiscent of the first of
the *Star Wars* epics, the film series brought to life by George Lucas,
the now multi-million dollar writer/director/filmmaker at its helm.
Here, too, the princess – this time, Princess Leia – is kidnapped. In
the *Star Wars* universe, evil incarnates as Darth Vader, who holds Leia
against her will. Artoo-Deetoo (R2-D2), an android instead of a talk-
ing vulture, carries a desperate cry for help. The princess, just prior
to being captured, managed to conceal a holographic message in the
droid's memory banks. Thus, through this futuristic robot, she asks for
the assistance of Obi-Wan Kenobi, a master among the mystical Jedi
Knights, hoping he would come to her aid. Luke Skywalker, a farmboy
from the planet Tatooine, is the one who initially receives this message, however, and it is he who apprises the otherwise retired Obi-Wan
about the mission to rescue the princess. Luke is reluctant to travel
into unknown territory, into a world of action and intrigue. After all,
he knows little beyond his simple farm. But brave Obi-Wan convinces
him to go, telling him that 'the Force' will protect him. The two team
up with Han Solo, a renegade space traveller, and Chewbacca, a 'half-
man/half-monkey'-type creature who devotedly assists them. By the
end of the original *Star Wars* trilogy, in the company of legions of bear
soldiers, they wage a war to end all wars – Darth Vader and his entire
evil empire are defeated and the princess is returned to safety.

The minutiae of the *Star Wars* stories is already discussed in the
prior chapter (and some of the Hindu texts are summarized in the next
one). But the reader will notice even in these short summaries that the
similarities are too specific to be coincidental. And since the *Ramayana* – as opposed to *Star Wars* – was written 'long, long ago', it is likely
that the modern epic, to one degree or another, was based on the older
one. Many other Indic texts are utilised in the *Star Wars* framework
as well – the *Upanishads*, the *Mahabharata* (including the *Bhagavad-
gita*), the *Srimad Bhagavatam* (also called the *Bhagavata Purana*), and
so on – and these too shall be explored throughout the present work.
While the literature of this ancient tradition and *Star Wars* naturally

are different in ways that cannot be ignored, they have enough in common – in the way of specific parallels – to warrant further exploration.[1]

Some examples: Princess Leia's full name is Leia Organa. The word 'organa' comes from *organic*, which means 'of the earth'. Interestingly, Princess Sita is described in the *Ramayana* as being literally 'born from the earth' and, at the epic's end, the earth mystically opens up for her to return. Or consider Yoda, best of the great Jedi adepts in *Star Wars*, who is reminiscent of a yogi or a spiritual master, his teachings quoted almost verbatim from the *Bhagavad-gita*. For example, Yoda tells Luke not to view him in terms of his size or outward appearance. He says that, in reality, we are 'luminous beings' – we are not the dull matter that we perceive with our crude senses.[2] In short, he tells Luke that we are not our bodies but are instead a spiritual spark within. This is one of the *Gita*'s central teachings: 'That which pervades the entire body

---

1   Major parallels between *Star Wars* and Indic traditions will be explored throughout this work. Parallels between the *Ramayana* and *Star Wars* are particularly numerous. Here's but one example: In the *Ramayana*, the wise and venerable Vashistha is attacked by a vicious forest-dweller who, it is said, was able to control 'mystical missiles of unlimited power'. The forest-dweller in fact used these missiles against the great sage. However, as the story develops, we find that Vashistha was able to destroy every last one of these missiles. He did this, according to the *Ramayana*, with the help of his Brahmanical staff: '...the Brahmanical staff raised in the hand of Vasistha blazed forth like the smokeless fire of universal destruction or like the second rod of Yama' (see *Srimad Valmiki Ramayana*, Vol. 1, p. 168. Quoted in Ramana Das, 'Two Epic Tales: The *Ramayana* and *Star Wars*', *Yoga Journal*, April 1978, pp. 37-39). The Brahmanical staff is graphically described in the *Ramayana*, and it sounds quite a bit like the 'lightsabre' of *Star Wars*, the cosmic weapon used in the battle between good and evil. Did the creators of *Star Wars* know about the Brahmanical staff? Some further thoughts: like Thor, who is the only living being capable of wielding his hammer, or Arthur, the only man able to pull his magical sword from its stone, Rama's ability to string Shiva's bow has mythical dimensions. We find a parallel in Homer's *Odyssey*, where King Odysseus, returning from the Trojan Wars, shows his strength and valour by lifting a miraculous bow as well. In Star Wars, Luke's lightsabre plays a similar role – it is a weapon that is properly handled only by a gifted master. Monomyth stories commonly include a magical weapon that in some way defines the central hero.

2   Interestingly, most analyses of Yoda acknowledge an Eastern component to his teachings. But it is usually Buddhism that is identified as Yoda's preferred model. Here, however, is a clear instance of Hindu teaching: Buddhists do not generally accept the idea of a 'luminous being inside the body'. Rather, they generally espouse the 'anatma' doctrine, that is, when the aggregate of material elements that make up this body is dismantled at the time of death, absolutely nothing remains – there is no soul, no future life – and certainly no 'luminous being'.

you should know to be indestructible. No one is able to destroy the imperishable soul.' (2.17) And further: 'As the sun alone illuminates the entire universe, so does the living entity, one within the body, illuminate the entire body by consciousness.' (13.34) Notice that the *Gita* also refers to the 'luminosity' so clearly expressed by Yoda.

Yoda also teaches Luke self-control, the importance of restraining the senses. Every Jedi, he says, must overcome desire and anger. The *Gita* must have been Yoda's sourcebook: 'A faithful man who is dedicated to the pursuit of knowledge – and who subdues his senses – is eligible to achieve such knowledge, and having achieved it he quickly attains the supreme spiritual peace.' (4.39) Again, 'By the time death arrives, one must be able to tolerate the urges of the material senses and overcome the force of desire and anger. If one does so, he will be well situated and able to leave his body without regret.' (5.23)

It is interesting, too, that Yoda locates the source of the Jedis' strength: it is not accessed independently but rather it flows from 'the Force', which he essentially defines as the ground of all being. Indeed, Yoda tells Luke that all ability comes from the Force, but that this is especially true of the Jedis' supernatural powers. The *Gita* also says that all power flows from the 'Force', i.e., the metaphysical source of all that is: 'Of all that is material and all that is spiritual, know for certain that I am both the origin and dissolution. . . .Everything rests upon Me, as pearls are strung on a thread. . . . I am the ability in man.' (7.6-8)

Yoda's name is closely linked to the Sanskrit *yuddha*, which means 'war'. Accordingly, he indeed teaches a chivalrous form of warfare, imbued with ethics and spirituality, to the Jedi Knights. The non-aggressive but valiant ways of these knights are exactly like those of Kshatriyas, ancient Indian warriors who emphasised yogic codes and the art of protective combat. In this, Yoda resembles Dronacharya from the *Mahabharata*, who, in the forest (again like Yoda), trains the Pandava heroes to be righteous protectors of the innocent. In the *Ramayana*, Vishvamitra Muni, as Rama's spiritual master, teaches the great *avatar*, or incarnation of a deity, to be adept in the art of war, but he also teaches him that fighting must always be based on yogic principles – he teaches Rama while they are living in the forest as well. Both Dronacharya and Vishvamitra seem like earlier incarnations of Yoda.

Some of the parallels between *Star Wars* and ancient Indian tradition are minor. Yet even these are thought-provoking. Consider the following nine examples: (1) In the first *Star Wars* prequel, Queen

Amidala is also known as Padmé, a word that comes from the Sanskrit *padma*, meaning 'lotus'. (2) In this same film, we are introduced to the Gungans, an amphibious species living deep in the waters of the planet Naboo. In India, the Ganges, also called 'the Gunga', is considered the ultimate body of water, a massive river known for its purifying properties as much as for its practical value. (3) At the end of the original *Star Wars* movie, the central characters 'pose for the camera' in typical Indian poster art fashion. Here they look remarkably like Rama and his associates: Luke and Han resemble the brothers Rama and Lakshman, as Leia does Sita; and faithful Hanuman, one of the heroes of the *Ramayana*, is represented by Chewbacca. As a side note, while some say that Chewbacca is based on the cowardly lion in *The Wizard of Oz*, and others say that he is in fact a re-working of Lucas's childhood dog – and both theories probably have more than a grain of truth in them – in narrative context he is clearly a Hanuman-like character. Interestingly, Chewbacca is described as being from the tree-covered planet of Kashyyyk. Monkeys, like Hanuman, are fond of swinging from trees, as we know, and Kashyyyk can be an allusion to 'coccyx', pronounced 'kok-siks', and derived from the Greek *kokkyx* – it refers to the small bone at the lower end of the spinal column, which is said to be the last remnant of our tail as monkeys (before our evolution to the human species). (4) Among the plethora of obscure *Star Wars* characters is one Admiral Ackbar, obviously named after the great Buddhist emperor. Queen Veda is named after the sacred texts of the East – the *Vedas*. And Durga the Hutt is obviously named after the Goddess of the material sphere, whose name is Durga. These characters, of course, are found in the secondary *Star Wars* literature and do not really figure into our discussion. (5) The term 'Jedi' might very well be related to the name of the ancient Indian province known as 'Chedi', over which Shishupala, Krishna's cousin and arch-enemy, reigned. (6) In Sanskrit texts, King Varuna is the demigod in charge of oceans; in *Star Wars*, he is a minor king on Padmé's planet, as revealed in Part Two of the prequels. (7) Shakti is the feminine energy of God, as we will describe in an upcoming chapter; Shaak Ti is the name of a female Jedi master. (8) In Indic languages, a *rishi* is a sage. The Rishi Maze is a section of the cosmos mentioned in *Star Wars* as being near the planet Kamino. (9) General Grievous, a hideous droid-like demon, shows his four arms in the last of the prequels, making him visually reminiscent of Vishnu, whose four arms hold a mace, a club, a lotus flower, and a conch. Grievous merely holds weapons, and while Vishnu is good and beautiful, Grievous is fearsome and ugly. But the four-armed parallel would definitely give a Hindu reason to pause.

Such similarities are numerous and are peppered throughout the *Star Wars* movies (and in related *Star Wars* literature and paraphernalia). Some of this is attributable to Lucas, and some is not. Some are clearly deliberate, while others are incidental. Some major, others minor.

Both major and minor parallels have one thing in common: they are sufficient to raise eyebrows, to make educated viewers (and readers) reconsider the source of Lucas's successful Star Wars franchise. How much of it was based on Indian myth? Was Lucas even aware of these myths? After all, *Star Wars* was not created 'a long time ago in a galaxy far, far away', but it wasn't created in India, either. Actually, it was born in Twentieth-century Hollywood, or, more specifically, in the mind of George Lucas.

A Plethora of Influences

Lucas brought many influences to bear in his creation. For example, much has been written about his brilliant adaptation of old Hollywood westerns in a space-age context; the Mos Eisley Cantina is a slightly transformed saloon from the old West, and Han Solo has the bearing and demeanor of an ornery gunslinger. World War II movies are also apparent in *Star Wars,* especially in Darth Vader's German-looking helmet and even in the use of the term 'stormtroopers', which was actually the name of Hitler's inner circle of bodyguards, to describe the soldiers of the Imperial Navy, the ruthless Nazi-like antiheroes of the *Star Wars* epic. Early science fiction and *Flash Gordon* serials of the 1930s and '40s, too, can be seen in almost every scene of Lucas's work, and in fact Lucas had opened his first film, a science fiction film released in 1971 entitled *THX 1138,* with a clip from a 1939 *Buck Rogers* serial. And, of course, Akira Kurosawa (1910-1998), Japan's renowned director, is a major influence. This becomes particularly evident if one views his 1958 samurai classic, *The Hidden Fortress.* The basic plot and visual direction of the original *Star Wars* film is almost identical, and even certain characters, such as R2-D2 and C-3PO, the two droids in Lucas's films, find their earliest incarnations as the two bumbling peasants who monopolise the Kurosawa movie. Lucas also made prodigious use of samurai-like costumes and other images from feudal Japan.

In other words, he drew on all his prior experience, his love of pop culture and his favorite films. His youthful years as a moviegoer were as influential in his making of *Star Wars* as was his later expertise as a filmmaker.

The concerns of the '70s, which, for some, are epitomised by fear of nuclear weapons and the struggle for women's rights, worked their way into his films: the Death Star, for example, is a masterfully constructed super-weapon that could destroy entire planets. It is the ultimate nuclear device, playing into the fears of a postmodern world anticipating technological disaster. Regarding women's rights, Princess Leia was Lucas's attempt to explore the burgeoning feminism of his day. In addition to being a princess, she was a high-ranking leader of the Rebel Alliance – at the time, such leading roles were played by few women in the real world, much less in film. Another concern of Lucas's generation was the tension between man and machine, the 'mechanical versus the organic', the exodus 'back to nature', a subject that made its way into the *Star Wars* movies as a consistent and underlying theme. This will be the subject of a later chapter in this book.

As a child of the '60s, Lucas also drew upon Carlos Casteneda (1925–1998) and the teachings of Don Juan, transposed, of course, in his own inimitable way.[3] The Jedi Knights are shaman-like warriors – Casteneda refers to Yaqui adepts, or 'men of knowledge', as 'warriors' as well. In Casteneda's work, all warriors have 'allies', mystical beings who come to one's aid in the quest for truth. This is almost like Lucas's concept of 'the Force', a divine energy (discussed at length in a later chapter) that assists Jedi Knights in their battle with evil. In a 1977 *Rolling Stone* interview, in fact, Lucas himself refers to the Force as 'a Casteneda *Tales of Power* thing'.[4]

One can see in *Star Wars* influences from *2001: A Space Odyssey, Dune, Lord of the Rings,* and even *The Wizard of Oz* – Leia makes one think of Dorothy, and Chewbacca and C-3P0 look as though they were modeled, at least visually, on the Cowardly Lion and the Tin Man. But to really understand where Lucas is coming from, especially in the context of our present work, one must look at what is arguably

---

3 For more information, see Leonard M. Scigaj, 'Bettelheim, Casteneda, and Zen: The Powers Behind the Force in *Star Wars*', in *Extrapolation* 22:3, 1981, pp. 213-30.

4 See the Paul Scanlon interview with George Lucas, 'The Force Behind George Lucas', in *Rolling Stone* 25, August 1977, pp. 40-48, 50-51.

his most dynamic and far-reaching influence: the writings of Joseph
Campbell (1904–1987).

From Campbell to Yoda

Lucas has been quite vocal about his reverence for the famed mythologist. *Times* film critic Steve Persall quotes a press conference in which
Lucas admitted, 'Yes, I consider him a mentor.'[5] The *Star Wars* creator
was so taken with Campbell, in fact, that he loaned PBS his studios
– studios usually reserved for his own work – to produce the now famous Bill Moyers/Joseph Campbell series, *The Power of Myth*. Further,
in 1985, Lucas delivered a speech in which he cited Campbell as one
of his main influences, particularly in relation to *Star Wars*, saying, 'To
conclude, I can only say: Joe, you've become my Yoda.'[6] In that same
speech, Lucas admits that he was 'entirely without direction' until he
came upon Campbell's most popular work, *The Hero with a Thousand
Faces* (1949).[7]

These are significant statements. In *Star Wars*, Yoda is the ultimate
Jedi master, a teacher of teachers. Referring to Campbell as 'my Yoda'
is the best of all possible compliments. Lucas's recognition of Campbell's
prominent place in his list of influences has profound bearing on our
thesis that *Star Wars*, at its core, was developed through an undercur-
rent of Indic ideas, for, as we shall see, Campbell openly mined the rich
resources of Indian myth, a mining endeavour that was inherited by
Lucas. Thus, it becomes apparent that while *Star Wars* is rooted in the
West, its seeds were brought from the East.

Let us look, then, at the person of Joseph Campbell, who, in many
ways, is as responsible for the *Star Wars* phenomenon as is its creator.
It should be noted, first of all, that Campbell had little formal edu-
cation in religious studies. His main fields of expertise, at least early
on, were Medieval European literature, Romance philology, American Indian culture, and modern literature from around the world. He
was especially interested in the novels of James Joyce (1892–1941) and

---

5   Quoted by Steve Persall, *Times* film critic, in 'Move Over, Odysseus, here comes
    Luke Skywalker', *St. Petersburg Times*, 16 May 1999, p. 1.F.

6   Cited in Tigue, J., *The Transformation of Consciousness in Myth: Integrating the
    Thought of Jung and Campbell* (New York: Peter Lang Publishing, 1994), p. 106.

7   See John Lyden, 'The Apocalyptic Cosmology of Star Wars', in *The Journal of
    Religion and Film* 4:1, April 2000.

their deeper implications. He was impressed with how Joyce had used Homer's *Odyssey* as the sole organisational principle for *Ulysses*: no plot, no narrative tension or appeal to dramatic sentiment – just an ordinary day in the ordinary life of an ordinary man. And yet, this day was seen as recapitulating one of the primary sagas of Western culture, and in doing so, it imbued that day with mythic resonance. *Finnegan's Wake*, also by Joyce, was even more important for Campbell. Based on themes already explored by Otto Rank (especially in *The Myth of the Birth of the Hero*, published in 1909)[8] and others, it was *Finnegan's Wake* that introduced Campbell to the word 'monomyth'. From this word – and the concept it implies – Campbell began to formulate his idea that famous stories from around the world are virtually the same, and that there is a pattern in the 'journey of heroes' as found in these stories.

Campbell discovered India early in life, though his passion for her culture and rich mythological tradition evolved gradually. Many say that his interest in India emerged on an ocean voyage to Europe in 1924, when the then twenty-year-old Campbell became a good friend of Jiddu Krishnamurti (1895–1986), the controversial '*avatar*' of the Theosophical Society. Long after this voyage, the two of them continued to have many long philosophical discussions about Indian texts and culture – this is a friendship that lasted for decades. Campbell's relationship with India reached new levels when he was called upon to edit the posthumous writings of Indologist Heinrich Zimmer (1890–1943), and grew further still as a result of his work with Swami Nikhilananda (1895–1973), with whom he translated the *Upanishads*. This was in the early 1940s. Nikhilananda was then pastor of the Ramakrishna Vivekananda Centre in New York City, and Campbell's view of Indian philosophy, from then on, bore the brand of Ramakrishna's neo-Vedanta. Campbell met Ananda K. Coomaraswamy (1877–1947), the great Indologist and art historian, during this period as well – his association with an aesthete of Coomaraswamy's stature left a profound influence on our young mythologist. Thus, by the 1940s, due to a series of inspirational meetings, Campbell found himself in the middle of a love affair with Hindu thought that lasted the rest of his life.

---

8 The hero pattern in Campbell's work is Jungian, whereas Rank's is Freudian. Therefore, Campbell's hero tends to begin in adulthood, but Rank's begins with one's origins. Lucas integrates both: Luke begins his journey as a young man, but Vader is said to have had a miraculous birth.

In fact, Campbell experts say that he tended to incorporate Indian mythological themes even when retelling the myths of other lands. He also referred to Sanskrit, the language in which most Indian holy books are written, as 'the great spiritual language of the world'.[9] He said this even though he was aware that Latin, Hebrew, Arabic and numerous languages are revered in other cultural traditions. If one views his PBS series with Bill Moyers, the Indian myths on which he draws clearly outnumber those of other cultures, and he expresses them with greater enthusiasm. In fact, his preference for Indian myth was noticed by the distinguished Harold Coward, Professor of Religious Studies and Director of the Calgary Institute for the Humanities at the University of Calgary, who wrote,

> While he used all traditions as grist for his mill, Campbell was particularly attracted to the life experience embodied in the Indian religions – especially Hinduism and Buddhism. . . It is not too much to say that the Indian melodies of the 'music of the spheres' (Campbell's definition of mythology) had an abiding influence on his life and thought. Indeed, it was in the Indian 'melodies' of the *Upanishads* and the Bodhisattvas that Campbell found the only mythology that is valid for today and for the future. In the Indian religions he found the template for fitting together the future myth of our planet. . . . To a great extent, Campbell's 'mono' or 'master' myth is the myth of India.[10]

Wendy Doniger, Professor of Religion at the University of Chicago Divinity School, whose work we will later draw upon, states it bluntly: 'So much of Campbell's work cites Indian sources. . . It was his preferred stock of myths.'[11] His preference for Indian thought, in fact, might be

---

9   See Joseph Campbell, with Bill Moyers, *The Power of Myth* (New York: Doubleday, 1988), p.120.

10 Harold Coward, 'Joseph Campbell and Eastern Religions: The Influence of India', in Daniel C. Noel, ed., *Paths to the Power of Myth: Joseph Campbell and the Study of Religion* (New York: Crossroad Publishing Company, 1990).

11 See Wendy Doniger's book review of Stephen and Robin Larsen's *A Fire in the Mind: The Life of Joseph Campbell*, in *The New York Times*, Sunday, 22 March 1992, p. 30. Interestingly, the book reviewed by Doniger is quite clear about Campbell's special relationship with 'Hindu' thought: '. . . contact with the world of Vedic philosophy made a profound impression on Campbell.' (p. 283) Campbell was 'steeped in the study of *Bhagavad-gita*'. (p. 307) 'Campbell would often tell the story of the *Gita*' (p. 308) Perhaps most impressively: 'He was reading the *Bhagavad-gita* every day . . . he really loved that book', said Jean [Erdman Campbell, his wife], and

summed up in his own words as follows: 'Clearly, Christianity is opposed fundamentally and intrinsically to everything that I am working and living for: and for the modern world, I believe, with all of its faiths and traditions, Krishna is a *much* better teacher and model than Christ.'[12]

His love affair with India turned into a sacred marriage when he discovered Swiss psychologist Carl Jung (1875–1961).[13] Though Zimmer had a passionate interest in India and an intuitive wisdom about her culture, he had never actually visited the subcontinent.[14] Jung, on the other hand, actually did travel to the land of the Ganges, as did the historian of religion, Mircea Eliade (1907–1986), another great Campbell influence (even if he was Campbell's contemporary, learning much from the mythologist as well). Neither Jung nor Eliade, however, enjoyed their journey East, preferring instead the India of their imagination. As we shall see, Campbell eventually adopted a similar attitude toward India, though he continued to be fascinated by the richness of her mythology. For now, it should be noted that, along with Zimmer and Joyce, Jung and Eliade were among Campbell's greatest influences. He especially liked the psychological spin that Jung gave to Eastern thought, and he was moved as well by Eliade's approach to comparative religion.

As a student of these four scholars, Campbell combined their thought in the following manner. From Joyce came the insinuation that our daily lives are unconsciously repeated timeless patterns, profound and banal at the same time. People always walk down the same paths, no matter where they come from or what time period they are born into. From Zimmer's work on the philosophies of India, Campbell received the idea

---

because of it 'Campbell felt himself gravitating back to Hinduism . . .' See Stephen and Robin Larsen, *Joseph Campbell: A Fire in the Mind – The Authorized Biography* (Rochester, Vermont: Inner Traditions, 1991, 2002, reprint).

12 The emphasis is in the original. Quoted in Stephen and Robin Larsen, ibid., p. 414.

13 One of Carl Jung's final works, *Flying Saucers: A Modern Myth of Things Seen in the Sky* (1958), seems to anticipate Campbell and even Lucas, psychologising man's journey into space (the final frontier?). Campbell, too, wrote a book called *The Inner Reaches of Outer Space* (1986), but it has little relevance in the present context.

14 Margaret Case, ed., *Heinrich Zimmer: Coming Into His Own* (New Jersey: Princeton University Press, 1994).

of cyclical rather than linear time, which favoured the reappearance of patterns as opposed to one-shot, here-and-gone reality. From Jung, he worked with the idea of the collective unconscious, the notion that the inheritance of humanity was not limited to one's particular historical lineage, but rather to the treasure house of the human race itself. Individuals accessed archetypal images from this realm through dream and reverie, and mythic narrative was seen as the dream of an entire culture. Finally, he found in Eliade's comparative approach to religion a way to amalgamate the myths of innumerable cultures.

Expanding on the thoughts of his impressive predecessors, then, Campbell held that the hero's journey is an archetypal monomyth, reenacted through diverse historical forms. The monomyth, or meta-myth, he tells us, is embedded in the consciousness of all beings, and for this reason, our expressions of truth throughout the world, in cultures as diverse as India and Greece, manifest in stories that are almost identical. Accordingly, the story of Jesus, for example, has uncanny parallels with the tale of Krishna, which is similar to the story of Odysseus, which has much in common with the story of Buddha, and so on.

Campbell's Soup

It has been argued that Campbell goes too far. It is true that his work is praised by laymen and by those who have a peripheral interest in world mythology. But others, particularly scholars of language and the mythologies of world cultures, take him to task for ignoring particulars in his effort to formulate universals. In other words, they say that Campbell's reductionistic method is uncritical, that he ignores the limitations of his proposed monomyth.[15] The same has been said of Jung and Eliade.[16] Wendy Doniger, the renowned scholar mentioned earlier, is particularly clear on the fallacy of Campbell's method:

---

15 For an elaborate critique of Campbell, see Robert A. Segal, *Joseph Campbell: An Introduction* (New York: Garland Publishing, 1987), and Robert A. Segal, 'Joseph Campbell's Theory of Myth', in Alan Dundes, ed., *Sacred Narrative: Readings in the Theory of Myth* (Berkeley: University of California Press, 1984). Also see Wendy Doniger, 'The King and the Corpse and the Rabbi and the Talk-Show Star: Zimmer's Legacy to Mythologists and Indologists', in Case, op. cit., as well as Doniger's book review of Stephen and Robin Larsen's *A Fire in the Mind: The Life of Joseph Campbell*, op. cit.

16 Ibid.

We must be grateful to him for making so many people aware of the existence of the great myths, and of the themes that myths from one culture share with myths from other cultures. But we must regret that he did it so slickly that no one was ever encouraged to go on to the second stage, to do the serious work done by other comparativists: the work of understanding what the myths really say, and the ways in which different variants of 'the same' myth are not the same. He cooked up the TV dinner of mythology so that everything tastes the same, instead of encouraging people to take the harder but ultimately more rewarding path of cooking up their personal mythologies 'from scratch', learning the context, learning the other related myths, maybe even learning the languages. He took other peoples's stories and turned them into easy-listening religion, Muzak mythology. He reduced great books to slogans. He made the myths he retold *his* myths, instead of letting them tell their own story.[17]

Later in the same article, Doniger sums up her critique of Campbell:

When thousands of people are walking around happy in their under-standings of Hinduism or the Navajos because of Joseph Campbell, who am I to point out that they don't understand Hinduism or the Navajos, because Campbell didn't understand them? Does it matter?

I think it does. It matters not just for the record – what else is schol-arship? – but, more important, for the sake of the Hindus and the Nav-ajos, who deserve to have their stories truly known. Out of respect for them, we must take the trouble to get the stories right. Buddhists did not struggle through two and a half millenniums in India, Japan, and China just so people in California could feel better about them-selves. The myths have other goals, and we must know and respect those goals, even if we do not choose to follow them.[18]

Doniger might be a bit heavy-handed here, but her central point should be understood: the sloppy universalising of the monomyth is only one of Campbell's faux pas. While he loved the depth and com-plexity of Indian mythology, his understanding of it was clearly a my-thology of his own making. As he once admitted, echoing his gurus Jung and Eliade, 'Nothing is quite as good as the India I invented at

17 From Doniger's *New York Times* book review, op. cit.
18 Ibid.

Waverly Place, New York.'[19] This he said after travelling to India and coming back disappointed: he wanted India to be something other than what it is. So he invented an India of his own. He did the same with her mythology.

Campbell's interpretation of Indian philosophy made use of Advaita Vedanta, or the more abstract forms of Hindu thought, but it was irretrievably commingled with his own Jungian ideas of internal psychological struggle and identification with the Divine. He completely discounted Indian theism, even while maintaining a healthy respect for Vaishnava theology.[20] Such ideas were inherited by Lucas.

This analysis of Campbellian interpretation is not meant to minimise him or his accomplishments. Rather, we explore his limitations (as a scholar of Indian tradition) solely because of its relation to our present discussion: as stated earlier – and it bears repeating – the India conveyed to Campbell by Zimmer who, again, never travelled there, must be considered suspect. Jung, as a psychologist, reduced the essentials of Indian religion to the intricacies of mental processes, while Joyce augmented this with a narrative that explicated the idea of a monomyth. Eliade, for his part, supported generalisations about

---

19 Ibid. His travels to India are detailed in Joseph Campbell, *Baksheesh & Brahman: Asian Journals – India* (Novato, California: New World Library, 2002, reprint). From this work it is clear that his disdain for India was as attributable to culture shock as to anything else. He was also disappointed by most Indians' preoccupation with *hindutva*, or 'Hinduness' – their focus on a national identity. 'I came to hear of Brahman', he said, 'and all I have heard so far is politics and patriotism.' (p. 12) Nonetheless, he visited Vrindavan (pp. 33-34) and Jaipur (p. 240) – two important Vaishnava holy places – and, upon visiting Jagannath Puri (p. 88), also holy to the Vaishnavas, praises it as 'the real throb of India'. He even mentions seeing Chaitanyaite *kirtaniyas* – those who glorify the holy name of Krishna – there (p. 88), and he describes them in a positive light. Moreover, when asked what he thought of Shankara's impersonalistic Vedanta, he answered that he preferred the *Bhagavad-gita's karma-yoga* to the monastic rejection of the world. (p. 194) That being said, however, his overall leaning does seem to be toward the impersonal form of Vedanta. Nonetheless, it is clear that he did experience India's most important holy places, and that, on a spiritual level, he deeply appreciated her culture: 'This wonderful art of recognising the divine presence in all things, as a ubiquitous presence, is one of the most striking features of Oriental life, and is particularly prominent in Hinduism.' (p. 309)

20 For more on Campbell's peculiar interpretation of Indic thought, particularly on how it relates to Advaita Vedanta and Jungian perspectives, see John C. Lyden, *Film As Religion: Myths, Morals and Rituals* (New York: New York University Press, 2003), pp. 60-61 & 217-218.

the overlapping of religious and cultural themes, with an emphasis on India. And now we find that Campbell himself created an India of his own liking. All of this was bequeathed, if on a subliminal level, to Lucas, and thus we find in *Star Wars* an amalgamation of composite heroes, mixed mythologies, and unclear spiritual messages.

Nonetheless, a close look at the entire *Star Wars* epic reveals provocative Indic influences, both subtle and direct. In absorbing Campbell's mythological perspectives and philosophical outlook, Lucas, oftentimes unknowingly, incorporates Hindu deities, names, ideas, and theological stances that originate in ancient Indian tradition, as pointed out earlier in this chapter. Because of Campbell's sources (as well as his own idiosyncratic method) as mentioned above, this Indian tradition is sometimes unrecognisable, especially to the layman. The present work thus seeks to uncover, or unmask, the many Indic underpinnings of the *Star Wars* saga, and to thus make them apparent to scholar and general reader alike.

Mythconceptions

As stated, both Campbell's peculiar view of Indian mythology and his insistence on an all-encompassing monomyth play an important part in Lucas's creation of *Star Wars*. Consequently, for the remainder of this chapter, we will define 'mythology' as Campbell understood it. But, more importantly, we will elucidate Campbell's conception of the monomyth in relation to the hero's journey – a journey that Campbell saw in Luke Skywalker, the central character of *Star Wars*.[21] It is a journey that Rama, too, embarks upon – '*Ramayana*' literally refers to 'the journey' of Rama – as do the Pandava brothers in the *Mahabharata*. All three journeys in relation to the monomyth schema will be briefly explored in the next chapter.

To begin with the touchy subject of defining *myth*, it should be pointed out that, for Campbell, a myth is not a myth. That is to say, a myth is not 'an untrue story', or 'a work of fiction', which is the generally accepted definition of the word today. Rather, for Campbell, a myth is the truest of stories. In his own words, '…mythology is the penultimate truth–penultimate because the ultimate cannot be put into words.'[22]

---

21 See Joseph Campbell, with Bill Moyers, *The Power of Myth*, op. cit., p. 18.
22 Ibid., p. 163.

Stated another way, to whatever degree mere words can express reality, or truth, to that degree it is best expressed by myth.

Campbell is not alone in this definition. That myths are profoundly true is commonly accepted in the scholarly world. Even *Webster's New Universal Unabridged Dictionary* defines myth as 'a traditional story of unknown authorship, ostensibly with a historical basis, but serving usually to explain some phenomenon of nature, the origin of man, or the customs, institutions, religious rites, etc., of a people.' This is *Webster's* first definition. It is not until the Dictionary's third that we see the first stirrings of myth as fictitious story. Perhaps the clearest definition of myth can be found in the *Encyclopedia Americana*:

> Myths may include elements of oral literature, such as fairy tales and legends, but myths are distinct from them in two ways: first, a myth is understood in its own society as a true story. (It is only when it is seen from outside its society that it has come to acquire the popular meaning of a story that is untrue.) A myth relates the most comprehensive and ultimate narrative about its subject, whether it be the origin of the world, the origin of death, the meaning of a gesture, or the structure of a temple. Second, it achieves comprehensiveness and intimacy, because it refers its society back to primordial reality, which is not merely prior in time but is a qualitatively different time, place, and mode of being. This primordial time is the reservoir and repository of the models on which all the significant knowledge, expressions, and activities of the present society are based. Although a myth may appear illogical and non-rational from the point of view of these later forms of intellectual and social order, it portrays its origins. In this sense, the myth exists as an expression of first principles...[23]

The root of the word 'myth' might itself be enlightening: It comes from the Greek *mythos*, which means 'word', 'story', or even 'plot', without so much as an innuendo that this word, story, or plot must be untrue. Interestingly, the idea that a myth refers to a fictitious story began 2,500 years ago with Plato, who was keen on contrasting actual history with fabricated tales. Some say that this enterprise of separating fact from fiction began even earlier, with the Fourth century philosopher Herodotus. As a result, today, in most European languages, 'myth' is indistinguishable from 'fiction'. Not so in the East, where myth is still used

---

23 Quoted to good effect in Robert W. Brockway, *Myth: From the Ice Age to Mickey Mouse* (Albany: State University of New York Press, 1993), p. 170.

in its original sense of mythos. In fact, all ancient cultures viewed their 'myths' as being rooted in ultimate reality. Eliade writes,

> Our best chance of understanding the structure of mythical thought is to study cultures in which myth is a 'living thing', constituting the very support of religious life – cultures in which myth, far from portraying *fiction*, expresses the *supreme truth*, since it speaks only of realities.[24]

Elsewhere, Eliade elaborates on this theme:

> Indeed, until about 1920 (and following the traditions of both Greek philosophy and Judeo-Christianity) myth was understood as 'fable', 'invention', or 'fiction'.
>
> But with the deepening of our understanding of the 'primitive', i.e., archaic societies, a new meaning of myth became apparent. For the 'primitives', what we call 'myth' – that is, a narrative having as its actors supernatural or miraculous beings – means a 'true story', and, moreover, a story that is sacred, exemplary, and significant.[25]

In other words, there are myths that are fictitious, like *Star Wars,* and there are those that are based on actual events, like the *Ramayana* and the *Mahabharata*. (Indeed, Indian tradition refers to the *Mahabharata* as *itihasa*, or 'that which really happened'.) The element that binds these sorts of stories together, however, is that they convey truths of 'mythic proportions'. That is to say, myths are stories that deal with ultimate realities, larger issues, their verity or falsity notwithstanding. Many of the world's ancient myths cannot be proven as historical fact, but, then, that is not their purpose. They speak to fundamental truths of existence, truths that have abiding value. The importance of these truths transcends whether or not they are framed in historically verifiable tales.

Campbell says that from time to time myths need to be re-framed, or updated; they need to be restructured so that they speak to people of today. The old stories may not work anymore, he says. Nonetheless, modern myths, to be effective, must draw on the standard outlines of

---

24　Mircea Eliade, 'Toward a Definition of Myth', in Yves Bonnefoy, ed., *Mythologies*, Volume 1 (University of Chicago Press, 1991, reprint), p. 3.

25　Mircea Eliade, 'Myth in the Nineteenth and Twentieth Centuries', in Philip P. Weiner, ed., *Dictionary of the History of Ideas*, Volume 3 (New York: Scribner's and Sons, 1983), p. 307.

the past, for the outlines themselves are coloured with mythic meaning and transcendent purpose.[26] The outer form of ancient myths – as much as their inner meaning – speak to people of all times, for they are structured on themes that are always true, in all circumstances. This is a subject to which we will soon return.

In a 1999 interview with Bill Moyers, Lucas addresses the perennial value of established myths, even though, with *Star Wars,* he was attempting to create a new one. The essence of mythic truth, he says, never changes all that much, even in outer form. This is because people never change all that much:

> With *Star Wars* I consciously set about to re-create myths and the classic mythological motifs. I wanted to use those motifs to deal with issues that exist today. The more research I did, the more I realised that the issues are the same ones that existed 3,000 years ago. That we haven't come very far emotionally.[27]

It needs to be pointed out that in the creation of new myths, one must exercise extreme caution. Doniger, quoted earlier, says that 'to create a myth on purpose for other people to use is an entirely different enterprise [than studying traditional ones that have time-tested value], and one that I distrust.'[28] Such mythology, she says, 'usually lacks the substance that traditional mythology draws from its tradition.'[29] Thus, while Lucas's creation of *Star Wars* must be considered an achievement, it is the underlying myths and original traditions upon which his modern myth is based that deserve close scrutiny.

Jungian analyst Steven Galipeau is also a supporter of traditional myths, saying that such time-tested capsules of wisdom can never be replaced by the shallow products of modernity. The 'unprovable but profound' stories of the past, he suggests, have many advantages over the 'truths' we today take for granted, even if such truths are couched

---

26 See the Arts/Cinema Section in *TIME* Magazine 26 April 1999, Volume 153, Number 16, 'Of Myth and Men: A Conversation Between Bill Moyers and George Lucas on the Meaning of the Force and the True Theology of *Star Wars*'.

27 Ibid. Interestingly, Lucas mentions '3,000 years ago', a time period that scholars usually attribute to the *Ramayana*, though tradition says it is much older.

28 Wendy Doniger, *Other People's Myths: The Cave of Echoes* (New York: Macmillan, 1988), p. 173, n. 29.

29 Ibid., p. 40.

in scientific terms. Galipeau expresses his skepticism of modern myth in the following manner:

> In some ways traditional religion has been replaced in our age by the 'myths' of science and technology, which have led us to overemphasise linear thinking, technological advancement, and material gain. The result is an enormous psychological imbalance that has become unsatisfying to those in tune with the deeper yearnings of the soul. Jung considered this issue to be the most pressing one now facing us.[30]

One has to wonder if in using the word 'myth' to describe science and technology – and particularly in relation to linear thinking, technological advancement, and material gain – we are not reverting back to the post-Platonic but pre-modern definition of myth: A work of 'fiction', or 'a tale that is simply not true', Or, more, as E. H. Rick Jarow, Professor of Comparative Mythology at Vassar College, says, 'In the East, myth has often been seen as history, while in the West, cherished history is often nothing more than myth.'[31]

The Monomyth Strikes Back

Before we begin our comparative analysis of *Star Wars* and Indian tradition, we should look a little more closely at Campbell's monomyth conception, especially since Lucas acknowledges that he used it in

---

30 Steven A. Galipeau, *The Journey of Luke Skywalker: An Analysis of Modern Myth and Symbol* (La Salle, Il.: Open Court, 2001), p. 59. Galipeau also notes, following David Noble in *The Religion of Technology*, that the technological myth 'is linked to ancient and medieval theological ideas rooted in desires for religious fulfillment. Rampant technology, however, is a signal that we, as its wielders, have lost contact with the deeper purposes it was originally intended to serve.'

31 Stated in personal correspondence, 8-25-01. 'Around this same time I also became familiar with the work of Vladimir Propp, whose brilliant structural analyses of folklore brought him international fame in the mid-Twentieth century. Propp explained folklore not in terms of the *dramatis personae* who performed various actions in a given drama, but rather in terms of the characters' specific actions themselves. He did this by assigning numbers and letters to each action, creating an almost mathematical way of analysing folktales. He thus universalised the essential story of each folktale in a monomythic sense.' See Propp's seminal work, *Morphology of the Folktale* (Austin, Texas: University of Texas Press, 1968 [1927]).

composing his space epic. Though it has been criticised as a theory in which stories have 'a beginning, middle, and end, and little more,'[32] it must be admitted that, as a basic outline, it has its virtues. In its simplest form, monomythic structure is summarised as Departure-Initiation-Return, which is why its critics tend to reduce it to a 'beginning, middle, and end' framework. As we shall see, however, it encompasses much more than a mere three-stage outline.

Although it exists in various versions, Campbell breaks down the journey of the hero in the following way: (1) The Call to Adventure; (2) Refusal of the Call; (3) Supernatural Aid; (4) Crossing the First Threshold; (5) The Belly of the Whale, or The Ultimate Challenge; and (6) The Triumphant Return and Boon for Mankind. There are often additional phases, too, such as miraculous birth; initiation;[33] interacting with the goddess (anima);[34] and a struggle with a father figure. Most if not all of these themes, says Campbell, will work their way into the hero's journey in one form or another. He admits, however, that not every myth contains every stage or every archetype, and that it is rare to see them neatly conveyed according to the traditional framework. The

---

32 See Steve Marcus, 'The Trouble with Campbell's Monomyth', in Ed Satchell, ed., *Myths of Our Time* (New York: Harod Publishing, 1989), p. 6.

33 Initiation usually occurs in the forest, which symbolises the great unknown. After a transformative experience there – or a series of such experiences – one emerges a new person, usually with the help of a teacher. A dark initiation occurs in *Revenge of the Sith*, when Palpatine finally succeeds in bringing Anakin to the dark side of the Force – he gives Anakin a new name (Darth Vader) and the young man responds by now calling Palpatine 'master', a term he had reserved only for Jedi adepts. A more traditional initiation is seen in the fifth episode, when Luke Skywalker goes to the swampy forest world of Yoda and becomes a Jedi. Similarly, in the Indian epics, Rama and his brother study with Vishvamitra in the forest, emerging as skilled archers who can defeat Ravana and his legions of Rakshasa demons; in the *Mahabharata*, we find the Pandavas entering forest life to study under Drona, becoming his most important pupils. These latter examples will be explained more fully in the next chapter.

34 The anima-animus terminology is used in Jungian psychology, usually in relation to one's own internal struggles. Originally, the words come from the Latin: *anima* = soul, *animus* = spirit. Jung used 'anima' to refer to the feminine images of men's dreams or fantasies, and he used 'animus' to describe masculine images in women's dreams or fantasies. Admittedly, the term anima usually refers to mother-like images, rather than sisters or lovers, especially in Campbell's work. In its broadest psychological application, however, the anima is merely a projection of one's own self when recognised in another person.

monomyth is fluid, he says, and one has to be flexible when observing the way it is applied to any given story.[35]

Traditionally, the journey of the hero is associated with several other standard motifs, such as 'the Myth of the Eternal Return', 'the Hero and the Dragon', and 'the Quest for the Holy Grail'. But make no mistake, these are all simply variations on Campbell's monomyth.

Briefly, the Myth of the Eternal Return (explored by both Joyce and Eliade) provides a metaphor for birth, growth, death, and rebirth, the cyclical view of time that ancient peoples inferred from the rotation of seasons, the phases of the moon, the cycle of the sun, and so on. Nowhere is this more recognised than in India, where reincarnation as a symbol of 'the Eternal Return' is accepted almost across the board. This motif of recurring reality is augmented by the idea of the Hero and the Dragon, which introduces moral purpose as an existential imperative. This moral purpose usually manifests in the conquering of evil in any of its forms (the dragon) or in the quest for the Holy Grail, which is itself a metaphor for achieving that which is valuable for mankind. On a more personal level, the Holy Grail can refer to one's own inner development – the holiest of grails.

Thus, in standard archetypal myths, the hero, after much ado, recognises his calling, defeats the dragon, rescues the maiden, and inherits the kingdom. Certainly this is the case in *Star Wars,* as it is in the Indic texts we will soon examine.[36] In fact, variations on these motifs can be seen in myths from just about every land, in every epoch of world history. Hence, Campbell's monomyth. The most important study of this phenomenon, particularly as it relates to *Star Wars,* is Mary Henderson's *Star Wars: The Magic of Myth,*[37] where she elucidates Campbell's monomythic format not only in relation to Lucas's

---

35 See *The Power of Myth,* pp. 52-3. The fluidity of the monomyth schema must be kept in mind when, in the next chapter, we see how it can be applied to the great Indian epics.

36 As a clear example of the dragon motif, students of the *Ramayana* will remember that the evil Ravana is described as having ten heads, much like the stereotypical dragon of common legend.

37 Mary Henderson compiled the companion volume to 'the *Star Wars* exhibition' at the National Air and Space Museum of the Smithsonian Institution. It was called *Star Wars: The Magic of Myth* (New York: A Bantam Book, 1997) and clearly outlined the monomyth in relation to *Star Wars* and other popular mythic traditions. This was followed by the Dorling Kindersley volume, *Star Wars: The Power of Myth* (New York: DK Publishing, 1999), which elaborates on Henderson's theme.

film series but also in most of the world's other mythic traditions, such as Greek, Roman, Norse, and so on. It is interesting, however, that her analysis de-emphasises Eastern traditions, particularly Hinduism, a discontinuity we hope this work will correct.

She also de-emphasises the monomythic structure in relation to important religious figures, though she does briefly mention them. As two examples, we need look no further than Buddha and Jesus, for their stories read like monomythic prototypes. Briefly, the Buddha is said to have been born of a virgin princess. Her husband, the king, did not want his growing boy polluted by the miseries of material life. For this reason, he kept his young son sheltered from the outside world, denying him the freedom to journey beyond the palace gates. Torn by his father's instruction and his own thirst for new experiences, the young Buddha, for most of his youth, reluctantly obeyed his guardians, never stepping foot outside his proscripted area. However, destiny eventually called, and the Buddha ventured beyond his father's protective walls. Once outside, he indeed experienced the harsh reality of material life: among his first experiences, he saw individuals undergoing birth, death, old age, and disease. He also saw a monk who had renounced the world. Asking his servant about the reality of these phenomena, he was told that such things occur in the lives of all people; but monks, the servant told him, while also going through birth, death, old age, and disease like anyone else, try to find resolution to these inevitable problems of life. 'Yes', Buddha said to his servant. 'I too will find resolution to life's dilemmas.'

Even at this early point in the story, an astute observer will notice the young Buddha's miraculous birth, his initial reluctance to take the journey of the hero, his tension with a fatherly figure, and a spiritual teacher (whether in the form of his servant, who first explained to him the miseries of material existence, or in the nameless renunciant, who indirectly inspired him to pursue higher truths) – four prominent features of the monomythic framework.

Next, the Buddha faces severe challenges. This begins when he marries and has a child. Looking upon the faces of his wife and newborn baby, he realises that he must make a choice between his quest for truth or a common life of material pleasure. He reflects on what he really wants, and which course of action will, for him, make a larger contribution to mankind – should he stay with wife and child, or should he try to live according to the principle of renunciation that he had come to believe in? He decides, though it is difficult, to tear himself away from those whom he loves most. He does this, he believes, for a greater good. But this is just the beginning of his journey (initiation). He sets out for the forest to live like a sage and to confer with like-minded people. As he sits under a now famous Bodhi Tree, he meditates deeply on the suffering of humanity and how such suffering could be overcome through spiritual practices.

At that precise moment, while contemplating these thoughts, he is attacked by the demon Mara, the god of desire. After trying to distract our hero in numerous ways, Mara decides a more subtle approach is in order: he sends his three beautiful daughters, Lust, Thirst, and Discontent, hoping that these obstacles would dissuade Buddha from his mission. After many such trials, temptations, and privations (the belly of the whale), the Buddha experiences transformation under the Bodhi Tree. He attains the enlightened state, sharing this new revelation with all who cross his path (the triumphant return and offering of a boon to mankind).

The traditional accounts of Jesus tell a similar monomythic tale. He is also born of a virgin. His birth is heralded by mystical signs and affirmed by 'the three wise men'. While still a child, his parents take him to Egypt in an attempt to flee King Herod, who wants to kill him. The wicked Herod felt threatened by the then widespread expectation of the coming messianic king – someone who would replace him as King of the Jews. In most monomythic stories, there is a special sign early on in the hero's life, something that distinguishes him even before his quest takes formal shape.

Although not much is known about Jesus's childhood, he eventually receives a calling from God and leaves home on a spiritual journey. John the Baptist functions as something of a guide for Jesus, as does God Himself. In the midst of Jesus's quest, he encounters both supernatural and human opposition, overcomes numerous trials, and meets several supporters along the way. His battle, of course, is with the Prince of Darkness, and, though Jesus is, like Buddha, tempted with pleasures uncountable, he eventually wins the battle and establishes a new law for anyone who will hear it.[38] In the course of his

---

38 As Buddha and Jesus are both tempted with unlimited sensual pleasures and emerge victorious, able to turn away the Prince of Darkness, so, too, do we find Luke Skywalker turning away from the alluring offers of Darth Vader and, later, the Emperor, both of whom promise Luke the galaxy.

journey, he goes to the land of Death for three days and then proceeds to Heaven. His church, it is said, is his holy bride (anima). Christian dogma asserts that because he voluntarily died for the sins of others, he is the ultimate hero. In the end, tradition teaches, he will return and reign forever. No monomythic commentary is needed – the basic outline should be apparent.

Though the complex stories of these religious personalities are here only summarised, the point should be clear: the monomythic structure so cherished by Campbell and his predecessors has an almost mystical tenacity, re-appearing in diverse cultures from around the world. As we shall see, *Star Wars* and the myths of India do not afford us an exception. Even the story of Krishna, who is described in many Indic texts as the Supreme Lord, or the chief cosmic *deva* (god), conforms to the monomythic journey. Though we will not explore the activities of Krishna here – for it would substantially distract us from our central point – their similarity to those of Jesus is nothing short of astonishing. This has been noted by scholars from the Eighteenth century onward.[39] Even just the birth and childhood stories reveal startling connections: as Jesus appeared in Mary's heart by immaculate conception, so too is it described that Krishna appeared first in the mind of his father Vasudeva and was then transferred to the heart of His mother, Devaki. The parents of both Jesus and Krishna were involved in paying taxes at the time of the divine births. Like Herod of Jesus's time, the evil king Kamsa ordered the death of all newborn babes, fearing that the immanent appearance of the great messiah, Krishna, would bring about his end. Consequently, in His youth, Krishna's royal identity was hidden from the world for His own protection, as Jesus's was – by the stables of Bethlehem and the carpenters' stalls of Nazareth – for the same purpose. There are many more such correlating features. For example, both Jesus and Krishna are said to have ended their sojourn on Earth when a sharp object pierced their flesh – the former suffered a spear

---

39 See P. Georgi, *Alphabetum Tibetanum* (Rome, 1762), p. 253, where he argues that Krishna worship was influenced by early Christianity. He based this on his belief that the Krishna tradition arose much later than it actually did. His work (and peculiar perspective) was developed by George Grierson and James Kennedy. To understand their point of view, see George Grierson, 'Modern Hinduism and its Debt to the Nestorians', in *Journal of the Royal Asiatic Society*, 1907, p. 323, and James Kennedy, 'The Child Krishna, Christianity, and the Gujars', in the same journal, 1907, p. 980.

in his side and the latter an arrow in His foot. And when we compare Krishna's teachings with those of Jesus, we find much in common as well.

These are just a few parallels, but they are enough to make one seriously consider the idea of a monomyth. Of course, one could instead attribute the similarities to a sort of intercultural 'copying' phenomenon, a 'borrowing theory', as historians have described it. Such a theory allows for the possibility that one cultural tradition may have influenced another, plain and simple. In our postmodern globalised world, this argument carries more weight than it would in ancient cultures, for there are examples of strikingly similar monomyths in traditions that had little or no communication with each other. Still, this explanation has its merits, and offers a pragmatic resolution to an otherwise baffling phenomenon.

If one proceeds with the 'borrowing theory' approach, the next question is, 'Who borrowed from whom?', a debate that was particularly lively in the Nineteenth century. Noticing uncanny parallels between the stories of Krishna and Christ, for example, many scholars argued over which cultural tradition might have come first. Did early Christians base their Jesus stories on the earlier Krishna traditions, or was it the other way around?[40] Other scholars opted for the theory of independent development – the idea that somehow, without one being influenced by the other, various peoples came upon the same sort of myths, which afforded their heroes the same sort of journeys. Clearly, the idea of the monomyth fits in neatly with this option of independent development. The monomythic framework merely offers a reason, following Jung, as to why diverse cultural traditions, from various time periods and from various parts of the world, happen to develop stories that are virtually the same: these stories, according to monomyth theory, are embedded in our consciousness. The religious contention, of

---

40 Early proponents of 'the borrowing theory', particularly in relation to Krishna and Christ, included such scholars as Albrecht Weber, F. Lorinser, and Edward W. Hopkins, notable Indologists who, of course, were all Christian. Naturally, they favoured the idea that the Krishna story had its roots in the Christian Gospels. Soon, however, Western scholars began to study Sanskrit, uncovering pertinent archeological evidence, such as the work of Megasthenes, the Heliodorus Column, the Mora Well Inscription, and so on, showing that it was more likely the other way around. The work of Auguste Barth, Christian Lassen, Richard Garbe, and R. G. Bhandarkar is significant here, as is the groundbreaking book by John M. Robertson, *Christianity and Mythology* (London: Watts & Company, 1910).

course, goes only one step further, saying that these stories are examples of ultimate reality and are therefore not only embedded in our consciousness but in our soul as well. The spiritual traditions of India hold this view.

To Campbell's credit, he acknowledges that all traditional myths have an esoteric dimension, that they are really about inner truths even if expressed in terms of an external narrative. Other scholars of myth have argued, too, that, '. . . these myths do not occur in outer space but inner space. They are really about the unconscious and its archetypal energies. The characters are unconscious energy representations brought to life in dramatic settings.'[41] The traditional cultures from which the world's established myths derive, however, tell us a slightly different story – they tell us that these myths occur in outer space *as much as* in inner space. And while there are definitely underlying messages and esoteric archetypal energies at the root of the world's great myths, the narratives themselves constitute essential truths, and thus, as stated earlier, are not to be discarded as merely outer coverings. Our current exploration of India in relation to *Star Wars* will bear this out. In India, the mythic stories themselves are held as sacred, not because they speak to some larger underlying truth but because, according to the tradition itself, they *are* truth. And, as Doniger stated earlier, we would do well to understand world myths as they understand themselves, in the cultural context in which they were originally transmitted. This context, at least in relation to the Hindu East, affirms that *Star Wars* is not the only myth to take place in 'outer space'.

One final point: the monomythic hero is not as removed or as distant from our everyday lives as we might think. Though this book will look at extraordinary characters, such as Lord Rama, the Pandavas, Krishna, Luke Skywalker, and so on, it should be noted that we all walk a hero's path to one degree or another, which is why monomythic journeys resonate so loudly for those of us who listen. In the words of George Lucas,

> Heroes come in all sizes, and you don't have to be a giant hero. You can be a very small hero. It's just as important to understand that accepting self-responsibility for the things you do, having good manners, caring about other people – these are heroic acts. Everybody has the choice of being a hero or not being a hero every day of their lives. You don't

41 J. Tigue, op. cit., p. 116.

have to get into a giant laser-sword fight and blow up three spaceships to become a hero.[42]

So, will we be heroes, or will we allow our more base instincts to take over? This question is one of the major concerns of the *Star Wars* movies. Luke Skywalker, the initial hero of the saga, chooses well, but his father (Anakin, Darth Vader) does not. This is not to say that Luke is good and Vader is bad. Things are not that simple, and Vader's early life proves this, as a viewing of the prequels makes clear. There is a little Luke and a little Vader in each of us, and this is the point. Interestingly, 'Arjuna', which is the name of the hero in the *Bhagavad-gita*, means 'Everyman'. The *Gita* thus asks us to identify with Arjuna's plight – with the choices he has to make between good and evil. We are all, in a sense, Arjuna. This is eloquently expressed by Antonio de Nicolas, Professor Emeritus of Philosophy from the State University of New York at Stony Brook:

> We must start with the *Gita*'s own initial situation: the human crisis of self-identity. This is Arjuna's concrete situation in the *Gita* – a situation which we human beings, in order to survive, must also consider at some time or another. We need to discover how our convictions function in our lives – a function so important that unless it is recovered, we cannot act. Our challenge is not only to understand Arjuna's plight, but also to understand that this plight is in many ways our own. . . . What is at issue is how we, as readers, decide to see ourselves in our critical situations. What makes us falter, doubt, stop on the path? What leads us to despair, inaction, abandonment, when faced with a determined crisis?[43]

Christopher Chapple, Professor of Theological Studies and Director of Asian and Pacific Studies at Loyola Marymount University in Los Angeles, elaborates on this same point:

> Arjuna, as a tragic heroic figure, represents the challenge of making difficult moral decisions. The human story often includes mysteries that

---

42 See the Arts/Cinema Section in *TIME* Magazine, 26 April 1999, Volume 153, Number 16, 'Of Myth and Men: A Conversation Between Bill Moyers and George Lucas on the Meaning of the Force and the True Theology of *Star Wars*'.

43 Antonio T. de Nicolas, 'Chapter One: Arjuna's Crisis', in *the Journal of Vaishnava Studies* 9, Number 2, Spring 2001, pp. 5-21.

do not lend themselves to easy resolution. In such circumstances, Hinduism offers a template in the person of Arjuna for finding 'one's radical orientation beyond the dictations of controlled situations and through these controlled situations'.[44] A literary tale can bring our human horizon beyond the strictly rational modality into a higher level of understanding, appreciation, and insight. In this, and in Arjuna's fulfillment of his destiny as a literary character, we are led to greater human freedom.[45]

I think this is where Lucas wants to lead us as well: he wants us to know that people who make bad choices are not all bad – that there is good and bad in each of us. *Star Wars* teaches us to deal with anger, to understand our fears, to live according to our faith; it teaches us to be disciplined, and to make righteous decisions – and to stick by these decisions; it teaches courage and loyalty, to live in harmony with nature, and to recognise powers greater than our own. In short, it teaches the ABCs of spiritual life. It does not explain these truths with the proficiency of the Eastern texts – Lucas is, after all, only a film-maker. He is not a prophet or a seer. But if we take the fundamentals of *Star Wars* and augment them with the elaborate analyses and guidelines offered by Eastern texts, we may well find ourselves on the road to becoming Jedis.

44 See Antonio T. de Nicolas, *Avatara: The Humanization of Philosophy Through the Bhagavad Gita* (New York: Nicolas Hays, 1976), p. 258.

45 Christopher K. Chapple, 'Arjuna's Argument: Family Secrets Unveiled', in the *Journal of Vaishnava Studies* 9, Number 2, Spring 2001, p. 30.

2

CLOSE ENCOUNTERS OF THREE KINDS: THE *RAMAYANA*, THE *MAHABHARATA* ...AND *STAR WARS*

*'The main motifs of the myths are the same,
and they have always been the same.'*
—Joseph Campbell, *The Power of Myth*

Using Campbell's monomyth as a basis to explore the similarities between Star Wars and various Indic texts, this chapter will focus on the hero's journey as it appears in the *Ramayana* and the *Mahabharata*, India's two most famous religious epics. In fact, our analysis throughout will focus on Vaishnava-Hindu texts such as these two epics, for here one finds the most pronounced parallels between *Star Wars* and Indian tradition.

Our approach is methodical if not simple: just as we have summarised the dramatic narratives of each of the *Star Wars* episodes in the Introduction, we here summarise, albeit more briefly, the *Ramayana* and the *Mahabharata*, without comparing them to Lucas's film series. Only after doing so will we briefly analyse them in terms of the hero's journey, and, specifically, in terms of *Star Wars*. More importantly, we will show several overlapping themes and points of departure, but not until after we complete our brief retelling of the epics. Though this method is somewhat circuitous, it serves a specific function: *Star Wars* fans will now get a working knowledge of Indian theology and culture, at least as they are depicted in the Vaishnava epics.

The *Ramayana*[1]

Unlike the *Star Wars* series, the Vaishnava texts of ancient India deal with personalities who are revered by millions. These texts, practitioners tell us, reveal esoteric truths and the realisations of historical sages. Moreover, embedded in these tales, one finds a wealth of philosophy and religion, as well as guidelines for a righteous life. The *Ramayana* and the *Mahabharata*, for example, have proven extremely valuable for countless people through the centuries, and continue to have meaning for the millions who embrace their teachings.

The *Ramayana* is ancient, and has the distinct honour of being called the first poem (*adikavya*) within the storehouse of Sanskrit literature. In terms of length, it is composed of some 24,000 couplets – 48,000 lines – eclipsing the well-known Western epics, such as the *Iliad* and the *Odyssey*, which have only 15,693 lines and 12,000 lines respectively. The *Mahabharata* is well over 100,000 lines.

The great epics of India have also been compared to the famous Greek epics in terms of style. This is primarily because they share certain underlying themes: Rama, for example, defeats the ten-headed villain Ravana and rescues his lovely wife Sita, bringing to mind the story of Menelaus, who destroyed Troy, facilitating the return of Helen.[2] The

1   The *Ramayana* is nicely summarised by Sadguru Sant Keshavadas, *Ramayana at a Glance* (Southfield, Michigan: Temple of Cosmic Religion,1976); F. S. Growse, *The Ramayana of Tulasidasa* (Delhi: Motilal Banarsidass, 1978); Satsvarupa dasa Goswami, 'The Glories of Lord Rama Chandra', in *A Handbook for Krishna Consciousness* (Philadelphia, Pennsylvania: Bala Books, 1979), pp. 16-39; H. Daniel Smith, *The Picturebook Ramayana: An Illustrated Version of Valmiki's Story* (Syracuse University, 1981); Philip Lutgendorf, *The Life of a Text: Performing the Ramcaritmanas of Tulsidas* (University of California Press, 1992); Ranchor Prime, *Ramayana: A Journey* (Great Britain: Collins & Brown Ltd., 1997); Krishna Dharma, *Ramayana: India's Immortal Tale of Adventure, Love, and Wisdom* (Los Angeles, California: Torchlight Publishing, 1998); and Bhakti Vikasa Swami, *Ramayana: The Story of Lord Rama* (Gujarat: ISKCON, 1999). Two complete translations are the two-volume *Srimad Valkimi Ramayana* (Gorakhpur: Gita Press, 1976), and the seven-volume *Ramayana of Valmiki* (Princeton: Princeton University Press, 1984). A 78-part adaptation of the *Ramayana* was also produced for Indian television in 1987-88, and has since been released on DVD with English subtitles. The summary here is based on my own readings of these sources and is a sort of amalgamation of Rama stories popular in the Indian subcontinent, incorporating regional accounts, like Tulsidas's *Ramcharitmanas*, as much as Valmiki's original Sanskrit *Ramayana*.

2   See W. L. Smith, *Ramayana Traditions in Eastern India: Assam, Bengal, Orissa* (University of Stockholm: 1988), p. 92.

commentarial tradition tells us that both Greek tragedy and Sanskrit epic often resolve problems in similar ways. One prominent example outshines the others: just as the pure and untainted Sita could not have really been touched by a demon such as Ravana, so, too, is it said that Helen never actually went to Troy with Paris – the Helen in Troy was a substitute apparition and the real Helen faithfully waited for her beloved Menelaus in Egypt. Similarly, the Rama stories tell us of a substitute Sita – a 'shadow' (*chaya*) or an 'illusory' (*maya*) Sita – who was kidnapped by Ravana, while the 'real' Sita existed in an unmanifest state, just waiting to be reunited with Rama.[3] Because of such similarities, scholars are currently researching the influence of ancient Indian epics on Western culture.

Despite its value as ancient literature, the *Ramayana's* strongest feature is its sheer beauty – beauty in terms of its sophisticated Sanskrit poetry, and in the provocative discourse that pours from the mouth of each major character. It is beautiful in terms of its exotic settings in the forest, and in terms of its magnificent cities, depicted in graphic detail – in terms of profoundly philosophical dialogue, and in terms of the morals and ethics it instills in its readers; in terms of *dharma* (duty) and the importance of doing one's duty, and in terms of the emotions it evokes; and, perhaps most of all, in terms of the characters one meets during a thorough journey through its pages. Chief among these, of course, is Rama himself. Tall, strong and righteous, he is the embodiment of virtue, a true hero who is not afraid to show his more human side, to love, to feel pain in separation when the woman so close to his heart is taken away from him. Sita, the woman in question, is not without virtuous qualities herself; she is the very emblem of chastity and all that is good and true. She is strong-willed, intelligent, and the single most important person in the entire story. Then there are Rama's younger brothers, chief amongst whom is Lakshman. Always at Rama's side, Lakshman is dearer to Rama than life itself – he shares all of Rama's noble qualities, as does Bharata and Shatrughna,

---

3   See C. Kirk, *The Nature of the Greek Myths*, p. 94, cited in W. L. Smith, ibid. For more on the concept of a 'shadow' Sita, see Wendy Doniger, *Splitting The Difference: Gender and Myth in Ancient Greece and India* (University of Chicago Press, 1999), pp. 8-79. The story of an illusory or shadow Sita does not appear in Valmiki's Sanskrit epic. However, it can be traced to the ancient *Kurma Purana*. It was also used as a device in Tulsidas's *Ramcharitmanas*, and it is certainly part of the larger Rama tradition.

his other two brothers. Hanuman, too, is among the most memorable
of the *Ramayana's* characters, half-monkey/half-human, and his devotion to Rama is so overwhelming that *bhakti* (devotional) cults have
arisen with this dedicated monkey-god as their central object of worship.

But to worship anyone other than Rama is to miss the point of the
Ramayana. Indeed, even Hanuman would shun those who worship
him, saying 'I, too, am merely a devotee of Ramachandra.' Hanuman
himself chants Rama's name – a name meaning 'the highest pleasure',
evoking thoughts of the Supreme Being and how the most intense bliss
comes from worshipping Him.

Elaborate though it is, the tale of Rama can be summarised as follows: millions of years ago, the Supreme Lord appeared on Earth as
a human prince named Ramachandra. Why does God incarnate as a
human? The story begins when a group of demigods approaches Lord
Brahma, their leader, with concerns about a demon-king, Ravana, who
is plundering the Earth. Brahma had given the demon a special power
– and the powers granted by Brahma always remain effective – saying that he 'could never be defeated in battle, not by god nor by any
heavenly creature'. Accordingly, Ravana had become nearly invincible.
However, Brahma's blessing did not mention humans, leaving open
the possibility that a highly qualified human, someone more powerful
than any heavenly being or demigod, could perchance conquer him.
Of course, Ravana thought that this was tantamount to being undefeat-
able, for how could a mere human ever supercede a higher being? Still,
the concerned demigods began to meditate on just how they could use
this loophole in Brahma's blessing to put an end to Ravana's reign of
terror. At that moment, Lord Vishnu descends, and he assures them
that he himself will incarnate as a human being named Ramachandra,
and by so doing he will destroy the evil Ravana.[4]

---

4   The 'loophole in the boon' motif is also found in the *Bhagavata Purana* (Seventh
    Canto), in the story of Lord Narasimha, the half-man/half-lion incarnation of
    Vishnu. Here, creator demigod Brahma offers the demon Hiranyakashipu the
    boon that he would not be killed by man nor beast; not during the day nor at
    night; not inside nor outside; not in the air nor on the ground. Hiranyakashipu
    thus thinks himself unvanquishable. Lord Vishnu honors the demon's boon by
    appearing as a creature that is half-man and half-lion (not fully man nor beast),
    killing him at twilight, in a doorway, and on His divine lap. There is another
    connection between the *Ramayana* and the story of Narasimha: tradition asserts
    that Hiranyakashipu is an earlier incarnation of Ravana himself. Thus, certain

By incarnating as a human, Rama not only enables himself to defeat the demon-king, but he sets an example for human behavior. He shows that the true hero is not some idealised symbol of perfection, but rather a loving, feeling individual with high moral character – one who also has 'imperfections', making him truly whole. As *Ramayana* scholar Ranchor Prime says of Rama:

> Rama is God incarnate, the seventh incarnation of Vishnu. He chose to become human, and for the duration of his human life to forget his divine identity, or so it seemed. He suffered physical hardships, and, when he lost his beloved Sita, a broken heart. On one level, Rama's journey is an allegory for the journey every soul must make. In becoming human Rama shared in our human suffering and enacted the drama of our own lives – each of us endures our own banishment, our own loss, faces our own disillusions, and hopes eventually to learn acceptance of our lot and to find ultimate redemption. Thus to hear or to witness Rama's struggles is to relive our own lives, but in a divine context. Each episode in the story is multi-layered, working through individual *karma*, or destiny, and the divine *lila*, or play, of Rama. In the same way, India's present-day Vedic sages point to life itself as being the working out, for each of us, of our own personal web of *karma*, desires and free will in accordance or in conflict with the will of God.[5]

Amazingly, Rama ultimately wins back Sita with the help of half-man/half animal-creatures, who are pious and who help wage a devastating war for the purpose of truth and righteousness.

The Story of the Pandavas[6]

The *Mahabharata* is considered the longest poem in world literature. Composed of some 110,000 Sanskrit couplets, it is seven times the

patterns emerge when the Lord descends to earth, and particular personalities, the Lord's associates, appear with him again and again.

5   Ranchor Prime, *Ramayana: A Journey*, op. cit., p. 7.

6   Good summaries of the *Mahabharata* include the ones by Chakravarthi V. Narasimhan, trans., The *Mahabharata* (New York: Columbia University Press, 1998, reprint) and Krishna Dharma, *Mahabharata*: The Greatest Spiritual Epic of all Time (Los Angeles: Torchlight Publishing, 1999). A complete translation is available as Kisari M. Ganguli, *The Mahabharata of Krishna-Dwaipayana Vyasa* (New Delhi: Munshiram Manoharial Publishers, 2004). In 1988-90, the *Mahabharata* was adapted as a 94-part television series for Indian television, and

length of the *Iliad* and the *Odyssey* combined or nearly three times the size of the Judaeo-Christian *Bible*. As an epic of immense proportions – both in terms of length and content – it has become the basis of Indian myth, religion, and philosophical thought. It is within the pages of the *Mahabharata* (1.57.74), in fact, that we first read of a work that sees itself on the level of the four *Vedas*, the oldest and most fundamental scriptures of the Hindu tradition; it proclaims itself 'the fifth Veda'.[7]

According to tradition, the *Mahabharata* was compiled some 5,000 years ago by the legendary Vyasa, who is seen as the 'literary incarnation' of God – meaning that he was empowered specifically for this task. After editing the original *Vedas,* he wanted to break down its basic truths in a way that the mass of people might understand them. Hence, he wrote the *Mahabharata*, a mammoth work that, as it is said, includes just about everything. As the text itself opines: 'If it is not found within these pages, it does not exist.'[8]

The *Mahabharata* contains a wealth of information about ancient Indian society, and, more generally, about what motivates people, toward both good and bad. The epic offers insights into love, hate, altruism, anger, suffering, and liberation. It teaches the importance of doing one's duty; of integrity; of harmlessness and non-aggression; it explains the futility of war, and of its occasional necessity; the

---

has since been released on DVD with English subtitles. For the Bhagavad-gita, please see His Divine Grace A. C. Bhaktivedanta Swami Prabhupada, *Bhagavad-gita As It Is* (Los Angeles: Bhaktivedanta Book Trust, 1972); also, the introduction to Winthrop Sargeant, *The Bhagavad Gita* (Albany: State University of New York Press, 1984); Barbara Powell, *Windows into the Infinite* (Fremont, California: Asian Humanities Press, 1996); and Ruth Katz, *Arjuna in the Mahabharata* (Columbia, South Carolina: University of South Carolina Press, 1989).

7   The *Mahabharata's* proclamation of itself as the fifth Veda might appear self-serving, as might similar claims made by several of the Puranas, or the established history books of ancient India. After all, the Veda is identified with direct revelation, and, therefore, any literature directly associated with it will automatically garner divine status. Be that as it may, there are quotations from within the Vedic corpus itself that legitimate the claims made by the Mahabharata and the Puranas. For example, Atharva Veda 11.7.24, Chandogya Upanishad 7.1.4, and the Brihadaranyaka Upanishad 2.4.10 – all suggest that the Epics and the Puranas are part of the original Vedic literature.

8   This bold claim is found near the beginning of the *Mahabharata's* central narrative and again toward the end of it (at 1.56.33 and at 18.5.38, respectively), underlining Vyasa's confidence that, indeed, all things are found in the epic's pages.

importance of honour; of how social roles commingle with transcendent ones; and how the pursuit of spiritual development is the zenith of all action.

The substance of the basic story, however, revolves around the furious quarrel between the Pandavas and the Kauravas, two groups of cousins who were nurtured from their earliest years in the chivalrous Kshatriya caste[9] – meaning that they were trained as warriors, administrators, and as protectors of the innocent. The quarrel between these two groups escalated into a full-scale civil war – involving gods, yogis, higher beings with magical powers, sages and royalty. Tradition holds that this war actually occurred – although certain commentators, like Mahatma Gandhi, see it more as a metaphor – and that it happened during the time of Vyasa, some 5,000 years ago. In the midst of it all, the character looming largest is Krishna, the Supreme Being – Vishnu in a more humanlike form. The *Mahabharata* depicts Him as a friend of the Pandavas, charioteer and confidante to the central protagonist, a Pandava leader whose name was Prince Arjuna.[10]

Although widely published as a book in itself, the *Bhagavad-gita* originally appears as an episode in the sixth section of the *Mahabharata*. It consists of 700 verses in eighteen chapters and is often referred to as the 'Gitopanishad'. In other words, it follows the literary style and philosophical conclusions of the earlier Upanishads, the esoteric books of knowledge appended to the Vedas. *Gita* means 'song', and *bhagavad* refers to 'God, the possessor (*vat*) of all opulence (*bhaga*)'. The *Bhagavad-gita,* therefore, is 'The Song of the All-Opulent One', embodying the essential teachings of Lord Krishna.

---

9 The word 'caste' is used here for convenience. Actually, the original socio-religious system of ancient India, known as varnashrama, was applied to individuals according to their intrinsic quality and vocational inclination. The contemporary caste system, on the other hand, is based on birth (jati), identifying one's status according to family heritage and social hierarchy. This latter deviated system has been one of the great banes of modern India.

10 Krishna is considered by most Hindus to be an incarnation of Vishnu, the Supreme Lord. However, the Bhagavata Purana (1.3.27), the Brahma-samhita (5.1), and other Vaishnava texts clearly grant a unique place to Krishna as the source of all Vishnu forms. Several Vaishnava groups who heed these texts, therefore, are more aptly called forms of Krishnaism than Vaishnavism, as their emphasis is on Krishna as the 'Supreme Personality of Godhead'. Traditional groups with this perspective include the Gaudiya and Vallabha lineages as well as the modern-day Hare Krishna movement.

On the eve of the great *Mahabharata* battle, with multiple armies arrayed on the battlefield at Kurukshetra, not far from Delhi in present-day India, Krishna spoke the *Bhagavad-gita*, the philosophical poem that, according to some, is the most important portion of the larger epic.

The text comes to us in the form of a dialogue: Prince Arjuna, putting aside his duty as an administrative officer, decides not to fight – though he is standing right there on the battlefield, and the battle is about to begin. His decision to desist will affect the lives of huge numbers. It is motivated by pragmatic if also emotional concerns: his kinsmen and teachers are in the opposing army. These particular family members, though noble and virtuous in numerous ways, have broken the law, and it is Arjuna's duty to bring them to justice.

Krishna, who has agreed to become the driver of Arjuna's chariot, is witness to Arjuna's reservation. He watches as the noble Prince turns from courageous warrior to a man with second thoughts. Arjuna's face reveals his ever-deepening realisation that he must kill relatives and friends, and he begins to question the entire militaristic enterprise that lay before him. Feeling compassion, Krishna eloquently reminds Arjuna of his immediate social duty as a warrior upon whom people are depending, and, more importantly, of his religious duty as an eternal spiritual entity in a relationship with God. Surprisingly, Krishna does not tell Arjuna to avoid the war and to adopt the life of a renounced spiritualist. Rather, He tells him to do his duty on the battlefield – that, in the long run, the battle would be the lesser of two evils. The relevance and universality of Krishna's teachings transcend the immediate historical setting of Arjuna's battlefield dilemma.

The dialogue moves through a series of questions and answers that brings Arjuna, along with subsequent readers, to an understanding of certain fundamental metaphysical concepts. These include the distinction between the body and the soul, or between matter and spirit; the logic of reincarnation; the principle of non-attached action, or how to work dispassionately and for a higher purpose; the virtues and mechanics of various forms of discipline and meditation (*yoga*); and the place of knowledge (*gyana*) and devotion (*bhakti*) in pursuit of the spirit. Krishna explains the modes of nature – goodness, passion, and ignorance – and how these qualities impact peoples' lives. He also explains the nature of God and the purpose of existence. Ultimately, Krishna teaches Arjuna that perfection lies not in renunciation of the world, but rather in disciplined action, performed without attachment to results. He urges Arjuna to fight, but with a sense of love and spiritual purpose.

In India, at the time, the *Bhagavad-gita* was revolutionary. The prevailing idea of spirituality had always been one of renunciation, of leaving the world behind to practice asceticism and contemplation in solitude. This, in fact, was Arjuna's inclination: when the question of battle became particularly poignant for him, he opted for retreating, for taking shelter of a more peaceful religiosity. Appealing though this option might have seemed, Krishna pointed out to him that it would in fact cause more harm than good. After all, as already stated, the lives of many would be on his head, and, clearly, his decision to renounce was made hastily, with self-centred motives. This is why the *Bhagavad-gita* is considered the *New Testament* of India: Krishna gave a new dispensation, a new approach to spiritual perfection, and He deemed it superiour to the traditional 'inactive' model of world-renunciation. Rather, He taught Arjuna that action is superiour to inaction, but only when it is done for the right purposes, i.e., when it is done for Him.

The Return of the Monomyth

The stories summarised above are complicated, and our attempt is necessarily incomplete, but we wanted readers to have a basic working outline. To see Campbell's monomyth at work in these stories, one is advised to get a *Ramayana* or *Mahabharata* of their own, if not a translation then at least a thorough summary of each. (Recommendations of good editions are given in the footnotes.)

Let us begin our monomythic adventure by recalling our summary of the *Star Wars* epic. Briefly, we learn (in the first of the prequels) that the hero's birth is supernatural, his father Anakin having been born of a virgin. (Incidentally, Anakin, who later becomes Vader, is also a hero of sorts, at least in the first two prequels. And Han Solo, too, may be considered a *Star Wars* hero. But we are here concerned with Luke.) The hero is called to adventure and, at least initially, refuses the call. He is then swayed by a series of events (largely the death of his aunt and uncle) and aided by supernatural forces (Ben and the Force), thus enabling the adventure to proceed. He is also given a magical weapon to accomplish his ends (the lightsabre). The hero then encounters the threshold (in the Mos Eisley Cantina and in the forests of Dagobah) and becomes determined to undertake his noble cause. For this purpose, he agrees to undergo proper training (by Yoda) as a Jedi Knight, which constitutes his initiation. Now focused on his goal, he is ready to enter the belly of the whale (by going to the aid of his friends and, later, fighting with Vader), more determined than ever to serve the goddess (or to rescue Princess Leia), his anima relationship. In the course of events, he loses his father figure (in terms of his Uncle Owen's and Ben's death, and, later, the deaths of Yoda and Darth Vader) but emerges as a victorious hero, helping to destroy the demonic forces (the Emperor, the Death Star) and bringing peace to all.

If we briefly look at the *Ramayana* – any thorough summary or translation will do – we will notice Rama's divine birth and his initial call to adventure when Vishvamitra comes to his home. Dasharath shows hesitancy, and so refusal of the call, in this case, comes from the father. Though Rama is acquiescent to his father's wishes, there is tension involving a father figure. Ultimately, Rama relents and journeys to the forest, a place of mystery and adventure. He conquers his demons (literally) and is initiated by a great teacher (Vishvamitra). Lakshman is his mystical helper. His magical Indra bow is his weapon, and he goes through a test, a challenge, when he comes to lift the bow of Shiva. This leads to anima resolution, his marriage to Sita, and they reign happily in Ayodhya.

The story has a second component, however, when Dasharath decides to make Rama king. The hesitancy here comes from Queen Kaikeyi, who creates obstacles for the hero's progress. He is banished to the forest, which again serves as a threshold for adventure and growth. His major tests come in the form of battling with the demonic Rakshasas and, ultimately, in dealing with the kidnapping of his wife, which suggests anima difficulty. In some ways, this is the belly of the beast – separation from Sita. Lakshman, Sugriva, Jambavan and Hanuman, among others, are his mystical helpers, who assist him through his next threshold: building a massive bridge to Lanka to retrieve his bride. They face the ultimate demon, Ravana, and his massive Rakshasa armies. Rama personally defeats Ravana, slaying the dragon, saving the princess, and goes back to Ayodhya as king.

In the *Mahabharata*, we find that the Pandavas are all born in miraculous ways, fathered by demigods. Dhritarashtra wants their kingdom for his own boys, the Kauravas, thus manifesting fatherly tension from the very beginning. Drona, a wise brahminical teacher who knows the art of warfare and yogic principles, trains and initiates the young Pandavas, and the Kauravas as well, in his forest hermitage. As time passes, the Pandavas are called to adventure by the iniquity of the Kauravas, who try to poison them, to burn them alive, and so on. The ultimate challenge, or threshold, comes when Yudhisthira is cheated in a game of dice, leading to the Pandavas' forest banishment. (The Kauravas also attempt to disrobe Draupadi, creating anima tension and fueling the animosity between them.) Emerging from their exile, the Pandavas are denied the land that is rightfully theirs, and they are plunged into the belly of the beast – a massive war taking millions of lives. But not before a firm dose of 'denying the call': though war seems inevitable, they are hesitant, for they know that any battle with the Kauravas will have devastating repercussions. On several occasions, they plead for peace. Eventually, however, war rears its ugly head. As the battle ensues, they are aided by many noble warriors and spiritual leaders, who bring otherworldly weapons and esoteric teachings onto the battlefield. The Pandavas prove themselves in combat, with courage, skill and wisdom. They learn many lessons about life (including those found in the *Bhagavad-gita*), and they come face-to-face with their own strong points, and their weak ones as well. They win the battle, avenging Draupadi's shame, and returning the kingdom to righteous rule.

Going back to *Star Wars* for a moment, we might observe that Han Solo also follows a hero pattern, one that overlaps with Luke's. This is not uncommon. It is not that only the central protagonist may follow a hero's path. Other characters might also embark on such a journey. As an example, let us briefly look at Solo: he is asked to make the Rebel's mission his own (the call). He is initially reluctant, and this hesitancy lasts for most of the first film (the refusal). But, deep down, he is clearly a heroic figure, risking his life to rescue Luke (acceptance of the call). He is aided by Chewbacca (mystical helper), and their adventures take them to Hoth, Bespin, and elsewhere. But more, it should be remembered, Solo flies directly into the belly of the whale – he and Leia find themselves in the body of a giant space slug (threshold crossings).[11]

---

11 Based on the biblical metaphor of Jonah's entrance into the belly of a whale, Campbell considers 'the belly of the beast' an important component of the monomythic journey. It represents a transformative experience whereby the hero comes into his own and is ready to accomplish his mission. For those familiar with Indic texts, the journey of Han and Leia into the mouth of the giant space slug is

He evades the Imperial Fleet on a number of occasions (tests), and proves his mettle throughout the film series. In the end, his love for Leia is clear (anima resolution) and his heroism eclipses his rough exterior.

The Composite Hero

An interesting part of Solo's journey is his love affair with Princess Leia, which will be echoed in the prequels as the forbidden love of Anakin and Padmé. In *Star Wars*, the anima-animus tension – the princess and knight who are drawn to each other – is resolved in an unexpected way, especially regarding Luke and Leia. Initially, the viewer thinks they will develop a romantic relationship. In due course, however, we find out that they are brother and sister. Consequently, Solo's tender feelings toward her start to seem natural, as if he were an extension of the Luke we have come to know through the first film of the series. And Leia's growing sentiments for Solo make sense, too, for he has certain masculine qualities that seem lacking in Luke. In fact, Solo's manly heroism, which at times makes him seem like Luke's necessary counterpart, allows him to overshadow our main hero in a number of ways.

This is significant because Luke and Solo then become a sort of 'composite hero', each compensating for the deficiencies of the other. This is a phenomenon that is more common in Indian myth than in those originating in the West.[12] Here, again, Lucas follows the Indian line of thinking. His syncretic imagination seems coloured by the *Ramayana* and the *Mahabharata*, at least on a subliminal level. He is certainly not basing *Star Wars* on the Greek epics, for example, where individual heroes take precedence over group dynamics. In *Star Wars*, Pricess Leia's relationship with the rebel heroes as a group is reminiscent of Draupadi's marriage to the Pandavas. Ultimately, Leia chooses

reminiscent of Krishna and his cowherd boyfriends marching into the mouth of the terrible demon Aghasura, representing, perhaps, the world's most literal 'belly of the beast' tale.

12 See R. P. Goldman, '*Ramah Sahalaksmanah*: Psychological and Literary Aspects of the Composite Hero in Valmiki's *Ramayana*', in *Journal of Indian Philosophy* 8:2 (June 1980), pp. 149-189. In his elaborate analysis of the composite hero in the Indian epics, Goldman explores, among other things, the anima-Draupadi character in the *Mahabharata*. He interestingly suggests that her group marriage to the Pandavas might be attributed to the fact that they are, in some sense, really only one person. See p. 151.

Solo as her preferred aspect of the composite hero, whereas Draupadi does not choose between her husbands. It should be noted, however, that there are other similarities between Leia and Draupadi: in *Return of the Jedi*, Leia is imprisoned by Jabba the Hutt, a loathsome demon who keeps her chained to his side. When she is with him, she appears in harem clothes. Obviously, she has been humiliated by being stripped and re-dressed in this uncharacteristic way. One familiar with Indic texts is here reminded of Draupadi's attempted disrobing by the Kauravas. Seeing Leia captured and violated, shackled in the lair of a cruel demon, is also reminiscent of Sita, who found herself among slave girls in Ravana's harem.

The composite hero concept also allows us to identify Lakshman with Han Solo, for, without it, how could Solo (Lakshman) be romantically involved with Leia, who is easily identified with Sita? It is true that in later versions of the *Ramayana* Sita alludes to Lakshman's 'desire for her', when Rama runs off to capture Sita's deer. But a romantic relationship between Sita and Lakshman is clearly beyond the scope of any dharmic parameters associated with ancient Indian texts. The composite hero motif resolves this dilemma: in the initial *Star Wars* episode, Solo is clearly a Lakshman-like character, and the viewer of the film would never think that anyone other than Luke could have Leia as his bride. But, in subsequent episodes, when it becomes evident that Leia and Luke are brother and sister, Solo becomes Luke's 'other side' and a relationship with the princess naturally ensues.

India's preference for composite heroes has been explored by the scholar of religions Robert Goldman,[13] who has thoroughly analysed this phenomenon in relation to Rama and Lakshman. These two are so clearly a composite hero, he says, that it is reflected in the way Valmiki refers to them in the *Ramayana*:

> Rather than always referring to Rama and Laksmana [separately], the poet has often relegated the latter's name to the status of an adjective modifying and subordinate to the name of the principle hero. Thus, throughout the epic Rama is described with adjectives such as *sahalaksmana* and *sahasaumitri*, which mean 'together with Laksmana'. …the inseparability of the heroic pairs Rama and Laksmana, and Bharata and Satrughna is a function of their forming psychologically

13 R. P. Goldman, Ibid.

complementary sets which make up what may be termed the composite hero of the epic.[14]

Moreover, Goldman argues that the composite hero is, in Sanskrit literature, more a rule than an exception. He cites the *Mahabharata*, referring to the five Pandava brothers as prime examples. 'The conjunction of these figures', he says, 'is so fully realised that it is in many ways difficult to isolate one of them as the principle hero of the epic.'[15] As evidence, we might remember that the eldest of the brothers, Yudhishthira, is hardly a satisfactory hero on his own – during the eighteen-day battle, he ran off, ostensibly as a coward. (He merely hated violence of any kind. Many see Yudhishthira's wise aversion to violence as a central teaching of the epic.) Arjuna and Bhima often seem far more courageous, with much of the outcome of the war falling on their shoulders. But they seem to lack Yudhishthira's wisdom. As Goldman observes, 'No one of the principle protagonists possesses all of the virtues required of an Indian hero and [one hopes] that somehow the deficiencies of one may be made good in one or another of his brothers.'[16] Goldman elaborates:

> For, in fact, we do not see in the *Mahabharata* a simple aggregation of heroes, the grouping together of similar figures of whom any one could stand alone. Instead the characters appear to be to a large extent complementary, forming, together, a group which itself functions as the hero.[17]

Ultimately, the epics show a 'composite preference' by indulging an almost formulaic fondness for twins – the *Ramayana* goes to great lengths to inform us that Lakshman and Shatrughna are twins; in the *Mahabharata*, we are consistently reminded that Nakula and Sahadeva

---

14 Ibid., p. 150.

15 Ibid.

16 Ibid.

17 Ibid. Regarding the composite hero, Goldman also points out that Krishna, for those who know his story well, is inseparable from his brother Balarama – tradition often asserts that the only difference between Krishna and His brother is the colour of their complexion and that of their *dhotis*, or dress. Theologically, too, Krishna is seen as inseparable from Radha, his female counterpart. They are considered the ultimate male and female Godhead, partaking of the same divinity. In these ways and many more, India favours the idea of a composite hero.

are twins; and now we are introduced to Luke and Leia, the twins of the *Star Wars* films. In all cases, the storylines indicate that the twins are interdependent. Finally, the composite hero syndrome is nowhere as strongly insinuated as in the story of Rama's demise: Lakshman is forced to leave Rama's side, and this separation causes the younger brother's death. Rama, for his part, cannot tolerate separation from the recently departed Lakshman (though, we may remember, he was able to live in separation from Sita), and dies immediately thereafter. The enigmatic sage Vasishtha had predicted that the two would leave the planet at the exact same time, their love for each other not allowing one to go on without the other.[18]

Another sense of composite structure, though manifesting quite differently than the one discussed above, can be seen in Luke's relationship with Vader. It has been said that Vader is symbolic of Luke's darker side,[19] which is why the boy sees his own face in Vader's helmet in the mysterious vision on Dagobah. This is also why he ends up with a mechanical hand, signifying his identity with his largely mechanised father. Stated another way, Vader is Luke's 'shadow', an archetypal concept with Jungian connotations.[20] This shadow, according to Jungian

18 See *Ramayana* 7.96.13-97.3 and also 7.96.8. See also Goldman, op. cit., who discusses this point in a footnote on p. 188. Maurice Phipps, in his interesting article 'The Myth and Magic of *Star Wars*: A Jungian Interpretation' (in *Viewpoints, report, Research/Technical. ERIC*, 1983) draws on the work of Dr. Paul Radin (cited in Carl G. Jung, *Man and His Symbols*, 1964, p. 112), saying that there are basically four developmental cycles in the hero myth: the final and most refined stage is known as Twins – the bringing together of the two disparate sides of human nature. I am indebted for this information to Shana J. Chrystie, whose 'Annotated Bibliography of Scholarly Works in English From May, 1977 to May, 2001 on the *Star Wars* Films (Episode IV, *Star Wars: A New Hope*; Episode V, *The Empire Strikes Back*; Episode VI, *Return of the Jedi*; Episode I, *The Phantom Menace*)' has been an invaluable resource throughout the writing of this book.

19 See Thomas Lee Snyder, 'Sacred Encounters: The Myth of the Hero in the Horror, Science Fiction, Fantasy Films of George Lucas and Steven Spielberg', unpublished Ph.D. thesis, Northwestern University, Evanston, Illinois, June 1984, pp. 88-91. It might also be mentioned here that the father figure in *Star Wars* is a composite character of sorts – Obi-Wan Kenobi is the good, authoritative 'father' that Luke never had; Darth Vader is the evil, authoritarian father, whom Luke gradually discovers. If we look at Vader himself, he is the evil anti-hero who appears throughout the film series, but he is also Anakin Skywalker, the embodiment of goodness. This is the same goodness, of course, that is eventually passed on to Luke. The Emperor is also a father figure, but not quite as developed.

20 Ibid.

psychology, is the part of our personality that we repress in favour of all we know to be right. Both good and evil exist in any given individual, but the ability to hold back urges for power, exploitation, manipulation, and so on, is what distinguishes the truly righteous from those who are given to more compromised behavior. The whole *Star Wars* series, in fact, seems to be saying that Luke already has the dark side of the Force within him, and that if he is not careful, he will turn out like Vader. Meanwhile, Vader, deep down, is a Jedi, with much good in him, not unlike Luke. This is all made clear in Vader's death scene.

The demons of the Indian epics, too, have both good and evil within them. For example, Ravana, in an earlier incarnation, is revealed to be Vijaya, a highly elevated being – a gate-keeper of the spiritual world. Another of the spiritual gate-keepers, Jaya, was born in a previous life as Hiranyakashipu, a demon who was killed by the divine man-lion, Lord Narasimha. This Narasimha story has many parallels with *Star Wars*. For example, the power-mad father, Hiranyakashipu, and his pious son, Prahlad, are like prototypes for Vader and Luke, the evil father repeatedly trying to kill his own flesh and blood. Reconciliation with a father figure is central to the monomythic journey. From a depth psychological perspective, *Star Wars* speaks directly to Oedipal fantasies – Luke fights with his father, defeats him, and, in the end, rescues him. The insurrection against father images, however, can be found throughout the film series: Luke rebels first against Uncle Owen, and then, for good reasons, Darth Vader. Later on, he acts against the good council of Obi-Wan and Yoda, for he leaves to rescue his friends even though his two well-wishers tell him he is not ready. Ultimately, though, Luke has high regard for Uncle Owen and both his teachers, while his tension with his biological father, we know, is resolved when the helmet comes off and we see a once-evil Vader redeemed, proud of his heroic son.

In Indian tradition, Hiranyakashipu is redeemed by Narasimha's sharp nails, which liberate him from his evil incarnation. Redemption of one's father is common in Indic sources: the story of Ajamila (in the *Bhagavata Purana*, Sixth Canto) is a good example of this. Though born a Brahmin, the most elevated caste in the Vedic system, Ajamila fell away from the path of righteousness. Nonetheless, he named his son 'Narayana', which is a name for God. Accordingly, he was shown special mercy when, at the time of death, he called out for his son. God took it that Ajamila was calling on him, and the errant Brahmin was thus saved. Clearly, he was redeemed by his love for his son.

Interestingly, the story of Krishna creates paternal tension by giving Him two sets of parents (Vasudeva and Devaki, as well as Nanda and Yashoda), but, further, by making His maternal uncle, Kamsa, also a father figure, one of the great demons of Vedic history. Krishna, of course, kills Kamsa for the benefit of everyone in the Braj area. Regarding Rama, we find Dasharath, though by no means a demon, banishing our hero from his kingdom, and while Rama does not see this as a betrayal, it does create tension with a fatherly figure. More tellingly, perhaps, later versions of the Rama story transform Ravana into Sita's 'real' father, thus making him Rama's father-in-law. This development is primarily found in Jain readings of the *Ramayana* and in South Indian versions as well.[21]

But our central point is this: just as Hiranyakashipu, who was born as a Brahmin, was not always evil, neither was Vader. Both are errant soldiers who took a wrong turn on the road of life. Dhritarashtra and Duryodhana also start out as valiant warriors and noble men. The *Mahabharata* describes their courage and skill, their character and determination. But then envy, jealousy, rage – something changes them. Let it be remembered that, in *Revenge of the Sith*, it becomes clear that Anakin's downward march to the dark side is extremely gradual, a long-term product of his ambition, his pride. It starts out as something relatively good, something to which we can all relate. It begins with attachment to loved ones – his anger over his mother's death and his intense desire to avert Padmé's certain doom. Chancellor Palapatine methodically seduces Anakin toward darkness by his seeming affection for him, by promises of power and knowledge. Ultimately, he is conquered by the misguided belief that the dark side of the Force could somehow save his wife – a belief whose fallaciousness should have been apparent to him by the end of the prequel trilogy, when his wife in fact passes away.

The rather simple message here is that we can all go to the dark side or to the side of light, depending on whether or not we allow ourselves to be conquered by our own lower nature – it all hangs on whether we

---

21 For more on 'father and son' explorations in early Vaishnava texts, see R. P. Goldman, 'Fathers, Sons, and Gurus: Oedipal Conflict in the Sanskrit Epics', in *Journal of Indian Philosophy* 6:4 (December 1978), pp. 325-392. For more on alternate readings of the *Ramayana* wherein Sita is seen as Ravana's daughter, see Ramesh Menon, *The Ramayana: A Modern Retelling of the Great Indian Epic* (New York: North Point Press, 2001), pp. 665-68.

think in terms of far-reaching, laudable goals, or if we submit to the lure of instant gratification, which often causes our own ruination in the end.

Campbell says that in the monomythic journey, the hero realises that he and his opponent are, in some sense, one. We have already mentioned how this is so in relation to Vader and Luke. This is certainly the case as well with Yudhishthira, who tries to avoid the devastating *Mahabharata* war because he sees that he and his enemies are not so very different. And Arjuna, too, feels this sense of harmony with his opponents, which is why he tries to avoid fighting, as in the opening of the *Bhagavad-gita*. In fact, the whole *Mahabharata* war shows that the 'good guys' and the 'bad guys' share much in common – toward the end of the battle, it is not only the Kauravas who start to compromise the etiquette of proper warfare. The Pandavas do as well. A major question is thus raised by the epic: does this mean that the Pandavas are any less virtuous? In due course, we find that they are indeed virtuous in any case. But we also learn that, in certain situations, the line between good and evil is indeed thin.

When we look at Ravana and Rama, we find the most interesting example of this abstract oneness. Ultimately, the epic tells us that Rama is God, and his actions are to be seen in that light, imbued with esoteric meaning. But in the *lila*, in the game of life, as conveyed in the many plots and subplots of the epic, there are lessons to be learned, instructions that can be gleaned from Rama's behavior and no less from Ravana's. Or, stated another way, can Ravana in some sense be the darker side of Rama? Clearly, for someone who is all good, Rama chooses some rather questionable courses of action. He kills Vali by ambushing him and shooting him in the back, and he banishes Sita – just to appease his subjects – when he knows that she is in fact faultless. *Ramayana* expert Jonah Blank considers this subject at some length:

> At the epic's end, Rama does not wish to bring Sita pain, but *dharma* says that a monarch must place his subjects' welfare above all else. As a king and as a husband, he must commit evil actions because the law of righteousness demands them....How could Rama, the very personification of good, commit an act of evil? How could Ravana, the Lord of Demons, behave like a true gentleman? These are questions that Indians debate every day, at the dinner table, at the temple, at the tea hut near the village well. Truck-driver philosophers and seamstress

theologians come up with many explanations, but never with an answer. There is no answer. Good and evil are not the separate entities we would like to believe.[22]

And, in many ways, this is one of the great teachings of the epics. They tell us that reality is not always what it seems to be, that illusion can engulf the greatest of souls, and that knowledge can sometimes be found in the heart of a tyrant. From an absolute perspective, yes, there is good and evil, the divine and the demoniac, and the epics do convey knowledge in this way. But from the point of view of our everyday experience, the world cannot be separated into neat compartments. And the epics explain truth along these lines as well. Though we would like clear lines drawn in the sand, demarcating the perimeters of the righteous and the unseemly, like the boundaries between the camps of the Pandavas and the Kauravas, the real world does not always afford us such a luxury. The epics ask us, therefore, to decide for ourselves, to make conscious choices about right and wrong, recognising that there is always a little wrong in what is right, and vice versa.

Star Wars, too, asserts the importance of making well-informed, conscious decisions about one's course in life. Lucas purposely blurs the boundaries of good and evil – Luke is not all good, and Vader is not all bad. *Star Wars* is a story that wants to provoke thought, if also to convey essential truths; it encourages debate about moral behavior; and it offers guidelines for ethical living. Like the Indian epics, *Star Wars* elaborates on the complex nature of good and evil, and, again like the epics, it does so in dramatic format. Vader goes with his impulse, seeking the immediate pleasures of the dark side of the Force. Luke, on the other hand, is able to conquer his lower self with his higher self – a teaching that he receives from Yoda but that can also be found in the *Bhagavad-gita* – and, because of this, becomes a more fully integrated person.

From a psychoanalytic perspective, then, *Star Wars,* much like the Indian epics, can be seen as a statement about integration, about reconciling the positive and negative forces in our own minds and hearts. Along these lines, Luke finds himself faced with an interesting conundrum: does he fight for what he knows is right, or does he surrender

---

22 Jonah Blank, *Arrow of the Blue-Skinned God: Retracing the Ramayana Through India* (New York: Doubleday, 1993), pp. 182, 185.

to his more base desires? The question becomes even more poignant when he realises that his evil opponent is in reality his own father, that he is actually making a choice between familial attachment and civic duty. A similar dilemma, it should be remembered, is central to the *Bhagavad-gita*, where Arjuna must choose between embracing a battle that he knows is just, or forsaking it because the opposing army consists of family and friends. Though these circumstances are extreme, we are all confronted with questions and situations that test our quality of character, that force us to choose between shallow, superficial responses to everyday urges, and thoughtful, well-considered actions that show integrity and self-respect. If we choose the former, we end up like Vader, a fragmented, tortured individual whose meaning in life comes from what he can get, or whom he can exploit. If, however, we opt for the latter, we have a chance to imbue life with higher meaning, to become a more fully integrated individual. *Star Wars* scholar J. Tigue brilliantly discusses this integration by looking at the name of Luke's mentor:

> The name 'Obi-Wan Kenobi' is itself rather fascinating: O-be-one/ Can-no-be; the idea of being and nonbeing, that is, of one who has integrated the opposites in his psyche. The name further suggests fulfilling one's potential or not. It is a matter of choice. Luke, like Obi-Wan, will choose the path of integration.[23]

In choosing to become a whole, integrated being, Luke is resolving the patriarchal dilemma established by Vader's poor choices in life. He is correcting the wrongs of his father, and, in so doing, liberating him. A son's ability to do this is nowhere as accepted as in Hindu culture. This is eloquently expressed by Jungian analyst Alfred Collins in a review of *Return of the Jedi*:

> This film suggests a redemption of the patriarchal problem with which our own culture so notoriously struggles, by way of an ancient mythologem, the mutuality of Self in father and son. This mutuality is one of the most central aspects of kinship in Hindu society. Several times the Upanishads have the father address his son with the words, 'Thou art the Self (*atman*) called Son', and the film's funeral rite is

---

23 J. Tigue, *The Transformation of Consciousness in Myth: Interpreting the Thought of Jung and Campbell* (New York: Peter Lang Publishing, 1994), p. 117.

remarkably similar to the Hindu rite, in which the eldest son consigns his father's body to the flames, that his spirit may be transported to the celestial world of the Fathers, where the father's soul will dwell in bliss with the entire male lineage. In the final scene of *Jedi*, Yoda, Ben Kenobi, and Darth Vader return as spirits who appear before Luke. Darth Vader has been transformed into Luke's young father Skywalker, the pupil of Ben Kenobi, and Ben Kenobi is beside his spiritual master Yoda. This patrilineage now includes Luke, its living representative, who is shown by the appearance of the 'fathers' that he belongs to an objective Jedi tradition that he cannot claim egoistically for himself.[24]

Thus, the transformative effect of fire and the well-intentioned love of one's son can bring ultimate liberation to a wayward father. The recognition here of a *parampara*, or a lineage comprised of spiritual masters and disciples, like the ones found in India, is also significant. *Star Wars* again points to truths found in Vedic literature. Using fire as a purificatory agent, teachers in well-established disciplic successions have spiritually purged innumerable souls throughout the centuries. In colourful initiation and marriage ceremonies, and through fire sacrifices involving the Vedic god Agni, Indian *sadhus* have for millennia helped people move forward in their spiritual quest. Western mystics refer to this use of blazing flames as *calcinatio*, an alchemical process of transformation through fire. An image of Luke near the end of *Return of the Jedi*, standing by the funeral pyre of his father, could be that of a Hindu boy, watching his father go to the land of the ancestors. But, more, it could be an initiation ceremony, where boy turns to man. It could also be Rama, watching Sita go through her trial by fire, to test her chastity. Ultimately, the auspicious fire is a symbol, a representation, of something greater, of transformation and love. For fire alone cannot make Vader all he should have been, and Rama's subjects were not appeased by Sita's fire ordeal, nor were Rama and Sita. It is love, and only love, that transforms Vader in the end, and which reunites Sita and Rama in the celestial Ayodhya.

---

24 See the 'At the Movies' reviews by Alfred Collins in *The San Francisco Jung Institute Library Journal*, Volume 4, Number 3, 1983, p. 55.

3

THE PERSONALITY OF GODHEAD: A FORCE TO BE RECKONED WITH

'I put the Force into the movie in order to try to awaken a certain kind of spirituality in young people – more a belief in God than a belief in any particular religious system. I wanted to make it so that young people would begin to ask questions about the mystery. Not having enough interest in the mysteries of life to ask the question, "Is there a God or is there not a God?" – that is for me the worst thing that can happen.'
–George Lucas, *TIME* Magazine

Toward the beginning of the first *Star Wars* film, Luke manages a narrow escape from the deadly Sand People. He accomplishes this with the help of the Merlin-like Obi-Wan Kenobi, a gifted Jedi Knight who initially tells Luke about the Force in passing. As Luke's curiosity is aroused, Obi-Wan explains some details, informing him that it is from the Force that the Jedi Knights get their power. He further explains that this mysterious Force is pure energy – that it penetrates and surrounds everything that exists, and that it holds the galaxy together. It can be accessed by all that is good – Luke learns that he must put aside lust, anger, greed, fear, and aggression, the usual meanness of the world, in order to feel the Force and to make use of its energies. He opens himself up to it by communing with nature – by just 'being'.

In *The Phantom Menace*, we also learn that the Force has a 'will' of its own. Will, of course, is a function of intelligence, which, in turn, implies consciousness and personality. The personal aspect of the

Force is highlighted in *Return of the Jedi*, where Yoda tells us that the Force is his 'ally', and alludes to 'the Force's love'. Thus, in *Star Wars,* the Force is a slightly impersonal expression of a personal divinity. At times, it also appears to be a form of pure energy. In this chapter we will look at various possibilities of Indic influence – is the Force personal, impersonal, or a mystic potency of some kind, and what do Vaishnava texts say about these three aspects of Godhead?

In conceiving the Force, Lucas brought to bear a wide range of influences, everything from his Christian upbringing to Casteneda's 'Life Force' concept, which is peppered throughout his published Don Juan explorations. Campbell, it has been argued, favoured a highly impersonal view of the Supreme, and this was incorporated into Lucas's Force as well. Taoism, too, played a role in Lucas's construction – in *The Phantom Menace*, we see Qui-Gon Jinn (played by Liam Neeson) emphasising the 'feel, don't think' component of Jedi philosophy, which is fundamentally Taoist. Qui-Gon Jinn's very name hints at where Lucas was going with this character – a *jinn* is a highly accomplished mystic, and Qui-Gon is an obvious take-off on Qi-gong, or Chi-kung ('energy-work'), referring to the *chi*, or vital energy, of Taoist philosophy. There is also a sort of cosmotheism, or pantheism, that makes the Force smack of Taoist teachings – the idea of seeing God in the universe, or in nature. In this sense, the Force might even be identified with the Indic idea of *dharma*, a word that is sometimes defined as 'a thing's essence', or 'its essential nature' – the *dharma* of water, for example, is liquidity.

The idea that the Force has positive and negative sides is reminiscent of another important aspect of Taoism and *dharma* – the unity of the world of opposites. In China, this is represented by the famous Tai Chi symbol of yin and yang, a circle that is half light and half dark. Taoism teaches that the dichotomy between these two is illusory, and that a practitioner must learn to balance each of these opposite dimensions of life.[1] In Indic thought, this is described as Bhedabhed, or unity

---

1   St. Augustine argues that negative qualities do not actually exist, since they are not positive expressions of reality. They are temporary, like a bad dream. To make this more clear: evil, he says, is merely the absence of good, as darkness is merely the absence of light. Flooding an environment with infinite light – if an infinite amount of light can be imagined – would disallow any darkness from engulfing that area. Similarly, for one who is fully absorbed in God, evil cannot exist. See Ed Mylow, trans., *The Collected Works of St. Augustine* (New York: Prower Press,

in diversity. This can also be understood on the level of the psyche. As Jungian psychologist Steven Galipeau writes:

> [This has] important psychological implications, especially if the Force is seen in terms of the collective unconscious. In the hands of a creative personality, relationship with the collective unconscious can have a positive effect as it has through great religious figures like Moses, Christ, and Buddha. It can also have a destructive effect when a person (like Hitler, for example) connects to the darker dimensions of collective psychology and has the ability to influence people accordingly.[2]

In *Star Wars,* however, the light and dark dimensions of the Force are represented as diametrically opposed and irreconcilable, and one must choose between them. In this sense, the Force engenders a more dualistic conception, like that of Gnosticism, or Zoroastrianism, where the lines between good and evil are clearly drawn. One must go toward the light, veering away from the darkness. In the Upanishads, it is said, 'Lead me from untruth to truth. Lead me from darkness to light. Lead me from death to immortality.' This is a prayer that would have had meaning for Luke Skywalker. It essentially asks to be saved from the dark side of the Force – to be established in the light of the Force's positive purifying energies. In this sense, the Force can ultimately be seen as an all-good spiritual energy that is filtered through positive and negative projections of consciousness. That is, as the ground of all being, it is inherently good. But it is seen as having various flavours or colours – good and bad – according to the individuals who relate to it.

Overall, the Force seems to be a divine energy field woven into the very fabric of the universe, sometimes acting as a personal God but more often coming across as something quite abstract.

Interestingly, some view this impersonal, abstract quality of the Force as an indication that Lucas was influenced by Eastern mysticism. Christian writers,[3] especially, have argued that the Force could

---

1965), p. 65. This is the Hindu view as well – where there is Godhead, there can be no nescience.

2   See Steven A. Galipeau, *The Journey of Luke Skywalker: An Analysis of Modern Myth and Symbol* (Chicago: Open Court, 2001), p. 36.

3   For example, see John Bradley Snyder, 'The Force of *Star Wars:* Is Luke Skywalker Jesus?', in *Report From the Star Wars Generation*, Volume 2, Number 1, July 1993, where he writes about the views of Marty Helgeson, a spokesperson for *Christian Science Fiction Fandom*: 'Marty didn't buy the Christian metaphor. He told me that

not have come from Western religion. They say that believers in the Judeo-Christian and Islamic traditions, *unlike followers of Eastern religions*, acknowledge a personal God. The Force, therefore, *must be based on Eastern thought* – for people in the East tend to view God as largely impersonal.

The premise here is simply not true, but before we explain why this is so, let us look more closely at just what Western critics think of Eastern thought.

A brief journey through any Internet search engine – typing in words like 'Star Wars', 'The Force', 'Hinduism', and 'impersonal vs. personal' – reveals a Western prejudice toward India's 'New Age' spirituality, claiming it has monistic leanings and a 'depersonalised' Godhead. For example, Eternal Ministries, Inc., a Christian site sponsored by evangelist Ron Bigalke, Jr., offers its readers an article called 'Eastern Mysticism'. This article contends that, 'Among [Eastern] mystics, God is not the personal Creator of the Bible. Mysticism states that there is an impersonal god-force (as in *Star Wars*) – the "force" or "God within"'.[4]

Faithworks, an on-line Christian magazine, gives us an article called 'Transgalactic Truth' by Sarah Diffenderfer. Here we learn that 'The Force is not God. The Force is impersonal; God is personal . . . No

---

"if one takes the Force seriously, it seems to represent Eastern religions, or a more pantheistic god". Marty thought that *Star Wars* presupposes an impersonal god, who is a force like gravity, rather than a personal god, like the one in Christianity.' Also see R. Albert Mohler, 'Faith vs. the Force', in *The World*, Volume 14, Number 20, 22 May 1999, where he says that 'the mythological structure of *Star Wars* is primarily indebted to the Eastern religions' and that 'we must not confuse Christian faith with the Force', for one is personal and the other is impersonal. The Internet is an invaluable resource in this regard: click on any worthwhile search engine and type in the words 'the Force' and 'Christianity'. Numerous articles and Web sites show up, each proclaiming in its own way that the Force is indebted to the impersonalism of Eastern religion – and is thereby different than Christianity, which claims to be the sole proponent of a personal God.

Regarding Christianity and *Star Wars*, also see Frank Allnut, *The Force of Star Wars* (1977), of which Snyder's article, listed above, is merely a review. Allnut sees in *Star Wars* a metaphor for the Christian tradition: for Allnut, God is 'the true Force'; Obi-Wan is Jesus and, sometimes, the Holy Spirit; Luke represents the Hebrew Christians, whereas Solo represents the Gentile Christians; Princess Leia is the Church, or Israel; Emperor Palpatine is Satan; and Darth Vader is Judas Iscariot. The book makes interesting reading and is a refreshingly light-hearted approach by a Christian author.

4   This can be found at www.eternalministries.org/articles/eastern_mystic1.html. Accessed 27 September 2010.

doubt there is a large dose of Eastern thought in *Star Wars*.'[5] Another article, entitled, 'Neopaganism, Feminism, and the New Polytheism', written by Norman L. Geisler, was published on-line in the *Christian Research Institute Journal*. Geisler writes: 'Hinduism has long sported a belief in one ultimate impersonal deity ("Brahman") with millions of personal gods as lower manifestations of it. It is at this point that the pantheistic polytheism of neo-paganism significantly overlaps with the New Age movement. George Lucas's *Star Wars* "religion of the Jedi" is a significant example.'[6]

To cite only one more instance of this Western chauvinism run amok, www.faithnet.org.uk sought to enlighten its readers in an essay called 'Religious Themes in the *Star Wars* Saga'. Here, we read, '[In Christianity] God is not an impersonal energy field but a personal Being. . . . In Islam, Allah is also seen as a personal being in a similar way. However, in Hinduism the Supreme Being Brahman is more like the Force in Star Wars. Although Brahman is sometimes referred to as having personal qualities it is often described using impersonal terms.'[7]

The point should be clear: Western thinkers, particularly Western religionists, view Hinduism as largely impersonalistic, and they also see the impersonalism of the Force as a direct result of Hindu influence. While I concur that the Force has certain Eastern characteristics, it is not for the reasons our Christian writers might think. Eastern conceptions of the Divine are not only impersonal but personal as well, as we shall see, and, more, 'the personality of Godhead' eclipses or supercedes the impersonal dimension.

It should be pointed out, perhaps as an aside, that we in the West, too, tend to think of God in terms of an otherworldly Force, as an abstraction more than as a person. Our religions teach that He is not a person in the usual sense. Rather, He transcends personhood, at least as it is commonly understood. Not only do we veer away from the idea that God is a person but we are taught to avoid anthropomorphism as well. In other words, we are uncomfortable assigning a form of any kind to God, what to speak of acknowledging His identity as

5   This article was no longer on-line as of 27 September 2010.
6   This can be found at www.iclnet.org/pub/resources/text/cri/cri-jrnl/web/crj0143a.html. Accessed 27 September 2010.
7   This article is no longer on-line, but is available through Google's Wayback Archive at web.archive.org/web/20050310045846/www.faithnet.org.uk/KS4/Religion+in+the+Media/starwars.htm. Accessed 27 September 2010.

a person. For us, God is totally Other; He is beyond anything we can conceive. 'For the spirit of the Lord fills the whole universe', say the Jewish prophets, 'and holds all things together...' (*Wisdom* 1.7); 'God is spirit' (*John* 4.24); 'God is light' (1 *John* 1.5) – there are many such statements, and each could be a reference to the Force in Lucas's films. These are Judeo-Christian descriptions of the Supreme Godhead, and they clearly lean toward the impersonal. And yet, despite this biblical tendency toward impersonalism, Western religion, we know, ultimately reveres a personal God. This work will show that the religions of India, particularly Vaishnavism, do the same.

Of course, it is quite natural, especially in Western countries, to think of Christianity as soon as one thinks religion. Indeed, which *Star Wars* fan who saw *The Phantom Menace* did not think of Jesus when we learned that Anakin Skywalker, soon to become Darth Vader, was born 'of a virgin'? In a 2005 *Rolling Stone* interview, however, Lucas is quite clear that viewers should not have such limited vision:

> *Rolling Stone*: Anakin has no father. Do Christ overtones –
> Lucas: Oh, it's not just Christ. Christ is one of a long, long, long line of heroes who don't have fathers. . .
> *Rolling Stone*: Can you name a few others?
> Lucas: There are a lot of Greek gods who came down [and impregnated mortal women], and so the heroes didn't have fathers. Whether it's Hindu, Chinese, or Middle Eastern, all the . . . heroes didn't have fathers. The fathers were the gods.[8]

Having been trained by Campbell, Lucas couldn't be more aware that the heroes of the *Mahabharata* were all fathered by divine beings, and so his allusion to a virgin birth in *The Phantom Menace* has implications far beyond Christ.

It should also be said at the outset that Lucas is purposely vague in his depiction of the Force. This is ostensibly to accommodate members of all faiths – so they can potentially find something in the Force to which they can relate. He hints at something higher, a mystery behind the universe, but tells us little more. Thus, even those without religion can view the Force as 'the animating power of life', a sort of Casteneda-flavoured energy found at the core of all things – without any reference

---

8   See Gavin Edwards, 'George Lucas, The *Rolling Stone* Interview: The Cult of Darth Vader', in *Rolling Stone* magazine, Issue 975, 2 June 2005, p. 46.

to God. From Lucas's perspective, this is a good beginning, because it gets people to look beyond their everyday life, to admit that there is more to reality than meets the eye. As we shall see, however, non-spiritual definitions of the Force, while a good starting point, necessarily fall short.

The Missing Force

Modern science recognises an all-pervasive energy at the core of existence – a Force – and divides it into four distinct categories: first, there is Gravitational Force. The weakest of the four, it has the power of attraction and can employ this power over large distances. The second division of energy, known as Electromagnetic Force, is more powerful, though it operates within the smaller domain of atoms and molecules, or those particles possessing electrical charges, which are divided into positive and negative. Next, we have the Weak Nuclear Force – this is the source of radioactivity, often found in nuclear decay processes that include neutrinos. The fourth category of energy is called the Strong Nuclear Force, or the force that allows particles to combine, to form solid matter. Together, these forces inform the theoretical dynamics of the material universe. However, they do not account for the subtle nuances of life itself – they do not account for consciousness – and so scientists still search for a Unifying Force, a Fifth Force, something that speaks to the larger issues underlying the mysteries of mind and heart. Thus, the four forces of material energy, while interesting, cannot be identified with the Force of Lucas's films, which clearly has a transcendent quality.

In an illuminating article, entitled, 'Bhakti: The Perfect Science', Dr. O. B. L. Kapoor – who is both a scientist and a religious scholar – traces the missing force of science to the principle of Shaktiman, i.e., that all energy (*shakti*) must have a source based on energy:

> The physicist, trying to discover the real nature of matter, found that the smallest piece of matter, smaller than even the point of a pin, was composed of millions of electrons. He tried to study the nature of electrons and found that they were 'disembodied charges of electricity', that is, electricity existing apart from matter. But though they were disembodied charges of electricity, they seemed to behave sometimes like a particle and sometimes like a wave. Eddington, therefore, suggested

that they should be called 'wavicles' to indicate their dual character, but their real nature remained unknown. If they were not any *thing* charged with electricity, but electricity itself, the question remained, what ultimately is electricity? The reply was that it is energy or *shakti*. Energy, it was further explained, was a process. But energy or *shakti* always pertains to the Shaktiman or possessor of energy, and a process is always the process of some *thing* moving or acting or doing something. What is that which possesses the energy? What is that thing of which the energy is a process? The physicist has not been able to answer these questions. And he will never be able to answer them, for he has reduced everything to energy, and nothing else remains to which he may point in answer to these questions. The real nature of matter thus remains unknown to him. He cannot say anything about it except that it is 'he knows not what'. Eddington says, 'Something unknown is doing we do not know what – that is what our theory amounts to.'[9]

If Kapoor had his way, the Fifth Force of the universe might be called Quantum Brahman,[10] which merges the concepts of physics with their underlying spiritual basis. In Eastern thought, Brahman is the eternal metaphysical foundation of the world we see around us. As such, it is a religious counterpart to what science would call the fundamental storehouse of variegated energies. The energies themselves are called *shakti*. The phenomena of energy and its enigmatic source is well known. Scientists such as Einstein, Eddington, James Jeans, and J. B. S. Haldane have already recognised this.[11] So Kapoor does not stand alone. John Boslough, in his best-selling book, *Stephen Hawking's Universe*, brings to light the fact that such things were known in India for millennia:

Recently, some physicists have come to see a relationship between their work and the ideas behind Eastern mysticism. They believe that

9   O. B. L. Kapoor, '*Bhakti*: The Perfect Science', in *Back to Godhead* Magazine, Number 53, 1973, pp. 17-21.

10 Kapoor used this phrase in a personal conversation with me. Coincidentally, it is also used by Robert E. Wilkinson as the title of his enlightening 1996 article (www2.eu.spiritweb.org), in which he analyses Quantum Theory in relation to Vedic Cosmology. See Robert E. Wilkinson, 'The Quantum Brahman', (c) 1994-2001 by SpiritWeb Org., Switzerland and America. *SpiritWeb* is no longer available, but the article can still be accessed at www.al-qiyamah.org/pdf_files/quantum_brahman_%28spiritweb.org%29.pdf (accessed 28 September 2010).

11 See Kapoor, op. cit.

the paradoxes, odds, and probabilities as well as the observer-dependence of Quantum Mechanics have been anticipated in the writings of Hinduism, Buddhism, and Taoism. Quantum Mechanics, these… physicists are fond of pointing out, is really only a rediscovery of Shiva or Mahadeva, the Hindu horned god of destruction and cosmic dissolution.

Shiva…takes several forms. One of them is Nataraja, the four-armed Lord of the Cosmic Dance pictured dancing on a prostrate demon. The god's dance symbolises the perpetual process of universal creation and destruction. Matter has no substance at all; it is merely the dynamic, rhythmic gyration of energy coming and going.[12]

This energy, again, is known as *shakti*, which, in the material world, expresses itself through three qualities, called *gunas*: *Tamas* (ignorance), *Sattva* (goodness), and *Rajas* (passion). The word *guna* means 'rope', implying that the various permutations of these three bind us to the world of matter – they tie us to conditional responses and further implicate us in material life. Briefly, the mode of ignorance consists of foolishness, madness, illusion, inertia, indolence, and sleep; the mode of goodness is characterised by relative purity, illumination, happiness, and freedom from sinful reactions; the mode of passion involves uncontrollable desire and longing, over-endeavor, greed, and attachment to the fruits of one's labour. The *Bhagavad-gita* explains these modes at some length, showing how they condition and bind the soul according to his individual tastes and needs. Each soul is unique, and so the modes are applied in different ways for each individual.

'The function of *Tamas* [the heavy, cold, or opaque principle of inertia] is to veil consciousness', says Sir John Woodroffe, in an insightful lecture about *shakti* and its various manifestations, 'of Sattva [the light, warm, or transparent principle of intelligibility] to reveal it.'[13] *Rajas*, the active, balancing principle – the thermostat, so to speak – determines how the other two will interact. These three states, which the person who is pure can perceive in his own inner being, are understood in many traditions: they are viewed as the destructive, creative, and the sustaining factors of the world; or the negative, positive, and reconciling forces whose dialectical action govern cause and effect.

---

12 John Boslough, *Stephen Hawking's Universe* (New York: Avon Books, 1985), p. 114.

13 See Sir John Woodroffe, *Shakti and Shakta: Essays and Addresses on the Shakta Tantrashastra*, 4th edition (Madras: Ganesh, 1951), p. 11.

Every particular form in the world we see around us is subject to, and is the consequence of, the interaction of these three forms of energy.[14] Clearly, in a *Star Wars* context, the mode of goodness leads to the positive side of the Force, whereas ignorance leads to the dark side. Passion, or the function that sparks one to action, will influence not only which way one goes, but the quality of action once one gets there.

Indic thought allows for Brahman, the metaphysical ground of all being, which is impersonal, and it also allows for Para-Brahman, or, as Kapoor called it, Shaktiman, the personal, energetic source of all *shakti* (energy). Lucas seems to accommodate both forms of Godhead as well. Descriptions of Brahman and Shaktiman fit in neatly with Lucas's portrayal of the Force. Even the conception of *shakti* has certain affinities with the Force, a subject to which we will soon return.

Bad Force/Good Force

But a problem arises. If the Force is identified with either impersonal or personal features of Godhead, how can the dark side of the Force have any substance? God, by definition, has no dark side. As St. Augustine said, 'Flooding an environment with infinite light – if an infinite amount of light can be imagined – would disallow any darkness from engulfing that area. Similarly, for one who is fully absorbed in God, evil cannot exist.'[15] So where does the dark side come from?

In the Gaudiya Vaishnava tradition, there is a certain negativity associated with the impersonal Absolute. For example, in Srila A. C. Bhaktivedanta Swami Prabhupada's translation of the *Ishopanishad*, Mantra Twelve, he offers an admonition against impersonalism: 'Those who are engaged in the worship of the gods enter into the darkest region of ignorance and still more so do the worshipers of the impersonal Absolute.'[16]

---

14 See Margaret Case, 'Shakti', in *Parabola: The Magazine of Myth and Tradition*, Volume XVII, Number 4, Winter 1992. The idea of 'passion' as a balancing kind of force is interesting from a *Star Wars* perspective: the Jedi await a powerful messiah-like personality who, they say, will bring 'balance' to the Force by his actions.

15 See note #1.

16 See *Sri Isopanisad*, trans., His Divine Grace A. C. Bhaktivedanta Swami Prabhupada (Los Angeles, California: Bhaktivedanta Book Trust, 1997, reprint). Another potentially negative aspect of the Force comes from the powers that one can develop by proximity: Vader, for example, is notably power-mad. He is able to control people's minds, to mentally move objects from here to there, levitate,

Vaishnava commentators say that impersonalists tend to fall into hellish consciousness because they deny God's ability to have personal features, implying that they have something that God does not. All of our greatest pleasures come from sensual experience, say the Vaishnavas, and God is not to be denied such pleasures. He can see, hear, speak, and love. In short, He can experience things as we do, but without the imperfections associated with a temporary and limited nature.

The *Ishopanishad* further informs us that God's impersonal feature is essentially an overwhelming white light, purely spiritual, and fully engulfing all who come in its path. It is composed of His personal bodily effulgence, which can be blinding, denying its viewers access to the personal form at its base. In Mantra Fifteen of this same Upanishadic text, the personified Vedas pray, 'O my Lord, sustainer of all that lives, Your real face is covered by Your orb of gold. Kindly remove that covering and exhibit Yourself to me, for I adore the Truth.' Vaishnava exegesis holds that the mysterious 'orb of gold' is the Lord's 'impersonal effulgence.' In Mantra Sixteen, we further read, 'O my Lord, O primeval philosopher, maintainer of the universe, O regulating principle, destination of pure souls, well-wisher of the progenitors of mankind, please remove the effulgence of Your transcendental rays so that I can see Your form of bliss. You are the eternal divine entity, and You are like the sun...'[17] For Vaishnavas, then, the impersonal aspect of the Lord is, in a sense, His dark side. For them – and, again, they are said to represent over 70% of Hindu India[18] – it is a less desirable manifestation. This is so not only because it is bereft of personal characteristics – characteristics that allow one to have an intimate relationship with God – but because it can actually interfere with the ability to relate to God's form.

---

and so on. The Indian equivalent would be *yogic siddhis*, or the mystic perfections associated with yoga. These are described in Chapter Three of Patanjali's *Yoga Sutras*. *Anima-siddhi*, for example, refers to the power by which one can become so small that he can enter into a stone. There is also the *siddhi* called *prapti*, or 'acquisition', wherein one can extend his hand anywhere and take whatever he likes. Another perfection is called *vasita*, by which one can control other people's minds. There are five additional *siddhis* as well. If a person has this much power over material nature, he may not only forget his quest for God – he may think he has become God. Such delusions of grandeur are what led to Vader's downfall, as they did to yogis throughout the ages.

17 Ibid.

18 See Klaus Klostermaier, *A Survey of Hinduism*, Second Edition (Albany, New York: State University of New York Press, 1994), p. 240.

Vaishnavas have at times gone still further, arguing that the entire impersonal enterprise is fundamentally suspect. They appeal not only to scripture but to reason. If God is an impersonal Force, they say, why is its most complex and highly developed emanation – man himself – distinctly personal? Drawing on Christian theology, they often ask us to reflect on what it means that we are made in God's image – is personal man made in the image of an impersonal God? They point to diversity in the cosmos – how could an impersonal Force create variety, something that exists apart from homogeneous impersonalism? Further, why would an impersonal Force create anything? Did this Force have desire, or the need for company? Was the Force just being creative? Does not creativity imply personality? Can an impersonal Force hear our prayers? Would it care? Would it relate to our sufferings? Does it have compassion?

Associated with the idea of God as an impersonal Force is the idea that one can merge with this Force. But the Vaishnavas question this as well: is it desirable to merge into a quantum of energy, to be dissolved into an amorphous void? Wouldn't the highest bliss, the ultimate attainment, be perfection in loving relationship, as opposed to forfeiting all that makes us individual people – character traits, identity, and unique behavior? Vaishnavas ask us to ponder these things, and to consider the folly of the impersonal conclusion.

This emphasis on personalism in relation to God is a fundamental teaching in the *Bhagavad-gita*. To be clear, the impersonal or monistic conception of the Supreme, or Brahman –wherein one envisions God as an inconceivable force, without form – is clearly a legitimate part of what the *Gita* teaches. But the idea of an abstract divinity is eclipsed by the idea of God as the Supreme Person. As Krishna Himself says in the *Gita* (7.24), 'Unintelligent people, who do not know Me perfectly, think that I, the Supreme God, was formless before and have now assumed this personality. Due to their small knowledge, they do not know My higher nature, which is imperishable and supreme.'

And yet, despite the *Gita*'s emphasis on God's personhood, in modern times the impersonalistic dimension of the *Gita* has become more popular, making its way into contemporary conceptions of Hinduism, and, in turn, into pop culture, as in movies like *Star Wars*. Teachers in the Vaishnava tradition suggest that the desire to depersonalise God comes, on a subliminal level, from the desire to avoid surrender. After all, if God is a person, then questions of submission and subservience come into play. If God is a formless abstraction, we can philosophise about Him without a sense of commitment, without the fear of having to acknowledge our duty to a higher being.

Krishna says, 'I am at the basis of the impersonal Brahman [the formless Absolute].' (*Gita*, 14.27) And when discussing the comparative value of the impersonal and the personal, He says, 'Those who focus their minds on My personal form, always engaged in worshiping Me with intense spiritual faith, are considered by Me to be most perfect.' (12.2) In other words, according to the *Gita* the conception of God as a person, to whom one may become devoted, is prior to and superiour to the conception of God as an impersonal force, into which one may merge.

Ultimately, Gaudiya Vaishnava philosophy says that all conceptions of God are included in the personal form of Sri Krishna. The impersonal Brahman, according to the tenets of Vaishnavism, is but an aspect of the Absolute, which by its very nature is endlessly qualified and perfect in unlimited ways. Vaishnavas dismiss the concept of the Absolute as merely impersonal, beyond all thought and speech. Such an Absolute cannot stand, they say, for it would cancel itself out. Our very language disallows it: even to say that Brahman is inexpressible or unthinkable is to say or think something about it.

Shankaracharya, an Eighth-century Indian philosopher, was among the first to emphasise the impersonal Absolute. While he accepted the undifferentiated Brahman as the sole category of existence, he failed to give a satisfactory explanation of the world of appearance, which implies distinct qualities (*vishesha*) in Brahman. In other words, how can a variegated world, with such diverse attributes, come from an undifferentiated Absolute? Impersonalist philosophers say that all variety in the material world is false and only the Supreme Brahman, or Spirit, is real. Vaishnavas counter that because the world emanates from Brahman, which is real, the world must also be real. For example, if a tree bears fruits, can anyone realistically claim that the tree is real but its fruits are not?

To sum up the Vaishnavas' personalist argument: to describe the Absolute as merely *nirvishesha*, or without distinct qualities and attributes, is to make Him imperfect by 'amputating' His divine limbs, as it were. Once we recognise the absolute, complete, and perfect nature of the Divine Being, we move beyond the philosophy of impersonalism. The Absolute Truth, say the Vaishnavas, is both personal and impersonal, or rather, it possesses infinite attributes and forms, including an impersonal dimension. According to the primary and general sense of the scriptures, at least as the Vaishnava reads them, the Absolute is essentially personal, because only in a personal Absolute, possessing infinite and inconceivable potencies, can the infinite forms of Godhead, including the impersonal Brahman, have their place.

Thus, contrary to what Western religionists – especially Christians – tend to think about Hinduism, the vast majority of the Hindu world views the Absolute as personal, though they acknowledge an impersonal aspect as well. But to see either God's personal or impersonal aspects as 'the dark side of the Force' is really a stretch of the imagination. This is so because, ultimately, both personal and impersonal are Divine, beyond good and evil. It is only when they are viewed in a comparative light that one is seen as inferior to the other. Otherwise, they are considered one and the same, beyond the dualities associated with dark and light. Rather, when God – whether personal or impersonal – manifests through His energies, or *shakti*, we see for the first time a legitimate distinction between good and bad, or light and dark. It is thus here that we may more accurately trace the Force of Lucas's films.

Yoga-Maya and Maha-Maya

If I had to choose one aspect of Indic philosophy that resonates most loudly with the idea of the Force – considering that the Force has both positive and negative, light and dark, components – I would have to opt for the principles of Yoga-Maya and Maha-Maya.

What is Maya? Briefly, it is the energy (*shakti*) of God. According to Vaishnava tradition, it is usually associated with the idea of illusory energy, and in the earliest Vedic texts it is defined as a type of magic. Originally, in the Vedic story of the churning of the milk ocean, Maya, or, more specifically, Maha-Maya, is depicted as a beautiful woman who deprives the demons of divine nectar. To extend the metaphor, Vaishnavas insist that if one flirts with her, one almost 'magically' loses one's clear vision and becomes disassociated with the reality of spiritual life. In other words, if one opts for materialism, one must bid adieu to the 'divine nectar' of ultimate reality.

This is the choice that confronts Luke Skywalker in *Star Wars*. He decides, of course, to give up the illusions associated with the dark side of the Force and to allow himself to be directed by the positive side, or, in Vaishnava terms, to be engulfed by Yoga-Maya instead of Maha-Maya. Interestingly, the qualities attributed to the dark and light sides of the Force seem to echo – almost point for point – Vaishnava descriptions of Maha-Maya and Yoga-Maya. To give but one example of each: the dark side in *Star Wars* is described as 'seductive'. Maha-Maya, in Puranic (the Puranas are also a form of sacred literature appended to the Vedas) and epic texts, is described in the same way. The light side is identified with 'reality'. This is the distinguishing quality of Yoga-Maya.

The word *maya* (translated as 'illusion') is interpreted by Vaishnavas as 'that which is not', implying that *maya* is 'that which does not truly exist'. And yet, it is also defined as 'that which is measurable'. Superficially, these two definitions appear contradictory. How can something be measurable if it does not exist?

Vaishnava texts explain that the material world exists, but it is temporary. Therefore, it exists like a dream – it has substance for some time, but eventually it fades. This speaks to the deep subject of reality and illusion: is something real if it is temporary, like a dream? In a sense it is, but, in another sense, it is not. So, when Maya is described as being 'that which is not', it refers to the underlying truth of material existence – that it does not endure, that it is temporary and limited. 'It is not' because it will soon fade into oblivion.

But Maya as 'that which is measurable' also pertains to material existence: only material things are measurable. Spiritual things are limitless, immeasurable by their very nature. Thus, both definitions of Maya point to the same truth – to the illusory, temporary, and limited character of material existence.

Maya, then, refers to illusion, deceit, fraud, deception – ultimately, it refers to a life divorced from God. Darth Vader, from a Vaishnava point of view, is engulfed by Maya – Maha-Maya – for he not only embodies the unsavoury qualities mentioned above, but his life revolves around conquering and controlling other people, the hallmark sign of one who is overtaken by the darker side of Maya. As the *Gita* (Chapter Sixteen) says, 'The demoniac person thinks: "So much wealth do I have today, and I will gain more according to my schemes. So much is mine now, and it will increase in the future, more and more. He is my enemy, and I have killed him, and my other enemies will also be killed. I am the Lord of everything. I am the enjoyer. I am perfect, powerful, and happy. I am the richest man, surrounded by aristocratic relatives. There is none so powerful and happy as I am." [The demoniac are] bewildered by ego, strength, pride, lust and anger, and they become envious of the Supreme Person. [They are] consumed by arrogance, conceit, harshness, and ignorance.' If this doesn't describe Vader, the epitome of the dark side of the Force, what does? Of course, demoniac nature manifests in degrees, and Vader is admittedly an extreme example. According to Vaishnava texts, all things material are representations of Maya, and can ultimately lead to a Vader-like mentality – *unless* one learns to use the accouterments of the material world in a godly way, to spiritualise them by using them in *seva*, or Divine service.

If the world of Maya is used in this more spiritual way, it becomes Yoga-Maya, that is to say, it becomes a positive, uplifting form of this same energy. After all, all energy originally comes from God – it is composed of the same substance. Vaishnava sages explain this as follows. Just as a sharp knife can be used in a harmful way, to kill someone, or in a positive way, as when a trained surgeon uses it to save a patient's life, so all of God's energies can be used in one of two ways. Scriptures, saints and sages of the past, and one's guru are all helpful in discerning just how to use this energy properly, with optimum spiritual intent. When so used, this energy is known as Yoga-Maya, and it allows one to have an intimate exchange with the Lord.

'But why Yoga-Maya?' one might ask. 'What is the *illusion* aspect of this Divine energy?' Vaishnava texts inform us that intimacy with God is impossible unless one is covered by a certain type of illusion, for how can an embodied person be intimate with an unlimited being? This particular form of illusion, or Yoga-Maya, allows transcendental exchange, forging a meeting between the limited and the unlimited, bringing one to a liminal border wherein one can relish association with the Divine. It is a special spiritual potency of which material illusion is only a perverted reflection. The literature of the Vaishnavas tells us that the spiritual realm contains all components of the material realm – but in their pure, original form. Accordingly, material illusion is the unnatural counterpart to a form of spiritual illusion that exists in God's kingdom, and it is this primordial potency that allows us to come into contact with God. This is called Yoga-Maya. To sum up: whereas material illusion (Maha-Maya) brings us down, spiritual illusion (Yoga-Maya) brings us up.

Putting a Face on the Force

Indian scriptures and iconography give us tangible images of both Maha-Maya and Yoga-Maya, and, in so doing, allow us to visualise the dark and light sides of the Force. A highly revered Vaishnava text, the *Brahma-samhita* (5.44), elaborates on the nature of Maha-Maya, identifying her as the Queen of the Material Cosmos:

> The external potency [of the Lord], known as Maha-Maya, who is of the nature of the shadow of the *chit* [or knowledge] potency, is worshiped by all people as Durga, the creating, preserving, and destroying agency of this mundane world. I adore the primeval Lord, Krishna, in accordance with whose will Durga conducts herself.

Here the presiding deity of the material world is identified as Durga, whom Vaishnavas understand to be a manifestation of Kali. In Indian tradition Kali is a goddess whose visual imagery is frightening, with protruding tongue, raw nakedness, a garland of human heads, spear, sword, and bloodthirsty stance, ready to kill. She is worshipped under different names and manifestations, such as Uma, Mahadevi, the Divine Mother, and so on. But what is interesting here is its correlation with the *Star Wars* material – she is merely the dark side, the 'shadow' of Ultimate reality; 'knowledge', or *chit* potency, is the domain of the Jedi Knights – soldiers who are immersed in Yoga-Maya. They are servants of the primeval Lord, or the positive side of the Force.

In India, Durga is identified with cosmic energy. She is seen as *prakriti* ('material nature') and, once again, *maya* ('illusion'). Indeed, two of her more popular names are Mulaprakriti ('the embodiment of Primordial Matter') and Maha-Maya ('the Great Illusion'). This is significant. As Krishna says in *Bhagavad-gita* (9.10): 'The material energy [*prakriti*] is working under My direction, O Arjuna, and it is producing all moving and unmoving beings.' Stated simply, all material existence is represented by Durga, of which Krishna is in complete control. When one doesn't acknowledge this simple fact, say Vaishnava texts, Durga becomes Maha-Maya – the Great Illusion.

Unaware of this, say the Vaishnavas, people prefer to worship Durga as opposed to the Supreme Godhead. Usually, they beseech her for material goods, or for power, much in the same way that one might be enamoured by the sensual pleasures associated with the dark side of the Force. As Krishna says in the *Gita* (7.20, 23): 'Those whose minds are distorted by material desires surrender unto the *devas* [which includes all gods or goddesses other than the Supreme Being]. . . Men of small intelligence worship the many gods, and the fruits of such worship are limited and temporary. Those who worship the gods, go to their planets, but My devotees ultimately reach My supreme planet.' For Vaishnavas, Durga is counted amongst the gods, and her 'planets' are comprised of the material world. In this sense, she is the 'Mother' of material creation. It is interesting in this connection that the words 'mother' (Sanskrit: *mata*) and 'matter' are etymologically connected through the Latin root. So the Goddess's identity with material nature is alluded to in the terminology itself.

Worshipping Krishna, on the other hand, involves eternal goals, knowledge, and pure devotion. One must see beyond the temporary fruits of sensuality and material pleasure, say the Vaishnavas, and aspire after more lasting spiritual pursuits. If one does this, one becomes engulfed in Yoga-Maya, having risen beyond the inferiour energy of the Lord (known as Maha-Maya). This, indeed, is the goal of the Jedi.

Yoga-Maya is personified as a beautiful woman, often with eight arms and quite alluring. She manifests as Krishna's sister and is the embodiment of auspiciousness. She resembles Lakshmi, the Goddess of Fortune, who offers opportunity and blessings. In another manifestation, she is Purnamasi, a warm, elderly cowherd maiden, who guides Vrindadevi, a young cowherd girl, in making Radha and Krishna comfortable in their forest retreat. She is saintly, beautiful, and dependable. In contrast to the vicious, heart-rending image of Durga, she is soft and loving. Clearly, she represents all that is good and nurturing.[19]

In *Star Wars*, the dark side embodies gross material qualities, such as selfishness and arrogance, as we have mentioned, while the light side is more often associated with characteristics of the spirit, such as knowledge and compassion. If Darth Vader has flirted with Maha-Maya, producing a hateful personality who, unwittingly, does himself as much harm as he willfully commits toward others, Luke Skywalker is an obedient pupil of Yoga-Maya, imbibing the finer qualities allied with a pious life.

---

19 For more on Yoga-Maya's manifestation as Purnamasi, see Donna Wulff, *Drama as a Mode of Religious Realization: The Vidagdhmadhava of Rupa Gosvami* (Chico, California: Scholars Press, 1984); and also see Amala-bhakta Dasa, *The Life of Tulasi Devi* (Sandy Ridge, North Carolina, The Bhaktivedanta Archives, 1997).

The Lord in the Heart

The one aspect of the Force that still needs to be addressed is the idea of 'The Lord in the Heart', which overlaps with the *Star Wars* concept of 'midi-chlorians', as we shall see.

In *Star Wars*, the Force sometimes seems synonymous with instincts, with listening to one's own inner voice. Of course, some people are more in touch with that voice than others. Where does this voice come from? Is it our conditional responses to the external world? Or is it something from another dimension? Is it material or Divine? Jedis are supposedly a race of beings who hear it in their heart of hearts; they are guided by the Force, who communicates with them in no uncertain terms. In theology, one's conscience or inner voice is often identified with God – but it can also be one's own conditioning. Generally, the world's religious traditions teach that one needs to cultivate an inner relationship with the Divine, and an inner awareness of how God communicates, before one can perceive God's voice in unmistakable tones. A pure soul can know God's communication by intuition. Otherwise, it is vague and uncertain. This is one of the many confounding question of religion: how does a practitioner know when God is speaking to him, or when the voice is one's own subliminal desires, one's own conditioning? Sometimes it is hard to tell.

In *The Phantom Menace*, Master Qui-Gon explains to young Anakin Skywalker that those people who recognise this voice from within are called Jedis. Further, he explains, their communion with the mystical voice inside themselves can be explained scientifically. He tells young Anakin about midi-chlorians – a microscopic life form that resides in living cells. For those with a high concentration of these midi-chlorians in their blood, the voice of the Force is loud and clear.

Anakin is shocked. He finds it hard to believe that these living creatures, however small, exist inside his own body.

Qui-Gon assures him that this is quite natural, and further explains that we are symbionts with the midi-chlorians, that we are all life forms co-existing for mutual advantage. Without midi-chlorians, he tells him, life would not exist. And we would be unable to communicate with the Force. Midi-chlorians are like bridges – they connect us with the higher realm. Qui-Gon explains to Anakin that when he (Anakin) learns to quiet his mind, he will hear the Force inside of himself, for his midi-chlorian count is higher than anyone else's.

This idea of the Force communicating with us through midi-chlorians has much in common with the Vaishnava idea of the Supersoul, or the Lord in the Heart. Interestingly, Vedic texts give much information about the Paramatma, or Supersoul – a form of God that exists not only in everyone's heart, but in every atom, and between every atom. This is where one might locate the Force as well. Yoda explains to Luke that we are luminous beings, spiritual in essence. He says that we are not matter, which is crude – we are subtle, consisting of a higher spiritual nature. But, more, he tells him that the Force is made of this subtle substance (Brahman?) too, and that it is present everywhere – in us, between us, in trees, in rocks, and so on. In terms of Vaishnava theology, this is clearly the Supersoul. And since we have already explored the Force in relation to Brahman and Shaktiman, let us now look at Brahman and Shaktiman in relation to the Supersoul, for these three together comprise the Vaishnava view of God. We can then see what, if anything, these three have to do with the Force.

Brahman, Paramatma, and Shaktiman

Vaishnava theology recognises three aspects of God: Brahman, Paramatma (Supersoul), and Bhagavan (Shaktiman) – or, more descriptively, the Lord's impersonal feature, His all-pervading localised aspect, and His supreme personhood. The three primary attributes of God – *sat* (being, or eternality), *chit* (full cognition), and *ananda* (unending bliss) – correspond to these three aspects. Bhagavan realisation represents the sum total of all God's qualities. Thus Krishna, Bhagavan Himself, has a distinct place in this stratification of divinity.

Brahman realisation (an understanding of God as an impersonal, mystical force) is a fundamental view of God, as we have already mentioned. This path is appealing to empiricists who are inclined to spirituality in general. By a process called *gyana-yoga,* a traditional discipline that focuses on the development of the intellect, one can achieve full Brahman realisation, or awareness of eternality (*sat*) in relation to God. Most current forms of yoga and religiosity bring adherents to this basic spiritual perception, at best. Persons who follow this path are known as *gyana-yogis.* Their quest for truth brings them to the Lord's personal effulgence, called the Brahmajyoti, into which they may merge after death. There is a tendency, however, to fail in this pursuit, because the vast impersonalism of eternality impels one to long for natural, interpersonal relationships. And so the practitioner may be born again to continue on the spiritual path.

After lifetimes of frustration, trying to achieve God realisation through Brahman, a *gyana-yogi* may raise himself to the next level and thus become an *ashtanga-yogi,* practicing the eightfold path of yoga as outlined in the *Yoga-sutras* compiled by Patanjali in the Second century BC. If such a yogi is successful, he may realise the localised form of God, who, again, is in every heart as well as within every atom. This manifestation of the Lord is called Paramatma, or Supersoul. Krishna elaborates on the Supersoul's nature in the *Bhagavad-gita*: 'He is the source of light in all luminous objects. He is beyond the darkness of matter and is unmanifested. He is knowledge, He is the object of knowledge, and He is the goal of knowledge....' (13.18) Krishna says that the Lord who dwells within is the source of the three modes of nature – goodness, passion, and ignorance – and is thus not affected by them. This Supersoul, says Krishna, is beyond the scope of the material senses. (13.13-17) He must be perceived by other means – by spiritual intuition. Upon realising Him, one achieves awareness of more than immortality: one attains the essence of spiritual knowledge (*chit*) as well.

Vaishnava teachers have attempted to clarify the position of Paramatma, the Supersoul, in the following way: as the sun may appear reflected in countless jewels, so the Lord within every atom may appear like many, though He is one, existing (in His original form) in the spiritual world.

An inherent danger in pursuing the path of Paramatma is misidentification of one's individual soul with the Supersoul, or the Lord in the heart. In *Star Wars,* this is translated as being seduced by the dark side of the Force. In other words, if one begins to forget the supreme position of God, trying to exploit God's energies for his own selfish ends, then one again falls into material life. This was Vader's miscalculation, and the danger that faced Luke. Indeed, there are Hindu writers[20] who predictably misinterpret the Force of *Star Wars* as somehow

---

20 One example should suffice: see Ashok Kumar Malhotra, *An Introduction to Yoga Philosophy* (Burlington, VT.: Ashgate Publishing Company, 2001), p. 97, where he makes the common Hindu error of identifying the life-force, or *prana*, with the Supreme life-force, or God, and then, by extension, identifying *prana* with the Force in Star Wars. Other than this, Malhotra's chapter 'The *Star Wars* Connection' is extremely insightful. He begins this section by saying, 'On examining themes and the message of *Star Wars,* I realised that Lucas has been greatly influenced by

representing *prana*, or the 'life-energy' of the individual soul, specifically because they misidentify this individual soul with the Lord in the heart.

The Vedic literature seeks to help practitioners avoid this danger by offering the following analogy. The Supersoul and the individual soul are like two green birds sitting in the same green tree. Because they are all of one colour, they may seem to merge, and it could become difficult to distinguish one from the other. But such a mistake would constitute dismal failure on the path of Paramatma realisation. All three – the Supersoul, the individual soul, and the tree – are quite different.

To extend the analogy, Vaishnava sages often say that the individual soul is enjoying the fruits of the tree, while the Supersoul stands by and watches, waiting for His companion to give up the pursuit of temporary pleasures. This, of course, may take many lifetimes. But when the living being finally turns to the Supersoul in love and devotion, the Supersoul agrees to direct him and purify him. At that time, He guides the living being from within, bringing him into the association of a pure devotee, one who is accomplished in Shaktiman realisation. When this occurs, one moves to the final stage of God consciousness.

Shaktiman realisation centres around developing a relationship with Bhagavan, the Sanskrit equivalent of 'God'. The word *bhagavan* literally means 'He who possesses all opulences in their most complete form'. The sages of the East have identified six primary opulences: strength, beauty, wealth, fame, knowledge, and renunciation. Only the Supreme Personality of Godhead possesses these qualities in full. One who becomes adept at worshiping Him becomes aware of eternity and knowledge – as in Brahman and Paramatma realisation – and develops a profound sense of transcendental bliss (*ananda*) as well. The person on the path of Shaktiman realisation attains intimacy with God, becoming absorbed in His personhood in a deep and meaningful way. Thus, Vaishnavism teaches that realisation of Bhagavan is the perfection of *gyana-yoga* and *ashtanga-yoga*, and, indeed, of all spiritual pursuits.

To make the three levels of God realisation more understandable, later Vaishnava commentators have supplied the following apt analogy. Three simple villagers and their guide are at a railway station,

---

the central ideas and mythology of Hinduism. His genius lies in his assimilation of the crucial ideas of the *Yoga Sutras*, the *Bhagavad Gita* and the epic *Ramayana*, and presenting them through the vehicle of *Star Wars*.'

waiting in great anticipation for the train to arrive, for they have never seen one. Observing the headlight on the front of the train, which is just visible in the distance, one villager asks what the light in the distance represents. The guide responds: 'That is the train.' Confident that he has seen the train, the first villager leaves satisfied.

When the train approaches the platform, one of the remaining two villagers exclaims, 'Oh! This is the train!' He has seen the series of cars pulling into the station – the form behind the headlights. He is now also confident that he has seen all there is to see, and he leaves.

The third man patiently remains behind. And when the train comes into the station, he has the opportunity to meet the conductor and see the various passengers on board.

The three villagers then went back to their small village and began to tell everyone what they had seen. Though it was an undeniable truth that each had seen the same train, their descriptions were diverse; their realisations were different. The third villager obviously had a more complete experience than the other two. He was able to convince the others of this, for he perfectly described what his two comrades had seen, and more.

Analogically, the big light represents the effulgent impersonal aspect of the Lord (Brahman). This light with something more concrete behind it conveys the idea of divine substance, a personality that pervades all existence (Paramatma). And the third villager's vision represents the most complete aspect of God realisation (Bhagavan), wherein one meets the Supreme Personality of Godhead, Lord Shri Krishna (Shaktiman), and develops a relationship with Him.

In the Vaishnava view, all three of the above are considered different aspects of the same Absolute Truth, and they all are valid. One views these different aspects of God according to one's level of spiritual advancement. Vaishnava teachers recommend meditation on the fullest truth: Bhagavan realisation. The other processes were developed for gradual elevation to this point. Under the direction of a spiritually accomplished Vaishnava, however, one can immediately pursue the path of Bhagavan realisation, surpassing the levels of Brahman and Paramatma.[21]

---

21 For more on these three levels of God realization see the *Bhagavata Purana*, Cantos One and Two. I elaborate on this issue as well in my work, *The Hidden Glory of India* (Sweden: The Bhaktivedanta Book Trust, 2002).

A Force to Be Reckoned With

Now that we have explained Paramatma in context, it would be prudent to again look at its relation to the Force in Star Wars. Paramatma is 'the source of light' and 'the object of knowledge'. It is a localised form of God, existing in and between every atom. This is also the way Yoda would characterise the Force. He specifically says that the Force interpenetrates all living beings – this is a defining feature of Paramatma as well. Both the Force and Paramatma have much in common with pantheism, too. This is the idea that God is a transcendent reality pervading all of nature.

The *Bhagavata Purana*, an ancient Vaishnava text, explains the Paramatma in the following way:

> The Lord, as Supersoul, pervades all things, just as fire permeates wood, and so He appears to be of many varieties, though He is the absolute one without a second.[22]

A. C. Bhaktivedanta Swami Prabhupada comments on this text:

> ...the Supreme Personality of Godhead, by one of His plenary parts expands Himself all over the material world, and His existence can be perceived even within the atomic energy. Matter, anti-matter, proton, neutron, etc., are all different effects of the Paramatma feature of the Lord. As from wood, fire can be manifested, or as butter can be churned out of milk, so also the presence of the Lord as Paramatma can be felt by the process of legitimate hearing and chanting of the transcendental subjects which are especially treated in the Vedic literatures like the Upanisads and Vedanta.[23]

This could be Yoda's description of the Force – a Divine substance that can be felt or perceived as an energy that pervades all of existence. But the Indic description goes further, putting yet another face on the Force. In describing Paramatma, the *Bhagavatam* (2.2.8-11) states:

> Others conceive of the Personality of Godhead residing within the body in the region of the heart and measuring only eight inches, with

---

22 See His Divine Grace A. C. Bhaktivedanta Swami Prabhupada, trans., *Srimad Bhagavatam*, First Canto, Part One (Los Angeles, California: Bhaktivedanta Book Trust, 1978, reprint), Chapter 2, verse 32.

23 Ibid., purport.

four hands carrying a lotus, a wheel of a chariot, a conchshell and a club. His mouth expresses His happiness. His eyes spread like the petals of a lotus, and His garments, yellowish like the saffron of a *kadamba* flower, are bedecked with valuable jewels. His ornaments are all made of gold, set with jewels, and he wears a glowing headress and earrings. His lotus feet are placed over the whorls of the lotus-like hearts of great mystics. On His chest is the *kaustubha* jewel, engraved with a beautiful calf, and there are other jewels on His shoulders. His complete torso is garlanded with fresh flowers. He is well decorated with an ornamental wreath about His waist and rings studded with valuable jewels on His fingers. His leglets, His bangles, His oiled blackish hair, curling with a bluish tint, and His beautiful smiling face are all very pleasing.

Though the description is surprisingly graphic – especially since it is a description of God's body – there are two aspects that are particularly interesting: One, that He exists in the region of the heart, and two, that He is eight inches in height.

First, let us focus on the fact that the Paramatma is in 'the region of the heart'. Indic scriptures also describe the soul itself (you, me, and all other living entities) as being located in this same region, and that the Paramatma is in the very centre of this individual soul. In other words, the Paramatma is in the heart of the soul, who resides in the heart of the material body. So the Paramatma is in the heart of hearts. What is interesting is that both the Paramatma and the soul itself use this location of the heart to pump the symptom of the life-force, or consciousness, throughout the entire body. This it does through the blood. Therefore, when blood does not reach a particular part of the body, we do not feel sensations there. We say it is 'asleep', for consciousness cannot be perceived in that particular location.

This, of course, tallies with the idea of midi-chlorians, for just as the life-force makes itself known through the blood, the Force makes itself known through this medium as well – it is perceived only through the symbionts travelling in our blood cells.[24] Moreover, this

---

24 This divine nature of blood is hinted at in other religious traditions as well. In the Judeo-Christian tradition, blood is considered sacred. The Hebrew word for 'blood' (*dam*) appears eighty-eight times in the book of *Leviticus* alone, a large number since this is not a medical text. In the Jewish tradition, *Leviticus* is where blood is identified with the secret of the soul, or the life-force: 'For the life of the flesh is in the blood...' (see *Genesis* 9.4; *Leviticus* 17.11; and *Matthew* 16.17). In the Christian tradition, the sacred meaning of blood was extended to metaphors

interrelationship between God and heart hints at the way in which God can ultimately be known – through activities of loving devotion, or, as it is referred to in Indic texts, through *bhakti*. Swami Prabhupada, in his explanation quoted above, emphasises the process of hearing and chanting, which manifests in various religious traditions as prayer, meditation, singing, reciting religious texts, and so on. The element that unites these activities is devotion, which also comes from the heart. This is perhaps the best way – maybe the only way – to understand the elaborate description of the Paramatma outlined above. How can a Force that extends to every bird, tree, human, and even rock be described as being merely eight inches in height? Perhaps this points to an even larger truth: that the Force is inconceivable, that God cannot be known, at least in His fullness, by any amount of mental wrangling. But only by a heart that is steeped in love.

---

associated with Christ's shedding of blood for all humanity. Christian tradition teaches that unless practitioners live as Jesus did, and are willing to sacrifice their blood, at least symbolically, they would have no real communion with him (see John 6.53-57).

4

Mechanised Metaphysics: The Battle Between Technology and Nature

'[Star Wars] shows the state as a machine and asks, 'Is the machine going to crush humanity or serve humanity?' Humanity comes not from the machine but from the heart. What I see in Star Wars is the same problem that Faust gives us: Mephistopheles, the machine man, can provide us with all the means, and is thus likely to determine the aims of life as well. But of course the characteristic of Faust, which makes him eligible to be saved, is that he seeks aims that are not those of the machine.'
–Joseph Campbell, *The Power of Myth*[1]

The tension between man and machine, between organic and mechanic, can be found in each of the *Star Wars* movies. The epic film series portrays technology as having a 'resistible allure', as it were, engaging us in what might be called 'a worried embrace'. It depicts technology as a gift with a catch. Traditionally, Western culture has always been ambivalent toward scientific advances, torn between a sense of wonder and a fear of its potential for destruction. Modern man tends to see science and technology as a source of endless opportunity, and as a bomb that might destroy us in a flash.

---

1   See Joseph Campbell (with Bill Moyers), *The Power of Myth* (New York: Doubleday, 1988), p. 18.

In a groundbreaking work entitled *A Distant Technology: Science Fiction Film and the Machine Age,*[2] author J. P. Telotte explores modern man's first flirtation with technological progress and his gradual awareness of its inherent dangers. Telotte focuses on the 1920s and the 1930s, often referred to as 'the Machine Age', or 'the moment at which the modern world first discovers its specifically modern character'.[3] He identifies the ethos of this age as emphasising the 'properties of the machine – speed, regularity, efficiency'.[4] The obvious advantages afforded by such qualities, argues Telotte, carry with them a certain alienation from 'the natural world and a traditional way of life'.[5]

These same truths are implicit in Aldous Huxley's *Brave New World*, also written in the 1930s, where technology is depicted as an instrument of evil, pandering to the human desire for comfort, vanity, and self-indulgence. In this view, technology takes us away from our humanity and situates us in an unnatural state of wanting more and more. George Orwell's prophetic novel *1984*, written in the 1940s, also views technology as a great monster, devouring man by controlling his everyday life. Here, technology intrudes, as 'Big Brother', into every personal detail, reducing the human race to little more than observed mice scurrying through a carefully prescribed habitat. Jeffrey Goldstein, Professor of Religion at Rutgers University, notes that '...we are living in a time when Huxley's and Orwell's nightmarish visions appear to be hypostasising in genetic engineering, psychotropic drugs, behaviour technology, and computerised dossiers.'[6]

In today's world, we can do little more than fearfully wait for the next logical step: the cyborg. This is a hybrid entity that is half-human/half-machine, and it has been on the horizon for decades, in actual scientific laboratories as much as in science fiction movies. The idea of a mechanised human plays into our desire for perfection. We want to make our bodies 'perfect' with artificial enhancements – not just in

---

2   See J. P. Telotte, *A Distant Technology: Science Fiction Film in the Machine Age* (Hanover, NH: Wesleyan University Press, 1999). Telotte has also written in direct relation to *Star Wars*.

3   Ibid.

4   Ibid.

5   Ibid.

6   See Jeffrey Goldstein, 'The Spiritualization of Technology: A New Vision for the 1970s,' in *The Drew Gateway,* Winter 1977, pp. 26-31.

terms of plastic surgery and prosthetic limbs but in the development of artificial intelligence, virtual reality, and neural network computers. As a result, we may soon be looking at a virtual replacement for human beings, one that is presumably free of flaws. Thus, in some ways, cybernetics is more disturbing than the nuclear bomb. After all, a bomb is ultimately only able to destroy the external body – by blowing it apart, or, if one escapes immediate destruction, by the gradual ravages of excessive radiation – but cybernetics can rob us of our souls. While it may make us supermen in terms of technical ability and longevity – at least this is the hype – it diminishes our quality of life, especially in terms of what we hold dear as humans. It replaces a thoughtful mind with a mechanical brain, a creative intellect with information processing, love with heartless programming.

Descartes had already compared humans and machines almost four centuries ago, but postulated that humans were superior because they had the power to reason. Futuristic technology may now offer that trait to machines, making the ability to reason no longer peculiar to humans. The cyborg, once thought to be merely a science fiction fantasy, could easily become a reality (if it hasn't already), transforming the world as we know it into a cold and alien place. For this and other reasons, technology has come to be frowned upon by large groups of thinking people. Goldstein explains that

> It wasn't until the sixties that students, fueled in part by Huxley and Orwell, revolted against the encroachment of technology. Earth Day, back-to-nature communes, organic foods, all had an inherent anti-technological message. The increasing visibility of pollution, the use of decimating technology against the Vietnamese people and their countryside, and the fright of the energy crisis in the seventies gave us the impetus to point the finger at technology.[7]

Enter *Star Wars* and Pop Culture

And then came *Star Wars*. Here was a movie that showed just how vicious technology could be – from the horrors of the Death Star to the callous hatred of Darth Vader. Lucas's cautionary tale about the dangers of scientific advancement, however, was not the first of its kind. A much earlier example is Mary Shelley's *Frankenstein* – which, as a

---

7   Ibid., p. 27.

novel written in the early Nineteenth century, predates Lucas's films by well over 150 years – where we are reminded that there are some things better left untouched by science. Interestingly, this has been a consistent theme in science fiction films since the genre's inception. Along the same lines as *Frankenstein*, a host of Godzilla films tell us that horrible consequences are the likely outcome of our relentless thirst for scientific knowledge, a knowledge we had hoped would bring us peace and comfort. This is the idea, too, in *Metropolis*, *The Invisible Man*, *The Man with the X-Ray Eyes*, ad infinitum. *Dr. Jekyll and Mr. Hyde*, which shares this message of self-destruction through science, makes the further point that man is made of good and bad, of light and dark – something that will later be seen in Luke and Vader, if in a more subtly nuanced way.

In the words of anthropologist Per Schelde,

> The main argument is that science, as depicted in the movies, threatens not only to destroy the physical world as horror movies such as Godzilla suggests, but, more to the point, science and technology are slowly invading our minds and bodies, making us more mechanical, more like machines. Science is robbing us of our humanity, metaphorically expressed as our soul: it threatens to replace the individual, God-given soul with a mechanical machine-made one.[8]

The same idea is expressed in one of Jung's earliest anthologies, *Modern Man in Search of a Soul*, and in Thomas Moore's bestseller, *The Care of the Soul* – both focus on the spiritual hunger of modern man, whose very soul, they say, is malnourished by the technological lifestyle of the modern world.

According to Schelde, the basic message of science fiction films – a message that in many ways reflects our society as a whole – is that we have reached a certain plateau, one that forces us to make critical decisions. Science and technology have now afforded us knowledge and power beyond our wildest dreams, giving us not only control over our environment but the potential to obliterate it. Indeed, the very existence of nuclear weapons makes a rational person think twice, for with this one scientific breakthrough we can destroy ourselves many times over. Science fiction films consistently warn us – as if one collective conscience was speaking to us as a species – that there are certain lines

---

8   Ibid., p. 27.

we should not cross, and that there is a price to pay if we thoughtlessly move from creation to creator. Just ask Dr. Frankenstein.

Schelde takes this further:

> Machines that humans have to operate and to which they must adjust their biological rhythms become the first step in the dehumanisation associated with the new scientific cosmology, where production and profit are the goals of all things.[9]

Basically, Schelde says that we are in the Belly of the Beast, to quote a familiar phrase, our technological advances causing us more harm than good. And he questions if we can remain human – if we can continue to make the right choices – in a world where more and more of our time is spent interacting with machines. This, he says, is not just the question of the science fiction film, but of our modern predicament. As J. Tigue writes

> The dramatisation of an advanced race of peoples, living in a highly technological world, cannot be overlooked, as today, many people, likewise, participate in a world of machines, robots, and computers. Much of the present environment is being destroyed by human beings, motivated by greed and power, using technology as their means to conquer nature. *Star Wars* addresses many of these same issues, albeit through a different scenario, but one which has the same underlying question: do humans first not have to gain control over their own lives, thoughts, feelings, and the innate forces which move them, before they think they are sufficiently prudent to inform nature how it is to act for them? And each time humans conquer nature, rather than make friends with it, does this not make it easier to then conquer each other, rather than to make friends and work out our own differences?[10]

Conquering nature as opposed to making friends with it: this is the difference between Vader and Luke, Ravana and Rama, Duryodhana and the Pandavas. Clearly, technology and material progress are not all bad, and this is made clear in the *Star Wars* films. But to exploit nature in the name of advancement, or to use scientific progress for selfish and egocentric ends – these are the dangers and, perhaps, unavoidable

---

9 Ibid., p. 11.

10 J. Tigue, *The Transformation of Consciousness in Myth: Interpreting the Thought of Jung and Campbell* (New York: Peter Lang Publishing, Inc., 1994), p. 109.

consequences of a world addicted to pleasure and comfort. If, however, we learn to cultivate the mode of goodness – with a broad-based concern for others and more noble goals – we then have a chance to befriend our environment, and even scientific advances can then be achieved and utilised with a modicum of dignity, without harming the world around us or the living beings who inhabit it.

Thus, early commentators on the *Star Wars* series were quick to notice its double-edged lightsabre known as technology:

> The good guys are on the side of truth, beauty and cosmic force, but they aren't opposed to machines. Nor do they fight missiles with stones. The real battle is between one technological society that supports a Lone Rider and praises his instinct, and a technological society that over-rules individuals and suppresses instinct…*Star Wars* played out our own Good News and Bad News feelings about technology. We want a computer age with room for feelings. We want machines, but not the kind that run us. We want technology, but we want to be in charge of it.[11]

Making Technology 'Work' For Us

Just as Lucas was not the first in pop culture to warn us about the dangers of scientific advancement, he was not the first to champion the idea that technology has a positive side as much as a negative one: Many came before him, but Robert Pirsig's popular book *Zen and the Art of Motorcycle Maintenance*[12] and Stanley Kubrick's movie *2001: A Space Odyssey* are among the best. Pirsig's book is basically a spiritual saga about man's relationship to technology, using the motorcycle as a case in point. The story's protagonist breaks down as a result of technology run amok, with its concomitant emphasis of 'quantity over quality', and he is only able to regain sanity when he 're-humanises' himself, reestablishing the importance of 'quality' and human values. He does this not by rejecting technology but by embracing it. In a

---

11 See Ellen Goodman, *Washington Post*, 30 July 1977, A15. Quoted to good effect in David Wilkinson, *The Power of the Force: The Spirituality of the Star Wars Films* (Oxford, England: Lion Publishing, 2000), p. 133.

12 Robert Pirsig, *Zen and the Art of Motorcycle Maintenance* (New York: Morrow, 1974). Goldstein uses both Pirsig's book and the film *2001*, among others, to show that pop culture, over the course of time, began to see a positive side to technological advances.

sense, he *befriends* technology – in this case, a motorcycle – allowing it to become a means rather than an obstacle to spiritual growth. As Goldstein says, 'Technology switches from a cruel God of fragmentation to a vehicle (the *'yana'* of Zen Mahayana) of spiritualisation.'[13]

In Stanley Kubrick's *2001*, technology is again seen as having two sides, depending on how it is used. Here, a computer – the very emblem of the modern machine – equipped with artificial intelligence to supervise a space mission grows fearful of its human masters, seizes control of the spacecraft and kills several of the astronauts before it is deactivated. In due course, however, the journey leads to the surviving astronaut's encounter with yet another machine, a 'monolith' built by extraterrestrials, which ultimately allows the hero to experience a form of spiritual rejuvenation.

Capturing this positive component of technological advancement, Lucas shows that technology is more than a necessary evil – it can be a catalyst for spiritual enlightenment. *Star Wars* does not construct an 'us against them' sensibility regarding man and machine, for, as modern-day philosopher Robert John Licuria notes, '[it is nonsensical to propose] a Romantic opposition between the organic and the mechanical, for there is much that is hybrid about its constructed elements.'[14] This is brought out further by the late Janice Hocker Rushing, who notes that not only does technology have both positive and negative sides, but that the natural world can at times overpower the seemingly unstoppable world of machines:

> Once again, technology, which plays a crucial role in all New Frontier stories, is a prominent sub-theme in the *Star Wars* films. A futuristic centaur, Darth Vader is (rather than half-man, half-horse) half-man, half machine. In his person, technology is evil; it is the half of himself Luke has given over to the Empire (the military/industrial complex) for violent and destructive purposes, Frankenstein's monster not only out of control, but bureaucratised. Joseph Campbell, upon

---

13 Goldstein, op. cit., p. 28. Goldstein also refers to Rudolf Otto's book *The Idea of the Holy* (1923), in which the esteemed philosopher acknowledges that 'the Holy' has two sides, one creative and the other destructive. Goldstein suggests that this might be indicative of our actual relationship to technology.

14 See Robert John Licuria, 'Man and Machine: An Essay on *Blade Runner*, *The Terminator*, *Terminator 2: Judgement Day*, and *Star Trek: First Contact*', 1999, available at www.ciampini.info/file/ferrari/4B_Man%20and%20Machine.doc. Accessed on 29 September 2010.

whose works Lucas claims to have based the trilogy, finds the Faus-
tian problem here: 'Is Mephistopheles, the maker of machines that
furnished Faust with anything that Faust needed…going to dominate
Faust or serve Faust? This is the modern problem'.…Technology as
evil is fought not only by Luke, as Campbell points out, but by the
furry Ewoks, the 'nature people' whose knocking out of the computerised weaponry with their Stone Age devices in *Jedi* is 'symbolic of
nature overcoming the machine'.…Technology is clearly not all evil
in this story, however. The Rebels, for instance, are accompanied in
all three films by the 'droids' (robots) R2D2 and C3PO who become,
despite the former's clumsiness and the latter's stodginess, as 'lovable'
to the audience as the human heroes.…The ever-present fraternity of
animal, machine, and human is a subtle reminder that the whole psyche contains both instinct (pre-consciousness), rationality, and when
guided by the Force, spirituality. Apparently, technology is only truly
evil when it is off on its own. When integrated with the rest of the
psyche, it is neither conquered nor conquering.[15]

Thus, absolute denunciation of technology is obviously an extremist
position. After all, technological breakthroughs are here to stay, and
they have given much good to the world as well, saving lives and afford-
ing conveniences that enable one to do good work. As Goldstein says,
'…if it does not blow us off the face of the Earth in nuclear holocaust,
we must learn to live with it despite the evil effects of its excesses.'[16]
This sense of proper utility, of use and misuse when it comes to science
and technology, is at the heart of *Star Wars*. And Lucas successfully
conveys this tension, showing that technology, like the Force, has both
positive and negative sides.

Jungian analyst J. Tigue has this to say:

Technology is at an incredibly advanced stage of development, in
some ways matching the subjective leaps of Skywalker and of Vader.
They each use technology in diametrically opposed ways, Luke for
the release of life and Vader for its bondage and ultimate extinction.
Vader has identified with technology to the point of becoming a par-
tial machine, himself being hooked up to a life-support system. Vader
needs technology for his own survival, and ironically uses it to destroy

15 Janice Hocker Rushing, 'Mythic Evolution of "The New Frontier" in Mass Mediated
    Rhetoric', in *Critical Studies in Mass Communication* (CSMC), Volume 3, Number
    3, September 1986, pp. 287-8.

16 Jeffrey Goldstein, op. cit.

the lives of others. Luke is not enslaved to the machine and demon-strates that technology is the servant and the human being its director. When Luke's hand is cut off and replaced with a mechanical hand to make his body function well again, technology does not determine how he will choose to use his new hand.[17]

Indeed, it is Luke himself who must choose. Technology, in other words, is benign. It is as good or bad as the person who uses it. Clearly, in *Star Wars* (as in life), technology is used for both good and bad pur-poses, since there are, essentially, good and bad people:

> The Sandpeople, least technologically sophisticated, manufacture their gaderffii sticks, breathe through metal sandfilters and weave cloth; the Jawas use energy guns, dwell in sandcrawlers and live by selling scavenged machines; Uncle Owen, the hardscrabble mois-ture farmer, exploits a range of technology to make life possible. The water needed to grow his crops is extracted from the atmosphere by machines which are tended by droids. Aunt Beru's kitchen is a small computer centre and Luke's garage is stocked with droid main-tenance gear, a skyhopper and a land-speeder. Kenobi may have little use for blasters, but his lightsabre is a marvel of technologic miniaturisation; and his mastery of technology is such that he can interpret the computer schematics of a space station he's never seen before and put the knowledge to work. Vader is even more depend-ent. Not only is his body a feat of technology, but he also wields a lightsabre and depends on his scanner and targeting computer in the climactic battle.[18]

Best Use of a Bad Bargain: An Indian Philosophical Look at Technology

Lest we go too far astray from the theme of this book, let us note that Indian philosophical texts, too, recognise both good and bad uses of technology. In Sanskrit, a machine is called a *yantra*, and it is re-ferred to in the earliest of Vedic texts. Many stories in Indian literature refer to a *yantra-purusha*, or a machine-man, elaborating on cyborg

---

17 J. Tigue, op. cit., p. 113.

18 Denis Wood, 'The Stars in Our Hearts – A Critical Commentary on George Lucas' *Star Wars*', in *Journal of Popular Film* (6), Number 3, 1978, pp. 262-3.

technology eons before it was conceived in the West.[19] Much like Descartes, ancient Indian thinkers compared the body to a machine. But they understood that this 'machine' was animated by a completely non-material entity, the Jivatma, or soul, endowing it with lifelike, sentient behavior. Also in this machine, say the sages of India, is Paramatma, or a portion of the Supreme Soul, who accompanies the Jivatma on his material sojourn. This Paramatma exists in the heart of the Jivatma's heart, as mentioned in the prior chapter. Thus, the *Bhagavad-gita* (18.61) says, 'The Supreme Lord is situated in everyone's heart, O Arjuna, and is directing the wanderings of all living entities. Both the Lord and the soul are seated in the body as on a machine [*yantra*] made of material energy.'

The renowned Sanskritist V. Raghavan, who writes on machines in ancient India, takes exception to this metaphor as used in the *Bhagavad-gita*. He worries that it might influence India to succumb to the Machine Age, eclipsing its deeply rooted spiritual culture.[20] While admitting it unlikely that India would ever forsake its spiritual traditions in favour of a mechanistic view of life, he laments that in other countries an overreliance on machines has indeed led to an imbalance, to civilisations that are overly dependent on technology.[21] India's elaborate philosophy of the soul, says Raghavan, may protect her from taking the body/machine metaphor out of context. 'Even writers who actually dealt with the *yantras*', he notes, 'like Somadeva and Bhoja, saw in the machine operated by an agent an appropriate analogy for the mundane body and senses presided over by the soul.'[22] And further, 'The wonderful mechanism of the universe, with its constituent elements and planetary systems, requires a divine master to keep it in constant revolution.'[23]

---

19 See Sadaputa Dasa, 'Imitators of Life', in *Back to Godhead* magazine, Volume 26, Number 2, March/ April 1992, pp. 13-14. Also see V. Raghavan, 'Yantras or Mechanical Contrivances in Ancient India', *Transaction* No. 10, Bangalore: The Indian Institute of Culture, 1956. Ancient Indian texts actually describe a plethora of 'man-made machines' that would be the envy of modern scientists. There will be more on this in the next chapter.

20 Ibid.

21 Ibid.

22 Ibid., p. 32.

23 Ibid.

Other writers feel that the machine is already taking over, even in India. Rabindranath Tagore (1861–1941), one of the great Hindu thinkers of our time, is one of them. He evokes the Luke Skywalker story, the *Ramayana*, and the problem of technology vs. nature – not directly, since *Star Wars* as such didn't exist in his time, but by implication – as follows:

> You know that fairy tale, the eternal story of youth, which is popular in almost all parts of the world. It is about the beautiful princess taken captive by a cruel giant and the young prince who starts out to free her from his dungeon. When we heard that story in our boyhood, do you remember how our enthusiasm was stirred, how we felt ourselves setting out as that prince to rescue the princess, overcoming all obstacles and dangers, and at last succeeding in bringing her back to freedom? Today the human soul is lying captive in the dungeon of a Giant Machine, and I ask you, my young princes, to feel this enthusiasm in your hearts and be willing to rescue the human soul from the chains of greed.[24]

But, again, it is not that Indian philosophy views technology as all bad. Only when modern amenities are utilised with selfishness or greed, as stated by Tagore, do we see their more debilitating side. But when engaged with positive attitude and long-range goals, another dimension emerges, one that is spiritual in scope. Though many are unaware of it, Indian spiritual traditions, such as Vaishnavism, actually encourage passionate use of material facility, even technology – but only in a God-centred context.

Most people are familiar with the Indian philosophical schools that teach silent meditation and renunciation – the worldview that promotes abandoning the material world in favour of ascetic practices and otherworldly goals. But there is also the school of positive engagement in worldly duties (*karma-yoga*). And this would include using modern technology for spiritual purposes. These two dimensions of spirituality are also found in Western philosophical traditions: In Christianity, for example, one finds via *activa* and via *contemplativa*, which manifest in the Roman Catholic Church as 'active' communities and 'contemplative' communities, though both share the same theological tenets. Active communities would generally make full use of technological

---

24 Amiya Chakravarty, ed., *A Tagore Reader* (Boston: Beacon Press, 1966), pp. 207-8.

advances, whereas the contemplative communities might have less inclination to do so. This two-sided aspect of spirituality is nowhere as developed as in the dialogue between Krishna and Arjuna.

In the first verses of the *Gita*'s Third Chapter, Lord Krishna introduces these two legitimate approaches to yoga (linking with God) for the first time. His teachings were revolutionary, for, when the *Gita* was initially spoken, the people of India were given to extreme acts of renunciation. Aspiring spiritualists of the age felt that only by shaking off the burden of active, worldly life could one approach a life of the spirit. The *Gita* seeks to correct this misconception. It takes the doctrine of *nivritti*, negation, so dominant in ancient India, and augments it with the principle of positive spiritual action. Thus, Krishna teaches Arjuna not so much about renunciation *of* action, as is commonly supposed, but about *renunciation in action*. In later Vaishnava terminology, this is the preferred *yukta-vairagya*, or 'renouncing the world by acting for the Supreme', as opposed to *phalgu-vairagya*, or the dry renunciation commonly associated with ascetic practices.

Krishna accepts both forms of renunciation, but he describes the active form as more practical and more effective as well. Whichever form or approach one chooses, says Krishna, detachment from sense objects is mandatory. The difference, then, lies only in one's external involvement with the outside world. Krishna asserts that contemplative, or inactive, yoga is difficult because the mind can become restless or distracted. He recommends the active form of yoga, which he calls *karma-yoga*. This is safer, he says, because one still strives to focus the mind, using various techniques of meditation, but augments this process with practical engagement in the material world. Krishna elaborates on how to perform *karma-yoga* in the *Gita*'s Sixth Chapter, again emphasising its superiority to mere renunciation and abstract philosophy:

> One who is unattached to the fruits of his work and who works as he is obligated is in the renounced order of life, and he is the true mystic, not he who lights no fire and performs no work. What is called renunciation is the same as yoga, or linking oneself with the Supreme, for no one can become a yogi unless he renounces the desire for sense gratification. (6.1-2)

Krishna's instruction here is applicable for us today, living in the Western world, and is also reflected in *Star Wars* (especially in the Jedis' positive use of technology). He is saying that, to be a yogi, we needn't go off to a forest to contemplate our navel. In fact, he says that such endeavours will most likely fail for most of us. Rather, we can achieve the goal of yoga by learning the art of 'detached action', one of the *Gita's* main teachings – and one of the teachings of the Jedi. Later in the *Gita*, Krishna will explain that art to Arjuna and, by extenuation, to the rest of us. The *Gita* teaches how we can, in modern terms, be in the world but not of it – how to use technology, like Luke, but how to not be overtaken by it, like Vader.

The *Gita* presents this in a hierarchical manner: first comes study, understanding, and meditation (*dhyana-yoga*). These lead to deep contemplation of philosophy and eventually wisdom that culminates in renunciation (*sannyasa-yoga*). Renunciation leads to the proper use of intelligence (*buddhi-yoga*), then to action with right motive (*karma-yoga*), and finally to action with love and devotion (*bhakti-yoga*). All of this involves a complex inner development, beginning with an understanding of the temporary nature of the material world. Realising that the world of matter will cease to exist and that birth all too quickly leads to death, the aspiring yogi begins to practice external renunciation and gradually internal renunciation, which, ultimately, means giving up the desire for the fruit of one's work (*karma-phala-tyaga*) and performing the work itself as an offering to God (*bhagavad-artha-karma*). This method of detached action (*karma-yoga*) leads to the 'perfection of inaction' (*naishkarmya-siddhi*), or freedom from the bondage of works.

One becomes free from such bondage because one learns to work as an 'agent' rather than as an 'enjoyer' – one learns to work for God, on His behalf, rather than for selfish purposes. This is the essential teaching of the *Gita*, and in its pages Krishna takes Arjuna (and each of us) through each step of this yoga process. The bottom line here is that while a fledgling spiritualist may reject the accouterments of modern technology in the name of spiritual progress, a more advanced spiritualist will use these same accouterments in the Lord's service. At least this is what the *Gita* teaches. In *Star Wars*, too, we see Jedi training in forests, preferring a life in the country, away from modern amenities. But then, as they develop their abilities, they go out into the world and use their newfound powers for positive spiritual purposes, even to the point of engaging modern technology.

The *Gita's* entire Sixth Chapter is about Arjuna's rejection of conventional yoga, the kind of yoga that prescribes renunciation of things like technological advancement. He describes it as impractical and 'too difficult to perform', as it certainly would be for us, too, in our current age of distraction and degradation (known as Kali-yuga). Since the goal of yoga is to re-connect with God, *bhakti-yoga* rises above all the rest. According to Krishna, Arjuna is the best of yogis because he has devotion to the Supreme Lord. Krishna tells his devotee directly, 'Of all yogis, he who always abides in Me with great faith, worshipping Me in transcendental loving service, is most intimately united with Me in yoga and is the highest of all.'

This, then, is the higher form of Indian spirituality: to take all that God gives us – even modern technology – and to use it in divine service. Otherwise, as the modern world has shown us, technology tends to lead one into hellish life, to distract one from life's real goals. And in such a condition, it is unlikely that one will become happy. To make this clear, we need simply look at Darth Vader: did all his power and technological advantage make him a happy person? What truly viable assets did technology afford him beneath his lonely mask?

After all, even from a material point of view, what is the purpose of technological advancement? Isn't it meant to make people happy, to give us a better life? Historian Charles A. Beard in his book *A Century of Progress* suggests that the real purpose of technological progress 'implies that mankind, by making use of science and invention, can progressively emancipate itself from plagues, famines, and social disasters, and subjugate the materials and forces of the Earth to the purposes of the good life – here and now.'[25]

It is certainly curious that with all his scientific advancement, modern man is today plagued by many of the same problems as those who came before him. We cure one disease only to discover another. We pollute our environment and make our quality of life recede – all in the name of material progress. But what can we do? Should we give up scientific advancement and go back to living without computers and cars? Beard says, 'When critics and scoffers, writing under soft lamps, or lecturing for fees to well-fed audiences, in comfortable rooms electrically lighted, venture to speak of an alternative, they can only offer a return to agriculture and handicrafts. . . . Are we merely to surrender the tractor and return to the steel plow? Why not the wooden plow? Or

---

25 Quoted in Ravi Gupta, 'Should We Reject Modern Science?' in *Back to Godhead* magazine, Volume 29, Number 2,

better still, to the forked stick hardened by fire? In the process of retreat are surgery and dentistry to go into the discard? . . . The problem is not one of retreat, but of ends and methods, of choices and uses.'[26] If something is used in positive and well thought-out ways, it naturally offers greater advantages for the people who use them. This is so much more the case when things are used spiritually.

By using things of this world in God's service, say Vaishnava philosophical traditions, they become spiritualised. This can become more understandable by considering the following example: if you place an iron rod in fire, it begins to take on fire's characteristics – it gives off heat and light, and it will burn you if you touch it. Similarly, if you take ordinary mundane things and use them in a spiritual way, these things then take on a spiritual quality. Consider a church or a synagogue, for instance. These are actually only buildings, structures made of brick and concrete. Yet, because they are used for spiritual purposes, they affect people spiritually; they can evoke transcendent emotions.

Such spiritual usage is actually the originally intended purpose of all things, since all things come from God. To illustrate this point, Swami Prabhupada, founder of the Hare Krishna movement, gave an appropriate example in a series of published lectures: 'When a thief steals your money, he will spend it. And if you had kept it, you would have spent it. So, either way, the money would be spent. Why, then, is he a criminal? Because your money should be spent for your purposes, and he has diverted it for his. Similarly, everything belongs to Krishna, God. So when we use it for Him, we are acting spiritually. But when we use it in any other way, we are acting materially and are thus like thieves. So when we change the focus of science from serving the body to serving Krishna, we straighten out the equation of civilisation.'[27]

Elaborating on this point, Prabhupada said, 'Sometimes people question the devotees of Krishna, asking, "If you condemn material life, why do you use modern conveniences such as automobiles, printing presses and computers?" But it is not the machines and technology of the material world per se that we reject. Rather, we reject the use of material things for any purpose other than the service and glorification of Krishna. And whatever is used in this way becomes glorious.

---

26 Ibid.

27 See His Divine Grace A.C. Bhaktivedanta Swami Prabhupada, *The Science of Self-Realization* (Los Angeles: The Bhaktivedanta Book Trust, 1977).

Thus, the devotees of Krishna neither condemn nor glorify computers and other such modern technological amenities. We understand that the purpose of human life is to know, love and serve Krishna, the Supreme Person. To devote one's life to this purpose is the ultimate goal.'[28]

The Conjunction of the Mechanical and the Metaphysical

Spiritual realisation dramatically changes the focus of human effort. The materialistic conception of life multiplies material desires, which lead to the overdevelopment of industry and technology, and to a ravenous, urban-consumer economy. Social scientists are nearly unanimous in warning us that the continuation of this trend will lead to ecological and social disaster – to a world of Darth Vaders. Therefore, the return to a simpler life (one in harmony with nature's laws, as *Star Wars* shows is the preferred lifestyle of the Jedi) has emerged as one of today's most significant priorities. Interestingly, the motto of Vaishnava civilisation, 'simple living and high thinking'[29] – a motto that, in the West, is often attributed to Emerson – should have much meaning for modern man. As Goldstein pointed out, technology need not be discarded, but rather engaged with a healthy respect for nature and the environment.

The *Srimad Bhagavatam*, in describing Krishna's opulent kingdom on earth, shows that ancient India's ideal of spiritual culture has much in common with the back-to-nature movement: 'The city of Dvaraka Puri was filled with the opulences of all seasons. Everywhere were

---

28 Ibid.

29 This 'motto' for Vedic civilisation was avidly utilised by Prabhupada and subsequently by various writers to describe the rural, bucolic and peaceful atmosphere of Vrindavan and the ideal civilisation described in Vaishnava texts. This civilisation is supposed to have existed in Earth's past as it exists eternally in the spiritual realm. Interestingly, the spiritual world is primarily envisioned in terms of a pastoral setting, with magnificent cows, large, shady trees, and beautiful ponds. Similarly, despite its acceptance of technology, *Star Wars* seems to point its viewers in the same direction: the narrative of all of Lucas' films takes its characters on a long archetypal journey, from the excessively technological world of spaceships to the forest home of the Ewoks – and on to the triumphant return of the heroes. This represents the long journey home, from madness to sanity, the journey back to Godhead. Along these same lines, it should be remembered that Leia's last name is Organa, indicating that her ideal world is an organic, pastoral one.

hermitages, orchards, flower gardens, parks, and reservoirs of water breeding lotus flowers.[30] There are many such descriptions of Krishna's city dwelling. And what always stands out is that while it was charming in terms of its homespun simplicity, it was also well-constructed by any standard, with elaborately planned roads, streets, and lanes. The city was replete with residential homes, assembly houses, and temples, all displaying varieties of architectural beauty – but with a deep respect for natural resources.

In commenting on Dvaraka, Swami Prabhupada notes that all its citizens depended on nature's gifts of fruits and flowers, without industrial enterprises forcing them into filthy huts and slums for residential quarters. Prabhupada writes:

> Advancement of civilisation is estimated not on the growth of mills and factories to deteriorate the finer instincts of the human being, but it rests on developing the potent spiritual instincts of human beings and giving them a chance to go back to Godhead....Human energy should be properly utilised in developing the finer senses for spiritual understanding, in which lies the solution of life. Fruits, flowers, beautiful gardens, parks, reservoirs of waters with ducks and swans playing in the midst of lotus flowers, and cows giving sufficient milk and butter are essential for developing the finer tissues of the human body.[31]

And this was Krishna's *city*. His country home, Vrindavan, was even more lush, with few modern amenities or other disturbances from the outside world. Renowned historian of religion David Kinsley captures the spirit and magical spontaneity of Vrindavan:

> In Vrindavana, Krsna is removed from the ordinary world and the necessity of acting according to pragmatic considerations. In Vrindavana he need not play a role but is free to express his essential nature in every action. In the cowherd village, removed from the world of his mission as an *avatara*, there are no inhibitions to acting freely. Vrindavana is a playground, a magic place, where Krsna can revel freely and continually as a playful child. Vrindavana is the Garden before the Fall, a place in which man and God may mingle freely and intimately

30 From Prabhupada's commentary to *Srimad Bhagavatam* (also known as the *Bhagavata Purana*). Quoted in Dharmadhyaksa dasa, 'Simple Living, High Thinking', in *Back to Godhead* magazine, Volume 11, Number 7, 1976, pp. 11-12.

31 Ibid.

in playful abandon. In this atmosphere God's essential nature, the divine, in the form of the beautiful cowherd Krsna, may express itself in play and self-delight.[32]

More to the point, Vrindavan is Krishna's *rural* abode, transcendentally resplendent with bucolic wonders and simple loveliness. As Vaishnava theologian Prabhodananda Sarasvati describes it:

> I have been enchanted by the flora of Vrindavana, the strangely beautiful varied trees and fruit- and flower-bearing creepers; by the calls and songs of beautiful peacocks, cuckoos, parrots, and other birds, their songs maddened by bliss; by lakes surrounded by green bowers; by the rivers and mountains. The golden fields of Vrindavana have also captured me. In Vrindavana the earth is made of transparent stones and gems of various kinds. Its trees and creepers are laden with flowers and fruits that diffuse bliss. Birds sing the sweetest songs of the *Samaveda*. The waters of rivers, lakes, and tanks are full of *rasa* of pure consciousness. Let my mind ponder them! The leaves are like emeralds in Vrindavana, the flowers are like diamonds, the sprouts and fruit are like rubies, while the trees in Vrindavana stand picturesquely with perpetually honey-shedding flowers, and the flowers are covered with large, black bees that look like shining blue gems.[33]

According to Vaishnava scriptures, both realms – the city, as exemplified by Dvaraka, and the country, perfectly represented by Vrindavan – have spiritual counterparts in the Kingdom of God. It is as if the texts were telling us that the spiritual world allows for both lifestyles, according to the preferences of those fortunate souls who go there. These scriptures emphasise devotional service to Krishna, informing us that this service can take place in the sophisticated environs of the city and also in the simplicity of the country. Thus, the scriptures talk of balancing city and country life, which coalesce in the service of Krishna. The importance of balancing these two lifestyle choices is recognised in less spiritual discourse, too. As well-known economist E. F. Schumacher writes:

---

32 See David R. Kinsley, *The Sword and the Flute* (Los Angeles: University of California Press, 1975, reprint, 2000), p. 76.

33 Prabhodananda Sarasvati, *Vrindavana-mahimamrita*, translated into Bengali by Haridas Babaji (Vrindavana: Bhagavandas Babaji, 1936), part 2, pp. 1-2. Quoted in Kinsley, *ibid.*, p. 31.

To restore a proper balance between city and rural life is perhaps the greatest task in front of modern man....Why is it so difficult for the rich to help the poor? The all-pervading disease of the modern world is the total imbalance between city and countryside, an imbalance in terms of wealth, power, culture, attraction, and hope.[34]

This imbalance, according to Schumacher, has brought havoc upon the world in which we live. The *Srimad Bhagavatam* and other ancient Indian literature explain that there is a complete arrangement in nature for human maintenance. The theological idea at the base of this conception is that God made everything perfect and complete. However, when we exploit nature for excessive material enjoyment, which is found to a heightened degree in the world's major cities, we disturb that natural arrangement, and the result is scarcity and the unfair distribution of wealth. The fact that many are today making their fortunes in the cities and retreating to the countryside in no way alleviates the situation: bringing their selfishness and exploitative behavior to their country homes only serves to quickly turn country into city, transforming a once peaceful environment into a replica of the maddening city they hoped to escape.

What is called for, again, is a transformation of consciousness. Vaishnava doctrine proposes that one can enjoy life only by dovetailing his desires and activities for the benefit of the complete whole, just as our hand is normal and useful only as long as it is attached to the complete body and serves the body's needs. If the hand were severed (as it literally was in the cases of both Luke and Darth Vader), it might still appear like a hand, but it would have none of its intended potencies. Similarly, we are parts and parcels of the complete whole (God, or Krishna), but if we detach ourselves from His interests, social chaos results. So how do we remain attached to God according to our individual tastes and qualities, as individuals living in today's world?

Vaishnava literature prescribes the *varna*, or the *varnashrama* system, which we will more thoroughly examine in a later chapter, as the means to integrate the various parts of human society with the complete whole, or God. Despite its bastardisation in the form of the modern caste system, *varnashrama* was originally intended to be a comprehensive social organisation designed to raise everyone to the

---

34 E. F. Schumacher, *Small is Beautiful* (New York: Harper & Row Publishers, 1973), pp. 203-4.

platform of spiritual understanding. First, to satisfy material needs, society has four main groups, or *varnas*: (1) learned intellectuals, (2) administrators and military men, (3) farmers and merchants, and (4) the assistants to the other three groups. And then there are the spiritual orders of life: the student, those who are married, the retired, and the renounced. Details on how to determine who is actually part of which group, and specifics on how to properly function as part of each group, is found throughout the literature of the Vaishnavas.

Ideally, the *varnashrama* system provides effective social organisation by fulfilling both the material and the spiritual needs of human society. Our modern world confirms the Vaishnava conclusion that without such a system, chaos and disorder will overtake us all. Therefore, Indian thinkers even today suggest that *varnashrama* would be helpful in establishing a sane social atmosphere for spiritual realisation, the stated goal of human life. Implicit in the *varnashrama* system is the acceptance of modern technology, for *varnashrama* is not about renouncing the world but rather about finding one's true place in it and acting accordingly. It is not about giving up the amenities of a progressive life, but about engaging those amenities in a spiritual way.

Star Wars, too, seems to suggest that social order is necessary for the proper functioning of society, and that the accouterments of this world can and should be used for the betterment of man. But its warning is that these accouterments can be abused, or misused, and so the knife that was meant to save someone in a delicate operation might instead be used for murder. Nonetheless, both Vaishnava literature and *Star Wars* suggest that the potential for abuse does not invalidate the obvious merits of technology, nor does it imply that modern amenities cannot be used in a constructive way. The sages of India and *Star Wars* further tell us not to renounce the world or to sit on our laurels, letting the world pass us by. Rather, one must learn to work passionately for a righteous cause – using all that this world has to offer. At times, this may mean engaging the dark side for purposes of truth and light, for both worlds are integrally connected.

How is this expressed in *Star Wars*? When Luke visits Yoda in his forest hermitage, the aged Jedi Master points to a nearby cave, telling Luke that it is an evil place, full of darkness and unwanted things. And, yet, he tells Luke that he, the young hero, must indeed enter that cave. When Luke fearfully questions his master as to what might be found in the cave, Yoda responds that the cave contains only what one takes with him. Luke enters and learns of that liminal meeting place of good and evil, the place that is otherwise known as his own heart:

> Yoda, it seems, lives in a place that contains both the light and dark sides of life, of the Force. To know oneself, one must know the dark side as well as the light. Metaphorically, it is as if Luke must face his own coldness and his own mortality. As an initiate Luke is to take nothing with him; he is to experience what is within himself....It is here we must go if we are to know the depths of life more deeply. Luke must come to terms with his worst fears and the depths of his own imagination.[35]

These modern perceptions echo the ancient truths of the *Ishopani-shad*, Mantra 11, wherein it is said, 'Only one who can learn the process of nescience and that of transcendental knowledge side by side can transcend the influence of repeated birth and death and enjoy the full blessings of immortality.' In other words, although the Vaishnava tradition recommends the spiritual pursuit as man's primary duty, it asks us not to be spiritualists with our heads in the clouds. Rather, we should cultivate awareness of *avidya*, the world of ignorance, as much as we passionately pursue *vidya*, or the world of knowledge. This is because we must live in the material world. If we were pursuing spirituality in some higher realm, things would be different. But we are not.

Thus, we need to know not only divine subjects but we need expertise in the mundane sphere as well. The *Ishopanishad* elaborates in Mantra 14: 'One should perfectly know the Divine. But one should also know the temporary material creation, with its *devas*, men and animals. When one knows these, he surpasses death and the ephemeral cosmic manifestation with it, and in the eternal kingdom of God he enjoys his eternal life of bliss and knowledge.' The idea is somewhat abused by Chancellor Palpatine in *Revenge of the Sith*. There, he convinces Anakin that light and dark, good and evil, must both be known, and that greater power exists in such dual knowledge, even the power to overcome death. While it is true that knowing the material creation, or the darker side of God's energy, is useful, especially in conjunction with spiritual knowledge, it is equally true that one should not let the darker side override the light. This was the one fact that Palpatine

---

35 Steven A. Galipeau, *The Journey of Luke Skywalker: An Analysis of Modern Myth and Symbol* (Chicago: Open Court, 2001), pp. 124-5.

conveniently neglected to tell Anakin. Working with the dark side includes working with modern technology. It is true. But if we learn to utilise the fruits of our technological civilisation in the service of the Supreme, rather than working for temporary gains in the material world as do the followers of the dark side, we will then have achieved the best of both worlds.

5

FROM *VEDA* TO VADER:
MODERN FLYING MACHINES
IN AN ANCIENT WORLD

'The general notions about human understanding...which are illustrated by discoveries in atomic physics are not in the nature of things wholly unfamiliar, wholly unheard of, or new. Even in our own culture they have a history, and in Buddhist and Hindu thought a more considerable and central place. What we shall find is an exemplification, an encouragement, and a refinement of old wisdom.'
–Julius Robert Oppenheimer, *Science and the Common Understanding*[1]

Until recently, human civilisation was seen as moving in a slow linear progression – from primitive Neolithic beginnings to the technological wonders of the modern world. This view of reality is the fruit of modern archaeological processes. At the beginning of the Nineteenth century, Napoleon was among the first to take archaeology as a serious science. He and his team of experts journeyed to Egypt, where they formally analysed and documented her now well-known monuments. Half a century later, European archaeologists began to look at Mesopotamia, and others would soon follow suit, using the newly found methods of archaeology to explore other lands. Gradually, as a result, our present worldview came into being, and the scholarly world

---

1 See J. R. Oppenheimer, *Science and the Common Understanding* (New York: Oxford University Press, 1954), pp. 8-9.

bequeathed to us the following 'reality': no sophisticated technology could have existed in the distant past, and human civilisation is now more accomplished than ever before.

An overabundance of contemporary literature, however, suggests that ancient man's attainment may have gone far beyond the grunts and groans of wild apes. Our distant ancestors may have been more advanced than we tend to think, their impressive achievements buried deep in the sands of our inaccessible past. Along these lines, there is much food for thought. Here are some examples: for several decades now, miners in the Western Transvaal region of South Africa have been finding oddly grooved metallic spheres embedded in deep rock. Experts say that these spheres unmistakably point to an advanced form of metallurgy. More than two hundred of these perfectly-cut spheres have been discovered so far – and our most sophisticated methods of dating tell us that they are over two billion years old. Roelf Marx, former curator of the Klerksdorp Museum in South Africa, where some of the spheres are stored, shows his tacit acceptance of the linear world view: 'They look man-made, yet at the time in Earth's history when they came to rest in this rock, no intelligent life existed.'[2] Mainstream scientists cannot explain these mysterious spheres.

More evidence of man's hidden past: the Great Pyramid of Egypt. The famous edifice weighs over six million tons, involving more stone-masonry than all the churches and cathedrals of medieval Europe combined. How was ancient man able to accomplish this, especially with the mathematical precision needed for its proper construction? The official explanation is that Egyptians used crude ramps and a huge army of workers to move the massive amounts of stone over many years. But this explanation cannot stand – and modern experts have admitted as much.[3] There is also the great pyramid at Cholula, which is near what is now known as Mexico City – the structure is three times the size of its Egyptian counterpart. Then, deep in the jungles of

---

2   Quoted in Michael Cremo, *Hidden History of the Human Race* (California: Govardhana Hill Publishing, 1994), p. 121. Many convincing evidences regarding the advancement of ancient civilisations can be found in Devamrita Swami, *Searching for Vedic India* (Los Angeles, California: Bhaktivedanta Book Trust, 2002), and I am referring to several of these evidences here.

3   See E. S. Edwards, *The Pyramids of Egypt* (London: Penguin, 1949), p. 220. Also see John Baines and Jaromir Malek, *Atlas of Ancient Egypt* (Virginia: Time-Life Books, 1990), p. 139.

Mexico's Yucatan Peninsula, exists the famous temple complex known as Uxmal, created by the Mayan people 1,500 years ago. Its design and construction show technical abilities that exceed what people from that period were supposed to be capable of performing.[4] There are literally hundreds of such examples, where ancient man appears to have had access to advanced technology.[5]

Most impressive of all, and perhaps most pertinent for our present study, are examples of an advanced culture thriving in India's remote past: in the early 1990s huge stone ports were found off the coast of Gujarat, India, on the Arabian sea[6] – these have subsequently been identified as Dvaraka, Krishna's ancient city as described in Vaishnava texts. According to the *Mahabharata*, Dvaraka was submerged by a great tidal wave soon after the battle of Kurukshetra. Now that the remains have been unearthed, they reveal more than the simple fact that Dvaraka actually existed: Previously unknown alloys were discovered that baffle modern scientists, and remains of city streets and elaborate temples continue to be uncovered showing signs of advanced technology.

Similar findings were announced by the Archaeological Survey of India, an important scholarly institution with ongoing government funding. The Survey has for many years sponsored a national project known as 'The Archaeology of *Ramayana* Sites', which seeks to verify the historicity of the *Ramayana*. This was the brainchild of B. B. Lal, Director-General of the Survey from 1968 to 1972. His work reveals that the cities described in the *Ramayana*, such as Ayodhya, have underground caves with ruins and artifacts suggesting an elaborately advanced civilisation. They boast sophisticated hydraulic systems and remnants of machines that indicate highly refined engineering processes.[7] These structures could not have been built with the backward

---

4   John Bierhorst, *The Mythology of Mexico and Central America* (New York: William Morrow & Co., 1990), p. 8.

5   Cremo, op. cit., also see Devamrta Swami, op. cit.

6   See David Frawley, 'On the Banks of the Saraswati: The Ancient History of India Revised', in *The Quest*, Volume 5, Number 3, Autumn 1992, pp. 22-30. Also see my own book, *Archeology and the Vaishnava Tradition: The Pre-Christian Roots of Krishna Worship* (Calcutta, India: KLM Firma, 1989).

7   B. B. Lal, 'A 2,000-year-old Feat in Hydraulic Engineering in India', in *Archeology* magazine, January-February 1985, p. 49. The Iron Pillar of Delhi may also be cited as an example of an ancient phenomenon that baffles modern science: this

technology we currently ascribe to ancient man, nor, in most cases, could they be built as effectively with the technology we have today.

So how did they do it? Again, a recent spate of literature suggests that material advancement in civilisation is cyclical, and that we have lost much of the technical know-how of our ancestors. How did our forebears lose vital information and the fruits of hundreds of years of research? Diverse cultures throughout the world mention a cataclysm or a massive war in ancient times.[8] This is one possible explanation. In India, for example, the battle at Kurukshetra was supposed to have taken the lives of millions, and it could have easily been responsible for wiping out much of ancient man's technological attainment. If we entertain this as a possibility, the theory would go something like this: man reaches a certain plateau of learning and knowledge, gradually destroys himself with the 'fruits' of his advancement, and, after watching civilisation slowly fall apart, starts to build it up anew, only to find that it again comes crumbling down around him.

Even if much of the literature describing this theory is New Age hype – the speculations of over-imaginative writers – there is nothing to say that it can't, at its root, be an accurate depiction of the way things are. For there are elements of this cyclical idea that ring true, especially if one considers the products of advanced technology mentioned above, such as the Egyptian Pyramid – technology that is inexplicable by modern calculation. This is so much more the case when one considers ancient Indian texts. How else could one account for the findings of the Archaeological Survey of India, not to speak of the elaborate details of sophisticated aircraft and nuclear-like weapons abundantly referred to in the Vedic literature? These prehistoric tomes not only describe the colourful outward appearance of these

---

solid iron shaft is centuries old, and, though exposed to inclement weather, even torrential downpours, it shows no signs of rust. Even the construction of such a massive pillar, made of pure iron, would be difficult to accomplish using current means. How, then, did the ancients manufacture it?

8   Author/archaeologist David Hatcher Childress writes, '. . . nearly every ancient culture in the world has myths and legends of an ancient world-before and the cataclysm that destroyed it. . . . The Mayans, Aztecs, and Hopis believed in the destruction of four or more worlds before our own.... The most widely known books in the world, such as the *Bible*, the *Mahabharata*, the *Koran*, and even the *Tao Te Ching* all speak of cataclysms and ancient civilisations that were destroyed.' See Hatcher Childress, *Technology of the Gods: The Incredible Sciences of the Ancients* (Kempton, IL.: Adventures Unlimited Press, 2000), p. 13.

technological wonders – for one can attribute such descriptions to an overactive imagination – but also plausible ways to build and use them, which is knowledge that should have been beyond the ken of ancient man.

Back to the Future?

Both the ancient texts of India and Lucas's films are set not in the future but rather in the past. It is curious indeed that all *Star Wars* movies make prodigious use of futuristic technology, such as spaceships, advanced weaponry, and so on. Why is this curious? Because each of these films clearly assert in their opening text that they are supposed to have taken place millennia ago, in a galaxy far away. The Vaishnava scriptures, too, come to us from a time deep in man's past, and yet, as in *Star Wars*, the accouterments of modern technology are an integral part of their narrative and teaching.

Both the *Mahabharata* and the *Ramayana*, for example, which are thousands of years old, refer to flying machines and weapons of destruction that not only rival but surpass those of modern man:

> The *Ramayana*, and its companion the *Mahabharata*, are something like a combination of George Lucas' *Star Wars* and J. R. R. Tolkien's *Lord of the Rings*. In texts thousands of years old, the combatants fly around in metallic flying machines that run on some sort of 'anti-gravity' mechanism and battle each other with particle beam weapons and horrifying explosive devices.[9]

Even a scholar as respected as the late J. A. B. van Buitenen, who was the George V. Bobrinskoy Distinguished Service Professor of Sanskrit and Indic Studies at the University of Chicago, recognises, in his translation of the *Mahabharata*, that these ancient texts definitely refer to advanced technology, though he admits he is not quite sure what to make of it.[10] In his commentary, he writes of the war of the Yakshas, wherein the aerial city of Shalva, known as Saubha, is mentioned in picturesque detail – Saubha, according to van Buitenen, was 'a huge

---

9   See David Hatcher Childress, *Vimana Aircraft of Ancient India & Atlantis* (Kempton, IL: Adventures Unlimited Press, 1999), p. 53.

10 Translated and edited by J.A.B. van Buitenen, *The Mahabharata*, Books 2 and 3 (Chicago: University of Chicago Press, 1975), pp. 202-3.

flying machine'. He also describes it as 'a spaceship', and the people who ride it, he says, are also known by a revealing name: the Nivatakava-chas, or those who are 'clad in airtight armour'. Van Buitenen remarks that this is a euphemism for 'spacesuits'. Thus, according to a respected Sanskritist, Arjuna is described as battling with spacemen.[11]

Along these same lines, we find that Ravana, in the *Ramayana*, kidnapped Sita in a chariot that could fly like the most versatile of modern aircrafts, and that much of the battle between Rama and the demonking took place in the sky. And while airbourne, they fought with technologiour superiour weapons. But we will discuss this later. For now, it should merely be added that Ravana, as depicted in the *Ramayana*, lived in an ornate 'aerial mansion' above his capital city of Lanka. When Hanuman searched for the kidnapped Sita, he came upon this magnificent structure, and the incident is elaborately described in the epic:

> That heroic son of the Wind-god [Hanuman] saw in the middle of that residential quarter the great aerial mansion-vehicle called Pushpaka-vimana, decorated with pearls and diamonds, and featured with artistic windows made of refined gold.
>
> Constructed as it was by Vishvakarma [architect of the demigods] himself, none could gauge its power nor effect its destruction. It was built with the intention that it should be superiour to all similar constructions. It was poised in the atmosphere without support. It had the capacity to go anywhere. It stood in the sky like a milestone in the path of the sun...
>
> It was the final result of the great prowess gained by austerities. It could fly in any direction that one wanted. It had chambers of remarkable beauty. Everything about it was symmetrical and unique. Knowing the intentions of the master, it could go anywhere at high speed unobstructed by anyone including the wind itself...
>
> It had towers of high artistic work. It had spires and domes like the peaks of mountains. It was immaculate like the autumnal moon.[12]

The idea that ancient peoples had access to advanced technological knowledge, particularly when we look at India's epics, such as the

---

11 Ibid.

12 Swami Tapasyananada, *Sundarakandam of Srimad Valmiki Ramayana* (Madras: Sree Ramakrishna Math,), pp. 46-48.

Mahabharata and the *Ramayana*, was articulated by Erich von Daniken in his now classic if controversial book *Chariots of the Gods*:

> . . . how did the chronicler of the *Mahabharata* know that a weapon capable of punishing a country with a twelve years' drought could exist? And powerful enough to kill the unborn in their mothers' wombs? This ancient Indian epic, the *Mahabharata*, is more comprehensive than the *Bible*, and even at a conservative estimate its original core is at least 5,000 years old. It is well worth reading this epic in the light of present-day knowledge.
>
> We shall not be very surprised when we learn in the *Ramayana* that *vimanas*, i.e., flying machines, navigated at great heights with the aid of quicksilver and a great propulsive wind. The *vimanas* could cover vast distances and could travel forward, upward and downward. Enviably maneuverable space vehicles!
>
> Even imagination needs something to start it off. How can the chronicler give descriptions that presuppose at least some idea of rockets and the knowledge that such a vehicle can ride on a ray and cause a terrifying thunder?[13]

What Exactly is a *Vimana*?

It is natural to ponder, like von Daniken, how ancient Sanskrit literature could refer to spaceships, aircraft, or 'aerial mansions'. Is it a matter of reading into the text meanings that are not actually there, or of mistranslating obscure Sanskrit words? In a word, no. Although the Sanskrit originals do not use the English terms, they are, nonetheless, quite clear. They generally use the word *vimana*, or variations thereof, which unmistakably refers to flying vehicles. Vaishnava scholars say that the word comes from the same root as 'Vamana', the name of the dwarf Brahmin, who was known in ancient India as an Incarnation of Vishnu. The story of Vamana may be summarised from Vaishnava sources as follows:

Millions of years ago, there was a pious Daitya King named Bali. He was the grandson of the famous devotee Prahlad, who was born in a family of demons. Through his good deeds, Bali eventually became ruler of 'the three worlds', a euphemism for the entire cosmos: upper, middle, and lower planetary systems. But the gods wanted their

13 Erich von Daniken, *Chariots of the Gods* (New York: Berkeley Books, reprint, 1999), pp. 70-71.

respective regions to rule; so they implored Vishnu to get their land back. To accommodate them, Vishnu appeared before Bali in the humble guise of a dwarf Brahmin named Vamana. He asked for merely three steps of land: 'Whatever I can cover with three strides, let that be my domain.' Bali agreed, and Vamana-Vishnu assumed a gigantic form. With two steps He covered both the heavens and the earth. Bali beseeched Him to put His final step on his head, to accept him as His surrendered servant. Thus, with three steps, Vamana covered everything in existence, leaving only the Netherworlds for Bali to rule.

The story is mentioned in the *Rig Veda* and retold with greater detail in later Puranas. What is interesting for our purposes is that the word *vimana*, if based on Vamana, already indicates a vehicle that can 'stride the cosmos'. It is not merely a conveyance for short-distance journeys; being related to the tale of Vamana, it potentially includes travel to all three planetary systems. And, as we shall see, *vimanas* are in fact described throughout Vaishnava literature as vehicles that can traverse the many universes in God's creation.

The literature on *vimanas* basically describe two different kinds: first, man-made conveyances that are comparable to airplanes, visually resembling birds; and second, odd-shaped structures that fly in inexplicable ways and which are constructed by supernatural beings. According to mathematician/philosopher Richard L. Thompson, 'The machines in category one are described mainly in medieval, secular Sanskrit works dealing with architecture, automata, military siege engines, and other mechanical contrivances. Those in category two are described in ancient works such as the *Rig Veda*, the *Mahabharata*, the *Ramayana*, and the Puranas, and they have many features reminiscent of UFOs.'[14]

Vimanas in Vaishnava Texts

In the Tenth Canto of the *Bhagavata Purana* (*Srimad Bhagavatam*), we find the ancient story of Shalva, mentioned earlier by van Buitenen in its *Mahabharata* context. Shalva was an ambitious earthly king who developed an intense sense of enmity toward Lord Krishna. Accordingly, he vowed to destroy Krishna's magnificent city of Dvaraka – and

---

14   Richard L. Thompson, *Alien Identities: Ancient Insights into Modern UFO Phenomena* (San Diego: Govardhan Hill Publishing, 1993), p. 257.

he used a vimana in an attempt to accomplish this end. His particular *vimana* is discussed by commentator Swami Prabhupada, mentioned earlier:

> The airplane occupied by Shalva was very mysterious. It was so extraordinary that sometimes many airplanes would appear to be in the sky, and sometimes there were apparently none. Sometimes the plane was visible and sometimes not visible, and the warriors of the Yadu dynasty were puzzled about the whereabouts of the peculiar airplane. Sometimes they would see the airplane on the ground, sometimes flying in the sky, sometimes resting on the peak of a hill, and sometimes floating on the water. The wonderful airplane flew in the sky like a whirling firebrand – it was not steady even for a moment.[15]

Interestingly, Shalva's *vimana* is described as being distinct among aircraft, implying both that there were other types of aircraft at the time and that this one was peculiar among them. The same story explains that Shalva had performed severe austerities, worshipping the demigod Shiva for a very long time, in order to procure this unique 'aerial city', as it is called elsewhere in the text. Pleased with Shalva's sense of sacrifice, Shiva ordered Maya Danava, chief among the humanoid beings of the planet Talatala,[16] to construct this 'flying iron city named "Saubha"' so that Shalva might use it in his fight against Krishna.

Such reference to flying machines is not uncommon in ancient Indian texts: '…*vimanas* are frequently mentioned in the Puranas and the *Mahabharata*. Apparently, they were as commonplace to people of the old Vedic culture as airplanes are to us today.'[17] Some examples: the timeless story of Kaliya Krishna, wherein Krishna defeats the huge venomous serpent named Kaliya, nonchalantly refers to Kaliya's flying machine – '[In my last life] I was very opulent and beautiful', said the serpent, 'and I used to wander freely in all directions in my

---

15 A. C. Bhaktivedanta Swami Prabhupada, *Krsna: The Supreme Personality of Godhead* (Los Angeles: Bhaktivedanta Book Trust, 1986), p. 649.

16 Though an ancient text, the *Srimad Bhagavatam* frequently refers to other planets and the kinds of beings who exist there. The Danavas are especially significant in the present context, for they are described as a species particularly known for expertise in technology – they are also associated with darkness and materialistic illusion. This, of course, further associates excessive technological advancement with the woes of a materialistic culture.

17 Richard L. Thompson, op. cit., p. 268.

airplane.'[18] In the original Sanskrit, Kaliya uses the word *vimanena*, generally translated as 'in my flying vehicle'. A similar story tells us that Krishna once freed a tormented soul from his destiny in the body of a lizard, awarding him instead a celestial body used for travelling to the spiritual world: 'Assisting him in his journey to his divine destination, Krishna sent an opulent aircraft (*vimana*) for King Nriga, the reptile in question, as others looked on.'[19]

Another story emphasises the importance of careful driving (!), when Vishvavasu, a divine pilot, falls from his *vimana* while ogling the beautiful Devahuti, the then soon-to-be bride of Kardama Muni.[20] Once married, Kardama decided to take Devahuti on a tour of the universe. To do so, he summoned the best of *vimanas* – an aerial mansion fully equipped with facilities for extravagant pleasures. By yogic power, he was able to manifest this elaborate sky-borne palace, resplendent with lush gardens and lakes, beautiful swans and endearing animals. It is described as being more like a city than a one-palace airplane.[21] The ancient text reveals that Kardama used this *vimana* to go to various planets: 'He travelled in that way through the various planets, as the air passes uncontrolled in every direction. Coursing through the air in that great and splendid aerial mansion, which could fly at his will, he surpassed even the demigods.'[22]

It should be noted that these *vimanas* are not 'spiritual' vehicles, either. These are mechanised aircraft made of material elements. To be sure, the ancient literature of India also talks about flying structures that are fully spiritual; they are known as Vaikuntha Vimanas. But these are very different from the *vimanas* mentioned above. The Vaikuntha Vimanas are usually said to be swanlike in shape; they are made of a spiritual substance known as *chintamani*, or 'gem-like particles of consciousness', like the one described in the story of Dhruva Maharaj.[23] Our analysis, however, will more properly be confined to

---

18 See *Bhagavata Purana* (*Srimad Bhagavatam*), Canto 10, Chapter 34, verses 12, 13.

19 Ibid., 10.64.30.

20 Ibid., 3.22.17.

21 Ibid., Canto 3, Chapter 22.

22 Ibid., 3.23.40, 41. In these verses, the demigods are referred to as *vaimanikan*, or 'those who travel in *vimanas*'.

23 The story of Dhruva is complex and need not be detailed here. Pertinent verses are in ibid., 4.12.19, 20.

mechanised *vimanas*, for these are more akin to the kind Lucas uses in his *Star Wars* universe.

In many ways the most important text on such *vimanas* is the controversial Sanskrit work known as the *Vaimanika Shastra*. Kanishk Nathan, who has studied *vimanas* in depth, writes that this book 'describes a technology that is not only far beyond the science of the times but is even way beyond the possible conceptual scientific imagination of an ancient Indian, including concepts such as solar energy and photography.'[24]

The origins of this text are shrouded in mystery. Some say that it was revealed in a trance to a man named Pandit Subbaraya Sastry in 1923; others that it is originally part of the *Yantra-sarvasva*, or *The Encyclopedia of Machines*, written in ancient times by the sage Bharadvaja. Because of its uncertain origin, many scholars dismiss it as a forgery. But even if we never determine the original source of the work itself, we do know that it contains greater technical knowledge than Sastry was known to have had, and that it was advanced in understanding even if we assume that it originated in the 1920s.[25]

How Do *Vimanas* Work?

In A. C. Bhaktivedanta Swami Prabhupada's commentary on the *Srimad Bhagavatam*, he mentions three processes known to ancient man for travelling in outer space.[26] Using Sanskrit terminology, he calls the first '*ka-pota-vayu*', which generally implied a mechanical conveyance: the word *pota* means 'ship', while *ka* refers to 'space' or 'ether' – the idea being that these are ships that move through space. *Kapota* can also mean 'pigeon', evoking a sort of double-entendre often used in Sanskrit literature. The second form of travel was called *akasha-patana*,

---

24 Kanishk Nathan, 'UFOs and India: Ancient and Contemporary', *MUFON 1987 UFO Symposium Proceedings* (Seguin, Texas: MUFON Inc., 1987), p. 71. Quoted in Thompson, ibid.

25 Though the scientific jargon of the *Vaimanika Shastra* would be inappropriate for our present work, this author recommends the following books for greater illumination on the construction and use of *vimanas*: G. R. Josyer, trans., *Vymaanika-Shaastra Aeronautics* by Maharshi Bharadwaaja, Propounded by Subbaraya Sastry (Mysore, India: G. R. Josyer, 1973); Dileep K. Kanjilal, *Vimana in Ancient India* (Calcutta: Sanskrit Pustak Bhandar, 1985); and David H. Childress, *Vimana Aircraft of Ancient India and Atlantis* (Stelle, Illinois: Adventures Unlimited Press, 1991).

26 A. C. Bhaktivedanta Swami Prabhupada, trans., *Srimad Bhagavatam* (Los Angeles: Bhaktivedanta Book Trust, 1982), Canto 4, Part 2, p. 182.

which referred to the fact that certain planes can travel at the speed of mind but also that there was an art of travelling *by* the speed of mind. In other words, by yogic discipline one could learn to move physical objects, including one's own body, with mental power. This is related to *laghima-siddhi*: the skill of levitation, or antigravity, by which one becomes virtually weightless, so that one can float in the air or on water. The third form of travel was called the Vaikuntha process, and this referred to a level of spiritual attainment whereby one could travel in swanlike *vimanas* directly arranged by the Lord, as mentioned earlier.

Regarding the *akasha-patana* form of travel, Richard L. Thompson has noted the following:

> According to the *Bhagavata Purana*, ether is the fabric of space, and all gross matter is generated by transformations of ether. This is an idea reminiscent of John Wheeler's theory of geometrodynamics, which holds that all material particles are simply twists or deformations of space-time. Both the *Bhagavata Purana* and Wheeler's theory imply that matter is directly connected to ether. Thus it should be possible to manipulate ether by manipulating gross matter. From this, we can see that it might be possible to build a physical machine that can manipulate space-time and provide for unusual modes of travel. . . . The *Bhagavata Purana* also states that the ether is the field of action of the subtle mind. This suggests that it may be possible to manipulate the ether by mind action, thus allowing for the *akasha-patana* system of travel.[27]

Some *vimanas* were propelled by the power of the mind, but others by more 'crude' methods. According to the *Samarangana-sutradhara*, written in the Eleventh century by Bhojadeva, the most common of these machines were made of 'a lighter form of wood' (*laghu-dharu*). They appeared like birds or modern planes in the sense of having wing-like formations on either side of a central structure, and they became airborne with the help of a complex 'fire chamber' involving heated mercury. Though many of the texts on *vimanas* describe sophisticated engines and methods of flight, including jet propulsion, the details of which, again, are beyond the scope of this book, it is the mercury vortex engine that has received the most attention.

---

27 See Richard L. Thompson, ibid., p. 286. Also see John A. Wheeler, *Geometrodynamics* (New York: Academic Press, 1962), quoted in Thompson.

The *Vimanika Shastra*, in Chapter Five, elaborates on this particular kind of engine – how it is made and how it is used. Briefly, the heated mercury generated the power needed to lift the craft, and a pilot would affect the direction by using a compound control panel inside the heart of the machine. It is interesting that the mercury method[28] is mentioned in the *Surya-siddhanta* as well, a text dealing with advanced astronomy – it describes a mercury-based engine that provided rotary motion for a mechanical model of the solar system. The text warns its readers to keep the mercury engine a secret, lest it would fall into 'the wrong hands'.

The sages who wrote these texts were probably not aware that Nazi Germany would one day come into being. Nonetheless, it is now well-known that SS leader Heinrich Himmler was interested in the secrets of the East[29] and that he had a team of Nazi scientists, known as the Ahnenerbe,[30] which had planned expeditions to India (and actually carried out expeditions to other places, such as Tibet) to unearth them. Luckily, these ancient mysteries were embedded in complicated Sanskrit texts and, even if one learned the language – as many of Himmler's men did – one must study for years under a qualified teacher, in an esoteric lineage, to unravel them. This is certainly our good fortune: imagine, for example, if the ancient *brahmastra*, which is described as being like a nuclear bomb, fell into the hands of Hitler's men. Swami Prabhupada tells us about this devastating weapon:

---

28 Interestingly, the mythical god Mercury, known as Hermes in Greek literature, was a messenger who was always depicted in flight – the idea being that if the gods wanted to convey a message over long distances, Mercury was the best way to get it there, efficiently and quickly.

29 In fact, Himmler was a great admirer of Hinduism and told his personal masseur, Felix Kersten, that he regularly studied the *Bhagavad-gita*, used it to justify his actions and carried it wherever he went. This is detailed at length in *The Memoirs of Doctor Felix Kersten* (Garden City: Doubleday, 1947), in which Kersten recounts his conversations with Himmler about India. For more on the interest of the Nazi leadership in Vedic philosophy, see Karla Poewe, *New Religions and the Nazis* (New York: Routledge, 2006).

30 The Ahnenerbe, which was itself a branch of the SS, carried out official expeditions throughout Europe, the Middle East, Antarctica, and also to Tibet. More information on the Ahnenerbe can be found in Heather Anne Pringle, *The Master Plan: Himmler's Scholars and the Holocaust* (New York: Hyperion, 2006) and Christopher Hale, *Himmler's Crusade: The Nazi Expedition to Find the Origins of the Aryan Race* (Hoboken: John Wiley & Sons, 2003).

The *brahmastra* is similar to the modern nuclear weapon manipulated by atomic energy. The atomic energy works wholly on total combustibility, and so the *brahmastra* also acts. It creates an intolerable heat similar to atomic radiation, but the difference is that the atomic bomb is a gross type of nuclear weapon, whereas the *brahmastra* is a subtle type of weapon produced by chanting hymns. It is a different science, and in the days gone by such science was cultivated in the land of Bharata-varsha [the ancient name for India]. The subtle science of chanting hymns is also material, but it has yet to be known by the modern material scientists. Subtle material science is not spiritual, but it has a direct relationship with the spiritual method, which is still subtler. A chanter of hymns knew how to apply the weapon as well as how to retract it. That was perfect knowledge.[31]

Interestingly, Dr. Robert Oppenheimer, quoted at the beginning of this chapter, was adept in Sanskrit and quoted the *Gita* (10.34) when he witnessed the first atomic blast in 1945: 'I am all-devouring death, the destroyer of all' (or, as he himself quoted it, 'Now I am become death, the destroyer of worlds'). When he was asked in an interview several years later if this was indeed the first atomic bomb ever to be detonated, his reply was, 'Well, yes, at least in modern history.'[32] In fact, a careful reading of the *Ramayana* and the *Mahabharata* reveals frequent use of nuclear-like missiles, as already stated. As a student of these texts, Oppenheimer would have been aware of this.

According to David Hatcher Childress, excavations at Mohenjodaro and Harappa indicate atomic explosions in India's distant past:

...they discovered scattered skeletons about the cities, many holding hands and sprawling in the streets, as if some instant, horrible doom had taken place. I mean, people are just lying, unburied, in the streets of the city....These skeletons are among the most radioactive ever found, on a par with those at Nagasaki and Hiroshima....Other cities have been found in northern India that show indications of explosions of great magnitude: one such city, found between the Ganges and the mountains of Rajmahal, seems to have been subjected to intense heat. Huge masses of walls and foundations of the ancient city are fused

31 A. C. Bhaktivedanta Swami Prabhupada, *Srimad-Bhagavatam* (Los Angeles: The Bhaktivedanta Book Trust, 1972), First Canto, commentary to 7.28.

32 Charles Berlitz, *Mysteries of Forgotten Worlds* (New York: Doubleday, 1972). Quoted in Hatcher Childress, *Technology of the Gods: The Incredible Sciences of the Ancients*, op. cit., p. 238.

together, literally vitrified! Since there is no indication of a volcanic eruption at Mohenjo-Daro, or at the other cities, the intense heat...can only be explained by an atomic blast or some other unknown weapon.[33]

Now, let us again consider the Nazis' interest in India: they even came to use the Swastika, originally an Indian symbol, as their trademark for the 'perfected race', or Aryan race. After the end of the Third Reich, some neo-Nazis even came to believe that Hitler was the final *avatar* (incarnation) of Vishnu predicted for the Kali-yuga.[34] Whatever erroneous theories the Nazis may have constructed after studying Indian texts, it seems possible that their main purpose in studying Vedic literature was not so much to find the secrets of elaborate weaponry as much as to find information on aeronautics.

Perhaps as a result of what Hitler's scholars brought back from India, the Nazis were in fact the first to develop the pulse-jet engine for use in the revolutionary V-1 and V-2 rocket bombs. The Nazis also used jet engines to create the first-ever fighter jets, the Messerschmitt

---

33 Hatcher Childress, ibid. These discoveries were originally reported by a Russian researcher, Alexander Gorbovsky, in a 1966 book (only in Russian), *Riddles of Ancient History*. There has also been evidence for the ancient use of nuclear weapons or nuclear energy discovered in the region of Rajasthan in India, where high levels of radioactivity have been detected in slag. A scientific study of this area has been published in an article by T. B. Pradeepkumar, et al., 'Uranium in Ancient Slag from Rajasthan', *Current Science*, vol. 94, no. 8, 25 April 2008, also available at www.ias.ac.in/currsci/apr252008/1031.pdf. Accessed 30 September 2010.

34 The idea of Hitler as an *avatar* began with a European woman of Nazi sympathies, who took the name Savitri Devi and lived most of her life in India. She wrote about this idea in many books after the Second World War, particularly in *The Lightning and the Sun*, which she self-published in Calcutta in 1958. This idea has since proliferated throughout the more esoteric elements of the neo-Nazi movement, most notably in the works of the Chilean author Miguel Serrano, such as *Adolf Hitler, el Último Avatāra*, or *Adolf Hitler: The Final Avatar* (Santiago: Ediciones la Nueva Edad, 1984). Serrano himself served as the ambassador from Chile to India between 1953 and 1962 and was very interested in Vedic philosophy. For more on the interrelationship between India, Hitler's regime, and post-war Nazi esotericism, see Koenraad Elst, *The Saffron Swastika* (New Delhi: Voice of India, 2001); Nicholas Goodrick-Clarke, *Hitler's Priestess: Savitri Devi, the Hindu-Aryan Myth, and Neo-Nazism* (New York University Press, 1998); and Nicholas Goodrick-Clarke, *Black Sun: Aryan Cults, Esoteric Nazism, and the Politics of Identity* (New York: New York University Press, 2002).

262. According to journalist Mukul Sharma, the Soviets, too, were aware of ancient India's advanced knowledge of aircraft: 'Curiously, Soviet scientists have discovered what they call "age-old instruments used in navigating cosmic vehicles" in caves in Turkestan and the Gobi desert. The "devices" are hemispherical objects of glass or porcelain, ending in a cone with a drop of mercury inside....'[35] Researcher Stephen Knapp details some of the positive ways in which knowledge of *vimanas* has been used in modern times. In a lengthy piece on what he calls 'the Vedic Ion Machine', he writes:

> It turns out that there are verses in the Tenth Chapter of the *Rig-Veda* that refer to the Art of Flight, and the means by which it can be achieved. The great Rishi Bharadwaja wrote a commentary, called *Yantra Vidya* (*Science of Machines*), in which he describes the mechanism which provides the impulse needed for propulsion, involving the combination of eight sub-assemblies and using the interaction principally of solar energy and mercury....The ancient text known as the *Vymaanika-Shastra* contains detailed instructions on building a mercury vortex engine. It turned out that a Sanskrit scholar, Shivkar Bapuji Talpade, used his Sanskrit knowledge and creativity to construct such an aircraft according to the *Rig-Veda* description. In fact, he demonstrated the capability of the aircraft on a beach in Bombay, India in 1895. The demonstration was attended by such people as Maharaja Sayajirao Gaekwad of Baroda, and was reported in a leading Marathi daily newspaper, called The *Kesari*. Let us remember that this was eight years before the Wright Brothers achieved their first flight at Kitty Hawk, North Carolina. Mr. Shivkar Bapuji Talpade used this flying machine, the Vedic Ion Engine, to reach an altitude of 1,500 feet.
>
> The basis of the Vedic Ion Engine is to use a stream of high-velocity electrified particles instead of hot gases to propel the aircraft. Interestingly, the National Aeronautics and Space Administration (NASA) was planning to send a space probe to meet with Halley's Comet in 1980 which was to be powered by such an Ion Engine. As Bhalchandra Patwardhan's article explains, 'The theory of the Ion Engine has been credited to Robert Goddard, long recognised as the father of liquid-fuel rocketry. It is claimed that in 1906, long before Goddard launched his first modern rocket, his imagination had conceived the idea of an Ion rocket.'

---

35 See Mukul Sharma, 'The "*Vimanas*" or Flying Machines of Ancient India', in *The Times of India*, 8 April 1999.

However, this is still after Talpade had already demonstrated what he could do by using the Vedic information to build a flying machine without additional research and development to perfect it. Nonetheless, as the article continues, 'The engine now being developed for future use by NASA, by some strange coincidence, also uses Mercury bombardment units powered by solar cells [much like the Vedic description].'[36]

The above strongly suggests that the Vedic *vimana* is not a fantasy. Still, it is natural to doubt that ancient texts could contain postmodern secrets of advanced technology: one might say that it is relatively easy to anticipate the direction of science and technology, as is done in modern science fiction, and to fantasise about the nature of inventions yet-to-be. Again, though an imaginative fiction writer might foresee futuristic flying machines and weapons of mass destruction, he or she would not be able to offer legitimate details for the construction and maintenance of these things, at least not before man actually discovers them. Indic texts, on the other hand, actually did offer such information, though it was encoded in Sanskrit verse, as described above.

But scholarship is a serious enterprise, and so there are scholars, no doubt, who would still feel the need to relegate all of this to science fiction fantasy, like a sort of *Star Wars* from ancient India. They would say that such stories must have been known to be fictitious when originally conceived but somehow, eventually, came to be accepted as literal fact. While an intelligent reader will necessarily consider such a conclusion, he or she must also consider just how something like this can happen. And further: could this ever happen with *Star Wars*? Lucas' films were known as a fable from the moment they were created and, in all likelihood, they will continue to be so known.

It might be argued that there are those who see India's epic and Puranic stories as mythological or as fictitious. But this is not how the tradition sees itself. From the original literature to the later commentaries by Vaishnava sages – the epics, the Puranas, and the *Vedas* are, internally, all seen as literally true. This is important. In other words, if one were to argue that *Star Wars*, in the distant future, might eventually be deemed a true story, we need simply ask ourselves how Lucas, the creator of *Star Wars* – or even how the early critics and commentators

---

36 Stephen Knapp, *Proof of Vedic Culture's Global Existence* (Detroit, MI.: The World Relief Network, 2000), pp. 34-35.

on the *Star Wars* film series – viewed his own creation. If we are even a little thorough in our research, it will be clear that all those involved knew that they were dealing with a fanciful and fictitious story – a very good fable, but a fable nonetheless.

Star Wars Vimanas

Because *Star Wars* was created in the modern era, Lucas was able to put modern technology to use, both in terms of the underlying theory behind the starships and other devices in his films, making them look real, and in the techniques he used to make them come to life on screen. As a consequence, *Star Wars* movies, as we know, delight us with futuristic-looking aircraft and believable depictions of interstellar travel.

It should not surprise us, then, that *Star Wars* films nonchalantly refer to Ion pre-cycle impellers, Ion turbines – and a variety of sublight engines that are based on the principle of Ion thrust, catalysed by reactants and accelerators from fuel that can take the form of pressurised radioactive gas, volatile composite fluids, or explosive liquid metal (mercury?). This is all explained by David West Reynolds, arguably the world's foremost authority on the aircraft depicted in *Star Wars*. He earned his Ph.D. in archaeology at the University of Michigan and wrote the book *Star Wars, Incredible Cross-Sections: The Ultimate Guide to Star Wars Vehicles and Spacecraft* (New York: DK Publishing, Inc., 1998), among others.

Reynolds, who was given unrestricted access to the extensive Lucasfilm archives at Skywalker Ranch in California, approaches the *Star Wars* universe as if it were a real 'culture from another time and place to explore.'[37] He worked with a team of artists, especially Hans Jenssen and Richard Chasemore, to recreate the ships in Lucas's head, ships that are not unlike the *vimanas* of ancient India. Together, they have reconstructed what the spacecraft engines would probably look like, what kind of fuel they would have run on, and so on. They depict with exacting detail the Star Destroyer, the TIE Fighter, the Death Star, the Sandcrawler, the Millennium Falcon, and others.

---

37 David West Reynolds, *Star Wars, Incredible Cross-Sections: The Ultimate Guide to Star Wars Vehicles and Spacecraft* (New York: DK Publishing, Inc., 1998), back cover flap.

When Reynolds tells us that the Star Destroyer carries 9,700 stormtroopers and has a full wing of 72 TIE Fighters, we are naturally reminded of the aerial mansions and anti-gravitational cities mentioned in the Vedic literature. When he writes that TIE (Twin Ion Engine) Fighters are made with engines that include 'the most precisely manufactured propulsion system in the galaxy' and that 'Solar Ionisation collects light energy and channels it through a reactor to fire emissions from a high-pressure radioactive gas',[38] we are reminded of what the *Vaimanika Shastra* tells us about *vimanas*: that they became airborne as a result of the interaction of solar energy and mercury. When we read that the Sandcrawler has 'a reactor that melts processed ore and metal into a superheated cascade', we can't help but think of the mercury vortex engine mentioned in ancient Indian texts.

The correlating factors are many, and it is not our desire to make too much of them. Suffice it to say that both *Star Wars* and Vaishnava literature depict a time in the distant past when man was not supposed to have knowledge of things like vortex engines and machines that fly. Yet, whereas *Star Wars* is set in the past but conceived in the present, ancient Indian literature is, in fact, ancient. This means that while it is far from miraculous that Lucas could bring these concepts into his movies – after all, with some sustained research, anybody living in the modern era could conceive of such things – it is indeed extraordinary that sages in India's past not only wrote about futuristic technology, but taught us how to use it with grace and perspective.

---

38 Ibid., p. 8.

6

JEDI WARRIORS:
THE CHURCH OF LATTER-DAY KSHATRIYAS

*'The Jedi are spiritual adepts – warriors who fight their own evil incli-
nations as much as they fight evil-doers in the external world. They are
noble, chivalrous, powerful, embodying all the qualities of the gods. In
Western traditions, one would have to look to myths to find their like.
In the East, such personalities existed in abundance in the Kshatriya
class, who are described in Epic and Puranic texts. Here, indeed, is
where one finds the prototype of the Jedi.'*
–Franklin S. Harrison, *Protectors of the Righteous: East and West*[1]

The Jedi are valorous warriors who adhere to a spiritual code of ethics. In the *Star Wars* milieu, they are considered the 'twice-born'
– a privileged group of individuals who are born not only to mother
and father, but who also undergo spiritual initiation, which is seen as
a second birth. The Kshatriyas of ancient India – can it be a coincidence? – lived by principles almost identical to those of the Jedi. They
were among the twice-born of Indian tradition, and they were mystic-
warriors of great integrity.[2] Thus, in this chapter we will look at the

---

1   See Franklin S. Harrison, *Protectors of the Righteous: East and West* (New York:
    Innerspace Books, 2000), p. 21.

2   Brahmins, Kshatriyas, and Vaishyas are called twice-born for a number of reasons,
    not least of which is the fact that they are considered 'spiritually evolved souls',
    as opposed to Shudras, who are generally not spiritually advanced. They are also
    called twice-born because, at roughly twelve years of age, they undergo a 're-birth'
    ceremony, which indicates their coming of age – they are now able to perform

similarities between these two groups of guardian-yogis, as well as the related concept of the guru-disciple relationship, which is indispensable for both Jedi and Kshatriya.

Second only to the Brahmins, the Kshatriyas were highly esteemed in the Varna social system of ancient India. Though we have briefly described this system in a previous chapter, we should here elaborate on its specific nature and practice. As an aside, the similarity between Brahmins and Kshatriyas, i.e., that they are both twice-born, makes it easy for the untrained eye to confuse the two – and to even claim that the Jedi might in fact be more closely aligned with Brahmins than with Kshatriyas. One glaring example of this confusion can be found in an otherwise insightful article by Cie Sharp.[3] Basing his work on an earlier paper by Rajan Rajbhandari ('*Star Wars* and Hinduism', 1994), Sharp writes, 'I see the Jedi as *Brahmins*.' He supports this contention by claiming that one's status as a Jedi is determined by birthright, and that, traditionally, one is identified as a Brahmin in this same way. He further argues that the Jedi engage in guru/disciple relationships, as do Brahmins. But, as already mentioned, these same phenomena exist for Kshatriyas: they are generally born into Kshatriya families and are accordingly identified by their peers. They also take initiation from gurus and take part in guru/disciple relationships, even though Sharp suggests that these things are peculiar to Brahmins.

Anticipating that some readers will disagree with his theory, saying that the Jedi engage in warfare, and that Brahmins simply do not fight, Sharp points out that Parashurama, an incarnation of Vishnu, and Dronacharya, the teacher of the Pandavas, were Brahmins, and that they, indeed, had many times engaged in battle. But if Sharp looked closely at the voluminous pages of Vaishnava history, he would admit that these two were exceptions rather than the rule, and, in general, Jedis have much more in common with Kshatriyas, as this chapter will make clear. Incidentally, the story of Parashurama has much affinity

---

religious rituals and take part in temple sacrifices. For more on this topic see G. M. Carstairs, *The Twice-Born: A Study of a Community of High-Caste Hindus* (London: Hogarth Press, 1957) and Louis Dumont, *Homo Hierarchicus: An Essay on the Caste System*, trans., Mark Sainsbury (Chicago: 1970).

3   See 'More Hindu Themes in the *Star Wars* Saga,' from the *Jedi Planet* Web site, 4 June 2002. It is no longer available, but is archived at Google's Wayback Archive: web.archive.org/web/20020624151256/http://www.thejediplanet.com/features/hindu2.shtml. Accessed 30 September 2010.

with that of Darth Vader, who, in his earlier life as Anakin Skywalker, was responsible for annihilating legions of Jedi warriors, in the same way that Parashurama is said to have exterminated generations of Kshatriyas.

Psychologist Jonathan Young, author and longtime associate of Joseph Campbell, has this to say: 'The Jedi are the high priests of the Force as well as the noble knights of their time. The Jedi began earlier as a theological and philosophical study group. Only after long consideration of the Force did they take up the idea of fighting for high principles and causes.'[4] In consideration of Young's perception, we may admit that the Jedi are more like a hybrid. In other words, the Jedi exhibit a merger of brahminical and Kshatriya sensibilities. Overall, however, they are more like Kshatriyas, for even their brahminical qualities of learning and introspection were often found in the Kshatriyas of Vedic times.

When Obi-Wan first presents Luke with his lightsaber, he informs him that the Jedi were the guardians of peace and light in the Old Republic. It is ironic, or perhaps telling, that it is the 'Old Republic' in which we first encounter the Jedi, for the Western world was first introduced to 'Kshatriya-like' ideals in Plato's book, also named *The Republic*. Here we read about the ideal society and the virtuous warriors that are a necessary part of it, not unlike the Kshatriyas and the Jedi in Vedic culture and *Star Wars*, respectively. In fact, it is often said that Plato's ideal society was based on the Varna system of ancient India, a subject to which we will now turn.

What Is the *Varna* System?

Varna must be distinguished from 'caste': the Sanskrit term *varna*, as used in early texts such as the *Rig Veda*, classified people according to their inherent nature, acknowledging the diverse and multifarious ways in which their distinct psychophysical makeup allowed them to function in society.

Varna is best translated as 'colour' – this is because it refers to one's personal proclivity, or the way one's natural disposition *colours* the way

---

4   See Jonathan Young, 'The Phantom Menace as Personal Mythology', in *The Quest: Journal of the Theosophical Society in America,* Volume 87, Number 5, September/ October 1999, p. 166.

he or she interacts with the external world. Such personal characteristics might arise because of one's birth in a particular family – it might be genetic – or it might be acquired in other ways, through conditioning, for example. However it comes into being, we are speaking here of character traits that are deeply embedded in the consciousness, defining, in a sense, who one is. In regard to the *varna* system itself, human society is divided into a four-tiered ideal, the *Chatur-varna*, or the 'four-coloured orders' of man: white, red, yellow, and black. To begin with white – which is symbolic of Sattva, or goodness and truthfulness – such people embody the qualities of purity, faith and detachment. They have a thirst for knowledge and often have a spiritual temperament. They are called Brahmins. The next *varna* is red – the colour of Rajas, which is energy or passion. This is characterised by action, determination, and aggression. Those who partake of this mode seek honour, power, and status. They are generally strong people with military and political leanings. They are called Kshatriyas. After this, we have the yellow *varna* – this is a person who shares certain Rajasic traits with those in the red *varna*, but he is devoid of martial tendencies. He is generally more family-centred and inclined to business, typically involving agriculture (but not always). Such people excel in communication, verbal exchange, trade, and commerce, and they are known as Vaishyas. Finally, black represents the quality of Tamas – that which is inert, or weighed down. People with this disposition are given to ignorance or dullness. They are usually dependent on the rest of society for motivation and direction. They are called Shudras.

Thus, at the highest tier of Vedic society, we find the Brahmins, or priestly intellectuals; slightly lower are the Kshatriyas, or the warrior class; the Vaishyas, who are generally businessmen and farmers, are next; finally, we have the Shudras, or the servants of the rest of society. Most forms of social stratification resemble the *varna* system to one degree or another. For this reason, ancient Vedic texts refer to this system as universal, in the sense that people tend to lean toward one or another of these characteristics and can thus broadly be defined as either Brahmin, Kshatriya, Vaishya, or Shudra.

While in India today the various classes are generally depicted in terms of highest to lowest in terms of power, wealth and status, the Vaishnavas emphasise the equality of all classes, noting that societal differences are merely external, existing for practical purposes, i.e., the interaction of people in day-to-day life. Vaishnava texts are clear that the soul, the core of one's being, is more important than any external designation, and, because of this, everyone is equal in the eyes of God. And all have important roles to play in the divine drama of life.

Though one fits into the various *varnas* according to inclination and disposition, in actual practice in India, birth status has come to preclude all other factors which once largely determined how an individual would live his or her life. As a result, today, familial associations and hereditary concerns have become major deciding factors in determining which *varna* a person will take part in: this compromised form of the original Vedic system is today known as 'the caste system'.[5]

Vaishnavas reject the modern caste system as a poor derivative of the original idea. While the *varna* system recognised social differences, it also claimed an underlying spiritual harmony for all people. Thus, while there was an implied hierarchy based on one's external designation, it was merely for the purpose of social order – beyond the hierarchy stemming from one's vocational identity, there was mutual respect for all members of society, all working for the shared goal of spiritual realisation. But as the modern-day caste system took hold, all of the symbols and customs of the classes of Indian society took on superficial meanings, devolving into petty competitiveness, interclass hatred, and strife.

Among the many catalysts for this devolution, perhaps, was the fact that the *varnas* were identified with colours – white for a Brahmin; red for a Kshatriya, yellow for a Vaishya, and black for a Shudra – though these colours were originally symbolic and had no relation to the hue of one's skin. Today, there are Brahmins who frown upon those Indians who look darker, claiming that they must be of lower birth status. In a similar way, Brahmins are allowed gold and silver ornaments, while Kshatriyas, also twice-born, can use the same kinds of ornaments but only if they are of an inferiour quality to those used by the Brahmins. Vaishyas are to use brass ornaments and Shudras can only use those made of iron. The Varnas were also associated with the four ages of time: Brahmins with the purest, Satya-yuga; Kshatriyas with the slightly less revered Treta-yuga; Vaishyas with Dvapara-yuga;

---

5 For more on the current system of *jati* and how it differs from the Varna system, see 'Varna and Jati', in Mircea Eliade, ed., *The Encyclopedia of Religion*, Vol. 15 (New York: Macmillan and Free Press, 1987), p. 188.

and, finally, Shudras are identified with the iron age, Kali-yuga, or the age of degeneration, in which we are now living.

In the *Rig Veda*, the *varnas* are associated with various parts of the body: the Brahmins are the head; the Kshatriyas are the arms; the Vaishyas are the torso; and the Shudras are the feet. Identification with these bodily parts gradually led to traditional modes of greeting according to one's station in life. The Brahmin stretched his right hand forward reaching the level of his ear; the Kshatriya held his hand to the height of his chest; and the Vaishya would hold it low, near his waist. The Shudra bowed down and stretched forward his joined hands in respect. Again, these customs and forms of civil interaction were meant to distinguish one class from another, but were never intended to be demeaning or judgmental in a negative sense. Today's caste system, however, throws a dark light on bodily differences, glorifying the Brahmin and maligning the Shudra.

This brings us to the much later concept of *jati*, a term that more accurately translates as 'caste'. Today, in India, it is used for the many 'sub-castes' found throughout the subcontinent, virtually replacing the original *varna* system.

Star Wars: Return of the *Jati*

Jati comes from the root *jan* ('to be born'), or *janma* ('birth'), and it implies 'begetting' or 'producing'. In terms of caste, it refers to the social stratum into which one is born. Thus, unlike *varna*, it refers to one's birth status and not to personal inclinations. For the modern Indian, *jati* is binding, and there are strict rules governing occupations, foods, marriage, and interaction with people born in other castes. Though there are only four *varnas*, there are literally thousands of *jatis*. Unfortunately, most Indians today feel duty-bound to honour their placement in one of these innumerable sub-castes – again, dictated by birth – as opposed to searching out their *varna*, which would enable them to best function in society by engaging their true psychophysical disposition.

In Lucas's films, too, we sense a tension between the idea that one must be born a Jedi, with large amounts of midi-chlorians in one's blood, and that one might just be a Jedi by inclination and training. In other words, one walks away from *Star Wars* with a question: 'Is being a Jedi merely about birth (which would align it with the conception of *jati*), or is it about one's inherent quality and work (one's *varna*)? Could I be a Jedi, or is it a position reserved for a select few?' Clearly, there is truth to both positions: a person can pursue Jedi *dharma* on his own and, through training and practice, achieve Jedi-like qualities. But being born with certain advantages, like a high midi-chlorian count, or to parents who have trained one as a Jedi from the very beginning, wouldn't hurt, either.

And this is seen in Vaishnava culture as well: while true Varna is more about an individual's qualitative traits and personal inclinations, it is well-known that parents who favour a particular field of work will direct their children to that same field. While this may not always hold true, it is a common enough phenomenon, making the family into which one is born a legitimate factor in assessing one's occupational direction. This, coupled with the fact that there are definitely metaphysical reasons – such as *karma* and destiny – why one is born in a particular family, makes the use of the *jati* idea understandable, if only from a particular point of view.

But rather than belabour this point, let us instead look at deeper similarities between Jedi and Kshatriya. We should perhaps begin by reassessing our conception of 'the warrior personality type', for we in the West tend to identify two basic 'warrior' models: first, there are those who are naturally aggressive, with an approach to life that is usually geared toward physicality and competitiveness. They need not be properly trained as warriors but rather simply have an inborn need for battle, argumentation, and the like. Such individuals may be manipulated by those who seek to utilize their power and determination for their own ends. However, there is also the more 'thoughtful warrior' -- the person who wisely engages his innate passion and physical prowess for higher purposes or to help others. This latter warrior type comes closer to the Jedi/Kshatriya version. Western legends tell us of glorious knighthood regimes, such as the English Order of the Garter, the Swedish Royal Order of the Seraphim, and the Royal Norwegian Order of St. Olav. There are many others as well. Such warrior types favor certain noble characteristics: Prudence, Temperance, Justice and Fortitude, in particular. They also traditionally value humility, compassion, courtesy, devotion, mercy, purity, and endurance. This points to the Jedi/Kshatriya model. In writing about the Jedi, Jessie E. Ayani states:

Our concept of the warrior must shift to pop us out of 3-D reality into realities of higher frequency. We will never lose our archetype of the warrior; it is part of the landscape of the human psyche, but aren't we ready to part with the barbaric behaviour we have inherited from our ancestors? The archetypal patterning of the warrior, the brutish and abusive Attila the Hun, the Roman gladiators, Medieval knights, soldiers, the warlords and even the new warriors of the men's movement will not work in the 5th dimension. All of the manifestations of this archetype, so graphically portrayed for us on film, the news, and everyday life, are born out of a false sense of courage that has, in no way, eliminated the deep fear that drives the warrior to conquer and kill.

Lucas is presenting us with an archetype that will work in higher dimensions, an archetype with a heart, a truly authentic man. The only mythic characters that have come close to this archetype have been the Grail Knights, the Knights of Arthur's Round Table. However, there were flaws in the round table that failed the evolution of human consciousness and a romanticism that could not possibly serve us now.[6]

Professor Ayani is obviously unaware of the Kshatriya kings of ancient India. They, indeed, existed on a 'higher frequency', far surpassing the 'barbaric warriors' of Western history. They would have been shining examples for the Grail knights and others like them – the Kshatriya works in 'a higher dimension', is 'an archetype with heart', 'an authentic man'. Ayani suggests that Western myth has given us similar heroes, though, she admits, examples of this are few. In the early days of the Crusades, there existed a group of idealistic monks known as the Knights Templar. They were considered 'holy warriors' in that they were never aggressors but sought only to protect pilgrims traveling to the holy land of Jerusalem. These specially-trained monks would undergo rigorous discipline and become skilled warriors for the faith. They were comparable to the Japanese samurai, or to certain contingents of Zen Buddhists, who were adept at the martial arts, combining meditation with fencing, archery, and jujitsu. But nowhere, East or West, can one find a concept of a noble soldier as akin to the Jedi as that of the Kshatriya. Ayani continues in her analysis of the *Star Wars* warriors:

6   Jessie E. Ayani, 'Virtue Transmutes Fear Into Love', August 2000, available at the *Heart of the Sun* Web site, www.heartofthesun.com/articles/Archives.html. Accessed 30 September 2010.

So, who are the Jedi Knights? The Jedi are spiritual warriors dedicated to maintaining peace in the galaxies. They poke holes in the egos of the powerful and controlling – those who seek personal gain at the expense of others. They try to bring things into balance wherever they find imbalance. These are the kind of high ideals that our armed forces and government would like us to believe they embrace, but the veil of this deception is thin. What is different about the Jedi is their integrity. They are trained to be impeccable and to exercise a high degree of discernment – what I perceive as a 6th sense, or knowingness, that allows them to choose right action in the moment. They must be focused in the 'Now' at all times. How different our lives would be if we could attain this degree of focus. They are a bit like the Shaolin priests of old China in that respect – using force only when it is used towards them, choosing every possible alternative to harming another.[7]

Ayani is describing the Jedi/Kshatriya model, almost point for point. Her focus, of course, is on the Jedi, which is, in turn, based on her viewing of the *Star Wars* films. But her words apply, with even greater force (pardon the pun), to the Indian Kshatriyas. If one reads Vedic texts, one sees that Kshatriyas are 'spiritual warriors dedicated to maintaining peace in the galaxies'. Moreover, 'they try to bring things into balance wherever they find imbalance'. Kshatriyas are 'trained to be impeccable and to exercise a high degree of discernment'. They embody 'knowingness' – indeed, they, like Brahmins, are possessors of great learning and intuitive wisdom – and they know how 'to choose right action in the moment'. Most importantly, they 'use force only when it is used towards them, choosing every possible alternative to harming another'. This was clearly seen in our earlier retelling of the *Mahabharata*, when the Pandavas went through great pains to avoid the inevitable war that was building before them. As stated in that same retelling of the *Mahabharata*: the etymology of the word 'Kshatriya' is itself revealing – *kshat* means 'hurt', and *trayate* means 'to give protection'. Thus, a Kshatriya is one who protects from harm or violence, not one who instigates it.

---

7   Ibid. It is interesting, too, that Lucas had originally intended to call his second film *The **Revenge** of the Jedi*. Promotional material, from T-shirts to bumper stickers, was issued with this title. But then it occurred to him that 'revenge' is not a Jedi concept, for Jedis engage in battle only as principled protectors of the innocent, never for unsavoury reasons, such as vengeance. See Steven A. Galipeau, *The Journey of Luke Skywalker*, op. cit., p. 173.

Ayani may have been a little hard on our own armed forces and government: she says they are attempting to deceive people when they pose as being righteous and noble. While this might generally be the case, there are certainly exceptions – individuals working for our government who live by a high standard of ethics and morals – and I think Ayani would support my contention here. But, overall, it is as she says: our system is more concerned with getting the job done than with exactly *how* we do it, endorsing an 'end justifies the means' sort of sensibility.

The Jedi/Kshatriya model, on the other hand, is just as concerned with the method as with the outcome. Surely, they fight to win. But they fight according to the strictest standards of fairness and dignity.

The Just War Concept[8]

Of course, even in the West, we appreciate these finer qualities, and we hope that protectors of the innocent adhere to them. Western history has shown us, however, that it is not uncommon for one to abandon principles of justice, or ethics and morals, when threatened by aggressors; we simply do what we have to do. Because justice has been so abused in the name of defence, some feel that violence is never justified. Such people adopt a policy of pacifism, an ideal in which human life is not to be taken under any circumstances.

The notion of pacifism invariably falls short, however, when one's life, values, and loved ones are threatened with extinction. Luke could have just let Princess Leia 'go to the devil', as it were; Rama could have abandoned Sita, letting her live out a dismal life in Ravana's kingdom; Arjuna and his brothers could have allowed the Kauravas their terrible reign. But courage and righteousness would not allow it. As the Irish politician Edmund Burke writes, 'The only thing necessary for the triumph of evil is for good men to do nothing.' Our heroes, the Jedi and the Kshatriyas, would never let evil triumph. In all of the above instances, violence had utilitarian justification, and our heroes knew it.

We in the West are painfully aware that such situations arise all too often. For the first three centuries of Christian history, pacifism was the preferred stance of all who called themselves Christian. Then, in

---

8   This small section is adapted from my edited volume, *Holy War: Violence and the Bhagavad Gita* (Virginia: Deepak Heritage Books, 2002).

the Fourth century, Christianity became a mainstream religion and had to systematically address questions of self-defence and public order – and the aggressive force necessary to uphold those values. As a result, pacifism was replaced by the 'just war' theory, which is based on the idea that pacifism is not absolute, and that there are other values that are just as important as the preservation of the lives of others.

After all, what is the value of life when existence is made intolerable, when our loved ones are killed or tortured? In such instances, we clearly have a right to engage in retaliatory action. In other words, the values that compete with the preservation of life centre around the principle of 'justice' – and when attempting to implement justice, we know, there are sometimes casualties. Within this context, the principle of pacifism is seen as an ideal for which people should undoubtedly reach. But they should simultaneously recognise its limitations.

Originally, the just war concept was meant to minimise the use of force, limiting it to situations where a wrong could not be undone by any other means. Further, if one indeed found that war was inevitable, one would have to fight that war in such a way that the least harm would be caused to the fewest number of people.

History informs us, however, that in due course of time the just war theory was exploited, especially by religious fanatics, who used its utilitarian stance to wage wars in religion's name – if not always in religious spirit. Words such as 'Crusades', 'Inquisition', and 'Jihad' give thinking people reason to pause, evoking suspicion and distrust for religious institutions. This is because innocent and sincere people have been victimised in the name of God for longer than anyone can remember. And we all know it to be true: believers with ulterior motives, supported by a superficial reading of religious tradition, have abused the just war concept from the beginning of recorded history.

Still, the abuse of an idea does not invalidate the idea itself. Sometimes, when there are no options left, war becomes inevitable. In such situations, all one can do is to fight that war with a measure of dignity and self-respect, and respect for one's opponent. After all, though he may have a differing point of view – though he may even be unjust and cruel – he is still a human being, if an errant one, and is worthy of consideration. 'Many of the truths we cling to depend on our point of view', Obi-Wan instructs Luke. A 'good' war must be fought with this awareness. Both Jedi and Kshatriya would never engage in battle without having this in the forefront of their minds. The *Mahabharata* war, especially, was fought according to sophisticated religious principles of fairness, though practically everyone involved compromised these principles as the battle wore on: 'In the course of the battle, if one fights with speech, he should be opposed by speech only. One who, for any reason, leaves the midst of the battle should not be killed. A warrior on a chariot may only be fought by a warrior who is also on a chariot. One must fight opponents in fair ways, and no one who does not wish to fight is to be so engaged.' (*Bhishma-parvan* 1.28-32) The rules of the *Mahabharata* battle are accurately summarised by *Gita* expert Winthrop Sargeant:

> The great battle was supposed to be fought according to certain rules of knightly etiquette, which were, in fact, adhered to in the very beginning. Fighting was to take place only in daylight. After sunset, everybody mixed in friendship. Single combats were supposed to be only among equals. Anyone leaving the field or sitting in Yoga posture was supposed to be immune from attack. Anyone who surrendered was to be spared. Anyone momentarily disengaged was prohibited from attacking one already engaged . . . Animals were not to be killed unnecessarily or deliberately.[9]

So What Exactly is a Jedi?

In summary: we learn from Lucas's films that a Jedi seeks harmony with the Force, with the essence of all that is. To tap into the Force, or to make use of its powers, a Jedi must learn to commune with it – he must feel an affinity with nature, with the will of God. To act in discord with the Force is to lose one's connection with it, to flirt with its dark side.

The Jedi is sworn to preserve life – he adheres to the principle of *ahimsa*, or nonviolence. In other words, he believes that it is wrong to kill. Yet, he is trained in the combative arts, for he knows that it is often necessary to halt those who are evil. Consequently, he supports a sort of 'just war' concept, as described above – a Jedi may kill only in self-defence or to defend others. Recall that when Luke tells Yoda that he is in search of a great warrior from whom to learn, Yoda responds, 'Great warrior? Wars not make one great' – this from someone who

---

9   Winthrop Sargeant, trans., *The Bhagavad Gita* (Albany: State University of New York Press, 1984).

has fought valiantly in wars himself, and knows that a warrior's first duty is to avoid war at all costs.

It is interesting, too, that a Jedi does not act for personal gain, for wealth or power. He acts out of a sense of duty. He seeks to defeat those who would impose tyranny and death upon others. Lucas makes it clear that a Jedi never goes into battle because of hatred, anger, fear, or aggression. Rather, the Jedi is equipoised, at peace with himself and with the Force. He fights merely to protect the innocent, because he has a great deal of compassion. In India, this would clearly be identified as Kshatriya *dharma*.[10]

Just to make clear that Vedic Kshatriyas actually embodied the qualities that Lucas attributes to his fictitious Jedi, we now offer three examples of Kshatriya leadership taken from the pages of ancient Indian texts: first, we have Maharaja Pariksit, a great king famous for having followed the traditional system of consulting a council of Brahmins (learned and saintly philosophers) on state affairs, respecting their collective wisdom above his own. While today's 'think tank' experts sell themselves to the highest bidder, the self-realised Brahmins who advised Maharaja Pariksit gave their services freely, without salary. They did this because they were, in fact, Brahmins – their inherent quality and natural disposition leaving them no choice but to do so. In other words, they were happy to serve the administration in the way that came most naturally to them. Consequently, they performed their tasks purely and flawlessly. Thus, they were above suspicion, as was the king who accepted their advice.

Though King Pariksit was famous for his impeccable administration, he is better known for his spiritual sensibility. Early in his reign he was cursed to die by a young *sadhu*. Although he could have nullified the curse, King Pariksit instead accepted it as God's will, deciding to fast until death. He seated himself on the bank of the Ganges, and an assembly of the greatest personalities of the day soon gathered to witness the event. During the seven days of life remaining to him, King Pariksit neither ate nor slept nor moved from his seat. His only activity was to ask Srila Sukadeva Gosvami, one of the great gurus of the

---

10 For more details on Kshatriya *dharma*, particularly in regard to the qualities we have here identified as belonging to the Jedi, see Harikesa Swami, *Varnasrama Manifesto for Social Sanity* (Zurich, Switzerland: The Bhaktivedanta Book Trust, 1981), especially Part III, Chapters 12 and 13, entitled, 'The Ksatriyas: The Arms of the Social Body'.

period, questions about transcendental subjects and to listen intently
to his answers – this series of questions and answers, once recorded,
is what gradually came to be known as *Srimad Bhagavatam*, or the
Bhagavata Purana ('The Beautiful Story of the Lord'), one of India's
most important theological texts. King Pariksit thus showed the example that a true warrior-king is deeply concerned with spiritual matters
and activities beyond the body.

Next, we have Maharaja Prithu. Unlike today's leaders and administrative officers, Prithu considered it his primary duty to enlighten
his citizens with spiritual knowledge. Though he was courageous and
was considered one of the greatest warriors of his time, he taught his
people that the spiritual pursuit was more important than anything
else. He rebuked the kind of leaders who simply exact taxes from
their constituency but neglect to inform them of the real mission of
human life. King Prithu advised the citizens: 'Dedicate your minds,
your words, your bodies, and the fruits of your labour for the service
of the Supreme Lord. Then you will surely achieve the final objective
of life [love of God].'

In addition, under the King's firm hand, all law-abiding citizens
were perfectly protected, not only from external dangers but from disease and famine. Because of his intimate connection with 'the Force', he
could mystically secure the welfare of his followers, making sure that
they were in good health and that the weather would suit their needs
in terms of allowing their crops to grow. When he travelled through
the world on his victorious chariot, appearing as brilliant as the sun,
all thieves and rogues would go into hiding, and all lesser kings would
bow to his supremacy.

Nonetheless, King Prithu always adopted a humble demeanour.
Moreover, even though he was very opulent due to the prosperity of
his widespread empire, he was never inclined to utilise his opulences
for the gratification of his senses. He remained unattached, and, like all
saintly kings of the Vedic age, King Prithu voluntarily gave up his rule
before death or infirmity overtook him, and he retired to the forest to
completely immerse himself in God consciousness.

Finally, King Yudhishthira, who was mentioned in a prior chapter,
was famous as 'the king whose enemy was never born' – he was so
pious that no one disliked him, not even his political enemies. Indeed,
the *Mahabharata* describes that his personal qualities were so alluring that his fame spread all over the universe, and his pure and saintly

character induced the Supreme Lord Krishna Himself to become his intimate friend.

Another epithet for King Yudhishthira was 'the personification of goodness', for by continuous service to Lord Krishna he was freed from all desire for sense gratification and personal wealth, fame, or power. This complete selflessness made him a worthy emperor, like an ideal Jedi Knight. 'All for the good of the citizens!' was his motto, and he lived up to it by always seeing to the social, political, economic, and spiritual benefit of the citizens of his kingdom. It is said that due to his perfect administration and his pure devotion to God, even the rivers, oceans, hills, forests, and so on, were all pleased with him, and they supplied their bounty profusely for all in his kingdom. Thus, during the reign of King Yudhishthira, the citizens of the world were never troubled by any lack or any necessity, nor by mental agonies, diseases, excessive heat or cold, or by any other material disturbance.

Again, like all saintly kings of India's mythic past, Yudhishthira renounced his kingdom at the end of life to devote himself exclusively to spiritual practice. After making sure that his kingdom would be properly cared for by his successor, he gave up his regal dress and departed for the forest. Thus, his administration culminated in his pursuit of spiritual ideals, a perfect legacy to those who followed him.

Such ideals are seen in Jedi Masters, who bequeath to younger Jedi an abiding spiritual sensibility, one that supercedes the thirst for action and adventure. Yoda, it may be remembered, was living in his forest retreat when Luke came to study under him. Lucas gives us a hint that he was modeling the Jedi master on yogi adepts by showing us that, like a guru or yogi, Yoda knew when his time had come. Like a removed observer, Yoda watched his own death approach, preparing a place to lay down and die as he casually conversed with his new pupil, Luke Skywalker. This is a common image in Vaishnava texts: an accomplished guru is so completely in touch with the Force that he knows his allotted span of time on earth, seeing death as if it were merely a change of clothes.

The Guru/Disciple Relationship

Luke first meets his master in *The Empire Strikes Back*, and we can immediately see in their alliance a traditional teacher/pupil exchange. For one familiar with Vaishnava literature, Yoda and Luke clearly represent a yoga guru and his student, for their connection is reminiscent of Krishna and Arjuna in the *Gita* – which is the prototype for all guru/ disciple relationships. That Yoda is many hundreds of years old (as is claimed of certain yogis in India), has powers like those of Indian mystics, and even has a name that sounds like the word 'yoga', only makes the connection with India more palpable. (In all probability, however, it is more likely that Yoda's name is related to the Sanskrit word *yuddha*, or 'war', for he is a Kshatriya guru teaching his pupil the art of spiritual warfare.)

The yoga teacher motif is enhanced by the fact that Yoda teaches Luke how to control his mind – and how to control material nature through his mind as well; this is at the heart of the yoga process. First, Yoda teaches him to levitate small objects, like a rock. Gradually, he goes on to lift his sunken ship! Yogis in India are well known for their practice of levitation.

Also like Krishna and Arjuna, Yoda's first teaching to Luke involves the distinction between body and self. This is traditional, for the expert guru realises the futility of trying to teach spiritual subjects to a student who still identifies with a body made of matter. Krishna makes this a major point in the *Bhagavad-gita*: 'As a person puts on new clothes, putting aside those garments that are old and worn, similarly, the soul accepts new material bodies, giving up the old and useless ones.' (2.22) Or, 'As the embodied soul continually incarnates, in this one lifetime, from childhood to youth to old age, the soul similarly takes on another body at the time of death.' (2.13)

Lucas conveys this teaching in an innovative way: he has Luke arrive on Yoda's planet with stereotypical preconceptions of what a Jedi Master, an adept spiritual warrior, should look like. The young hero expects to see a massive, well-built example of perfect manhood, a bodily form that is enviable and attractive. Instead, when he finally meets the diminutive, gremlin-like Yoda, he cannot even imagine that this is the great teacher about whom he had heard so much. And Yoda decides to play with Luke, to keep secret who he really is until it becomes abundantly clear on its own:

Yoda looks down; he's dejected and disappointed, too. 'Size matters not', he responds. 'Judge me by my size, do you? Hm?' Luke shakes his head in recognition of the fact that he doesn't judge Yoda this way. 'And well you should not', the Jedi Master continues. 'For my ally is the

Force. And a powerful ally it is....Luminous beings are we ... [Yoda pinches Luke's upper arm] ... not this crude matter.'
Luke has made a judgement based on a superficial observable factor. ... We might recall that when he first came to Dagobah he was looking for a 'great warrior'. He imagined someone larger than life, not the Jedi Master he found. While he has come to accept Yoda as the teacher he was seeking, he is still caught up in the issue of 'size'.[11]

There are more connections to the *Gita*, and we have alluded to them before: Arjuna, we will remember, must choose between sentimental feelings toward familial relations, and his obligation to the legions of innocent people who will be killed if he does not fight. Likewise, Luke must choose between familial affections and civic duty – for he realises that his evil opponent is in reality his own father.

But the Krishna/Arjuna and Yoda/Luke comparisons have their limitations. The relationship between Yoda and Luke is in fact more reminiscent of Drona and Arjuna: though Krishna enlightened Arjuna with transcendental knowledge on the battlefield of Kurukshetra, it was Drona who earlier served as his martial guru, training him in combative arts and Kshatriya *dharma*. In this sense, Vishvamitra and Rama, too, can be seen as early archetypes for the Yoda/Luke relationship. In the above instances we find a teacher/student model that has been popularised in yoga texts for centuries. Sociologist William Sims Bainbridge elaborates on Yoda and Luke as yoga teacher and student, respectively, illuminating how the master is basically training his disciple as a Kshatriya:

Yoda proves to be a deceptively tiny creature who has the spiritual power to levitate Luke's spacecraft. In the weeks that follow, he gradually teaches Luke how to levitate objects as well, and instills in him the first rudiments of Jedi philosophy. ... [He tells Luke that] A Jedi must have deep commitment and a serious mind, never craving excitement and adventure, even though he will be surrounded by them. A Jedi's strength [comes] from the Force. But beware of the dark side [Yoda tells him]. 'Anger ... fear ... aggression. [This is] The dark side of the Force. ... [Qualities that come] Easily... . [O]nce you start down the dark path...it [will] dominate your destiny.' A Jedi should use the Force for knowledge and defence, not for attack, and should remain

---

11 See Steven A. Galipeau, *The Journey of Luke Skywalker*, op. cit., p. 132.

serene. Strong emotions lead to the dark side of the Force ... [And for this reason] the Jedi must seek peace.

After preliminary instruction, Yoda brings Luke to a gloomy, damp cave, a place where the dark side of the Force is strong, where he must confront the evil that is within him. Deeper and deeper Luke presses into the darkness, his lightsabre drawn and ready. With a sudden hiss, Darth Vader leaps at him, and Luke desperately swings his sword, decapitating his nemesis. The severed head rolls until Luke can see the face, and he discovers that it is his own. Only when Vader fades away does Luke realise it was a vision, created by his own, tormented mind.

[In a later episode] He [Luke] arrives just in time to be with the nine-hundred-year-old Jedi Master as he dies. In his last words, Yoda tells Luke to beware the power of the Emperor.[12]

In other words, Yoda helps Luke from the ground up. He gives him positive spiritual knowledge, teaching him to be aware of the Force and to tap into the latent spiritual energies within his own body and mind. He trains him, too, to be aware of the negative, showing him how it can get in the way of spiritual attainment. He tells him what to watch out for – the dark side of the Force, the evil Emperor, and his own negative qualities.

What Exactly is a Guru?

A guru is a teacher. In all serious areas of endeavour, we require teachers. Whether you want to be a doctor, a priest, or even a plumber, if you are serious you will find a teacher. Indeed, it has been said that anyone who claims to be his own guru has a fool for a disciple.

---

12 See William Sims Bainbridge, 'May the Force Be with You!' in *The Sociology of Religious Movements* (New York: Routledge, 1997), pp. 395-403. The idea that Jedis could levitate, and also move heavy objects from a distance with the power of their minds, is clearly derived from yoga and the mystic powers that a yogi eventually achieves. However, yogis, much like Jedi, are warned not to abuse such powers, lest they be victimised by the dark side of the Force: 'In the Yoga system, students are given a stern warning not to be lured by these unusual powers because they will impede their progress towards spiritual realisation. Those who give in to these powers become egotistical and might employ them to hurt others and themselves. While others use the same powers to heal and comfort those who are undergoing pain and suffering.' For more on this subject, see Ashok Kumar Malhotra, *An Introduction to Yoga Philosophy*, op. cit., p. 96.

Spirituality is no exception. The Vedic literature informs us that: 'To learn the truths of the spirit, one must approach a spiritual master [guru] who also has such a teacher. This preceptor must be fixed in the Absolute Truth' (*Mundaka Upanishad* 1.2.12). Thus, the Upanishads inform us that one who wants spiritual knowledge must approach a genuine guru who comes in a lineage of self-realised teachers. After lifetimes of material conditioning, say the Vedic texts, doesn't it make sense that we would need help in approaching God? Moreover, if we are actually serious about the goal, why would we deny ourselves that assistance?

But just what is a genuine guru? How can one distinguish saints from swindlers? In an attempt to understand how a Vaishnava would answer these questions, let us look more closely at the above verse from the Vedic literature. In Sanskrit, a genuine guru is *srotriyam brahma-nishtham*. *Srotriyam* indicates that the actual guru is one who has fully absorbed his own guru's teachings. In other words, if everyone must approach a guru for spiritual knowledge, then the guru must have received knowledge in the same way. Thus, there exists an historical succession of teachers, and a genuine guru must belong to that line. Further, the guru's teachings must agree with those of the previous spiritual masters, as well as with the holy scriptures. If they don't, something is amiss.

Here, then, is a sort of 'check and balance' system whereby one can ascertain if one's guru is genuine. Most people in India are unaware of this objective system, but a careful reading of Vedic texts makes it clear that this system exists. What's more, the authoritative disciplic lines are mentioned by name in the *Padma Purana* – the Sri, the Brahma, the Kumara, and the Rudra – and important modern-day teachers in these lines are purportedly predicted as well: Ramanuja, Madhva, Nimbarka, and Vishnu Swami. The lines that have these titles and that include these great teachers are considered bona fide according to Vedic/Vaishnava tradition.

Another essential qualification of the genuine guru is *brahma-nishtham*: he must be fixed in transcendence – a virtual storehouse of transcendental knowledge. While this may be a little more difficult to ascertain, it becomes easily observable when considered in tandem with the above qualities and/or affiliations. In other words, a genuine spiritual master is not about an outward appearance of holiness but is, rather, about speaking philosophy that does not contradict established predecessors. He must actually demonstrate realised knowledge while belonging to a traditional lineage. In addition, he must be completely devoted to God with body, mind, and soul.

Thus, spiritual knowledge, which originates with God, descends to a sincere spiritual aspirant via the guru. One might question whether or not a line of teachers can accurately pass the message from one teacher to another without change or addition. Is it possible to deliver, as does a good mailman, an unchanged and thus reliable message? The Vaishnava scriptures assure us that indeed it is. For not just anyone can presume to speak spiritual knowledge in succession from the past masters. Only a person who possesses the rigorous qualifications given in the Vedic literature, as mentioned above, is fit to be accepted as a guru. By assuring the qualifications of the transmitter, the Vaishnava process assures the pure transmission of spiritual knowledge.

A sincere student can thus receive the pure Vaishnava message in the same way a person might receive a mango from a number of men sitting on the branches of a mango tree. The safest way to get the most succulent mango, which is always found at the top of the tree, is to have the man at the top pick the fruit and pass it down carefully to the man below. Thus, it comes down from man to man and reaches the person on the ground undamaged and unchanged.

Conclusion

The *Star Wars* movies are overflowing with guru/disciple relation-ships: Obi-Wan and Luke, Yoda and Luke, Yoda and Obi-Wan, and on and on. In *Attack of the Clones*, we see the guru/disciple relation-ship at work. Anakin repeatedly calls his teacher 'Master' – as does the traditional Indian student, who refers to his teacher as 'Prabhu' (the Sanskrit version of the same word). It might be argued, how-ever, that novitiates in many ancient traditions refer to their teachers in this way, and that is certainly true. But *Attack of the Clones* goes so far as to depict Anakin with a *sikha* (!), a tuft of hair that dangles from the upper portion of the back of his head. Indian students in the Vaishnava tradition have for centuries either shaved their heads completely or cut their hair in such a way as to leave a *sikha* on the back of their heads, marking them as servants of God. Of course, the tuft of hair, too, can be found on the heads of monks in Chinese and Japanese traditions, and in others as well. But when viewed in conjunction with the many other factors outlined in this book, the inescapable conclusion is that ancient India was a central resource for Lucas's epic.

In other words – and this is true for the *Star Wars* series as a whole – if you look at one or two elements of the Skywalker saga, you may attribute its influence to many different sources. However, if you look deeply, taking the whole panorama of *Star Wars* into account, you find that there is a vast gamut of Indic influences permeating the series. Thus, one can only conclude that Lucas owes a debt of gratitude to Indian tradition, either as a direct influence or as a subliminal one, coming from Joseph Campbell and others.

AFTERWORD

After reading this book, it should be evident that there is a deep and abiding connection between *Star Wars* and ancient Indic texts. Is it a stretch to say that Lucas was directly and/or indirectly influenced by the *Ramayana* and the *Mahabharata*? This author thinks not. If the reader has doubts, look again at what we have determined thus far: although Lucas's influences can be traced back to a staggering variety of Westerns, World War II movies, early science fiction, pop culture, social contemporary issues including women's rights, and even a Japanese samurai classic, his primary influences were the mythologies of the ancient world – specifically the work of the legendary expositor of *The Power of Myth*, Joseph Campbell.

Since Campbell's primary influences were, as we have shown, the myths of India, the connections and resemblences between *Star Wars* and the Indian epics are considerable, and, throughout this work, we have provided both major and minor examples of this. The basic monomythic structure found in *Star Wars* was earlier evident in the *Ramayana* and *Mahabharata*. Of this there can be no doubt. The abduction or mistreatment of a beautiful princess, a heroic effort to reclaim her with the help of partially human creatures – the Chewbacca character and the bear-like Ewoks make comparisons with the *Ramayana* unavoidable – and a devastating war between good and evil, is clearly more than coincidental. And there are a number of other interesting parallels specific to the Indian epics, as we have pointed out in some detail.

We have seen the Indian preference for a composite hero work its way into *Star Wars*. Human complexity, embodied in the fact that each person has both good and evil within them, is also a prominent feature of the Indian tales, as it is in *Star Wars*. Another common theme is the tension between familial affection and civic duty, and the son's redemptive role in saving his errant father – as we have shown, all are elements of *Star Wars* as they are in the age-old Indic scriptures.

We have also shown that the Force is more easily identified with Eastern theological concepts than with those in the West. First of all, the Force seems to have both personal and impersonal characteristics, something that mystics in the East have explored in some detail. The conception of Brahman in many ways tallies with Lucas's conception of the Force. However, given that the Force has both positive and negative sides, the divine energies known as Yoga-Maya and Maha-Maya seem more closely related to what Lucas had in mind. All these concepts come from India. Finally, Paramatma, or God as the indwelling spirit located in the hearts of all living beings, has much in common with Lucas's Force, accommodating even the midi-chlorian idea found in *Star Wars*.

Lucas also explores the tension between technology and nature – an idea that is easily identifiable with the East. His epics seem to be saying that technology is not inherently bad – it is all in how one uses it. This is the philosophy of *karma-yoga* found in the *Bhagavad-gita*. Or, stated another way, the tension of a spiritual being (man) in a material world (machine) can be reconciled in the concept of *yukta-vairagya*, in which one utilises the energies of matter in the service of God, or Krishna. All of this is found in Eastern texts.

Significant parallels, too, can be seen in the fact that Lucas's films are supposed to depict incidents in the distant past, a time when, according to conventional wisdom, man had no access to aircraft or other advanced technology. Still, the characters of *Star Wars* use elaborate flying machines, intricate weaponry, and so on. Why assume that distant galaxies had access to these things when we know for certain that we on earth did not? Most science fiction writers who want to depict characters using advanced technology simply set their stories in the future. Could Lucas instead be taking his cue from ancient Indian texts? These texts, written thousands of years ago, proffer the existence of *vimanas*, ancient but sophisticated aircraft, with Ion-mercury engines, as we have described. They mention futuristic weapons, aerial mansions and anti-gravitational cities. In short, they described the *Star Wars* universe eons before Lucas had conceived it.

And what of the Jedi/Kshatriya parallels? Again, these are too many to be coincidental. In addition, the stress on a lineage of teachers that passes on esoteric art and wisdom to dedicated disciples is characteristic of the *Star Wars* stories, and it is basic to Indic wisdom as well.

The above is not meant to bore the reader with a rehashing of what has already appeared in this book. Rather, it is a summary for the purpose of reflection. We ask the reader to think deeply about all the evidence in this book: that there are parallels between *Star Wars* and Indic texts is certain – it is not in question. We see the parallels loud and clear. The question is *to what degree* was Lucas consciously and/or unconsciously influenced by the Vaishnava texts. It is this question with which we would like to leave you.

Let us emphasise that throughout the *Star Wars* series, Lucas uses specific names that come from the Sanskrit, the language of ancient Indian tradition, as we have shown (largely in Chapter One). This can also be seen in the following: two central songs in the *Star Wars* soundtrack are sung in Sanskrit. In *The Phantom Menace*, we find the songs, 'Duel of the Fates' and 'Qui-Gon's Funeral' (the former song also appears in *Attack of the Clones*). These sound like Vedic *mantras* chanted by sages on the bank of the Ganges. John Williams, the musical director of the *Star Wars* movies, claims responsibility for the use of the Sanskrit songs,[1] but he admits that nothing goes into Lucas's movies without Lucas's direct approval and consideration. What is one to make of this? We leave that to you, the reader, to decide.

In concluding, we would also like the reader to ponder the overarching theme of the entire *Star Wars* enterprise. These movies are not ultimately about saving a princess, the use or abuse of futuristic technology, the man/machine dilemma, the path of the Jedi, good guys versus bad guys, or even about the guru/disciple relationship – though, in individual *Star Wars* episodes, these ideas may appear as central or dominating issues. Overall, if one looks at the series as a whole, the principal theme is the life and struggle of Anakin Skywalker and his personal choice between good and evil.

This is made clear in an insightful article by *Star Wars* expert Scott Chernoff (contributing editor to *Star Wars Insider*, an authorised *Star Wars* fanzine), in which he interviews Lucas himself. Chernoff tells us

---

1   See the Frequently Asked Questions page at *The John Williams Web Pages*, at www. johnwilliams.org/reference/faq.html. Accessed 30 September 2010.

that, '[The prequels] … revolve around a key character question: what makes a bright, gifted and good-hearted Jedi-in-training turn to the dark side?'[2] And then he quotes Lucas:

> This whole story turns on the psychology of Anakin Skywalker, and how he turns to evil.…Why, and what are the emotions that caused that? It's an interesting story. His redemption is interesting [in the latter three parts of the *Star Wars* series], but at the same time, how somebody with good intentions goes bad, and that we all have good and bad in us, is a good story to tell. It's not as powerful as the redemption part in certain ways -- it ends up being a tragedy. But I think in the end the audience will recognise bits of themselves in it. This one is just somebody struggling with himself and how that happens.[3]

The *Star Wars* story is really about Everyone, and this is also true of the *Bhagavad-gita*. The very first Sanskrit word in the *Gita* is *dharma*, or 'duty', and the last is *mam*, which means 'my'. Tradition thus tells us that everything that comes between those two words is 'my duty', or the duty of Everyman. As already stated, we are all, in a sense, Arjuna, the warrior who is perplexed on the battlefield of life, and we are approaching Krishna for direction. We are all the innocent Anakin Skywalker, and we are free to choose: will we become Darth Vader or not? As Chernoff tells us:

> It was the larger picture that led Lucas to set the tone for Episode I as the lightest of all six movies. 'The first film', he said, 'simply sets up Anakin as a sweet kid, which is what we have to do – say, "First of all, he's just like you and me. He's a nice little kid and he wasn't evil." A lot of people got very upset and wanted him to be an evil little kid that went around pulling wings off flies, as if that would explain everything. But then where does the story go?
>
>   'The point is not that you are born evil – the thing that makes the film work ultimately is the fact that he is a good kid, trying to be a good kid, and he grows up to be a good kid. It's simply that his emotions take him places he can't control. He becomes evil out of his own ambition and greed, and revenge and hatred – all those things that

---

2   Scott Chernoff, 'The Plot Thickens', in *Star Wars Insider*, No. 60, July/August 2002, pp. 54-61.

3   Ibid.

kids face. Kids can see how their fears can cause them to do things that will turn them evil, even if they don't want to be evil. . . .'[4]

This is precisely Arjuna's dilemma, and, in the last part of the *Gita's* Third Chapter, he asks Krishna: 'What causes a person to act sinfully, even if they are not willing, as if engaged by force?' Krishna answers that it is lust (material desire), which He says is the 'destroyer of knowledge and self-realisation'. After locating the problem for Arjuna, He prescribes the method for overcoming it: sense regulation inspired by spiritual knowledge. The senses, mind, and intelligence are the three 'sitting places' of lust. Knowing the self to be transcendental to these three, 'one should control the lower self by the higher self and thus – by spiritual strength – conquer this insatiable enemy known as lust.'

This is an important teaching. And, like Arjuna, both Anakin and Luke struggle with it. But while Anakin succumbs to his lower self, Luke emerges victorious, conquering his more base desires. *Star Wars* asks us to consider whether we, as individuals, are following the path of Anakin or that of Luke. Are we being 'conquered' by our own conditioning, or are we rising to the challenge, becoming whole by battling with the demons inside ourselves?

In this sense, the *Bhagavad-gita* may be the ultimate guidebook for aspiring Jedis: lust, anger and greed are deeply embedded in our consciousness. Just ask Anakin. And deep-rooted habits are not always easy to overcome. Nonetheless, in the *Gita*, Krishna helps us through the darkest of battles by explaining the source of our dilemma, the gradual steps by which we delude ourselves, and by putting us in touch with the spiritual element lying dormant within our hearts. He tells us that those who are enamoured by materialistic life begin simply by contemplating the objects of the senses. Again, just ask Anakin. Such contemplation naturally leads to self-interested action and, finally, attachment. This, in turn, gives rise to anger. Why anger? Because everything in the world is temporary, and so we eventually lose the objects of our attachment. Anger, Krishna says, leads to bewilderment, and bewilderment to loss of memory. At this point, intelligence is lost. We can watch the initial stages of this happening to Anakin in *Attack of the Clones*. It totally overtakes him in *Revenge of the Sith*, where Yoda expresses these teachings almost verbatim from the *Bhagavad-gita*. He

---

4   Ibid.

talks about passions born of lust and how they bring a person to his knees.

According to Krishna, intelligence means good memory and fine discretion – both of which fall away when we adopt a materialistic and self-centred approach to life. This vicious cycle puts us in a non-spiritual frame of mind, in which we forget who we are and what life is really all about. Krishna refers to this as 'a material whirlpool' that drags people ever lower; it is a complex downward spiral that begins, as He says in the *Gita*, simply by one's contemplating the objects of the senses. (2.61-64) Krishna thus tells Arjuna not to be distracted by sensorial involvement and, instead, to control his senses for a higher purpose. This, indeed, is the teaching of the Jedi and a lesson that is valuable to each and every one of us.

Other Books by Steven J. Rosen

Krishna's Other Song: A New Look at the Uddhava Gita
(Westport, CT.: Praeger Publishing, 2010)

Sonic Spirituality: A Collection of Essays on the Hare Krishna Maha-Mantra (Vrindavan, UP, India: Ras Bihari Lal & Sons, 2009).

The Yoga of Kirtan: Conversations on the Sacred Art of Chanting (New York: FOLK Books, 2008).

Ultimate Journey: Death and Dying in the World's Major Religions, ed. (Westport, CT.: Praeger publishing, 2008).

Essential Hinduism (hardcover, Praeger, 2006; paperback, Lanham, Maryland: Rowman & Littlefield, 2008).

Krishna's Song: A New Look at the Bhagavad Gita
(Westport, CT.: Praeger Publishers, 2007).

Black Lotus: The Spiritual Journal of an Urban Mystic (Capital Hill, Washington D. C.: Hari-Nama Press, 2007).

Hinduism –Volume 6 of Greenwood's Introduction to the World's Major Religions (Westport, CT.: Greenwood publishing, 2006).

Holy Cow: The Hare Krishna Contribution to Vegetarianism and Animal Rights (New York: Lantern Books, 2004).

From Nothingness to Personhood: A Collection of Essays on Buddhism From a Vaishnava-Hindu Perspective (New York: FOLK Books, 2003).

The Hidden Glory of India (Korsnas Gard, Sweden: Bhaktivedanta Book Trust, 2002).

Holy War: Violence and the Bhagavad Gita (Poquoson, VA: Deepak Heritage Books, 2002).

The Four Principles of Freedom: The Morals and Ethics Behind Vegetarianism, Continence, Sobriety, and Honesty (New York: FOLK Books, 2002).

Gita on the Green: The Mystical Tradition Behind Bagger Vance (New York, NY: Continuum International Publishing, 2001).

The Reincarnation Controversy: Uncovering the Truth in the World Religions (Badger, California: Torchlight publishing, 1998).

Diet for Transcendence (Badger, California: Torchlight publishing, 1998). A reprinting of *Food for the Spirit: Vegetarianism and the World Religions* (New York: Bala Books, 1986, preface by Isaac Bashevis Singer).

Vaishnavism: Contemporary Scholars Discuss the Gaudiya Tradition (Delhi: Motilal Banarsidass, 1997). A reprinting of New York: FOLK Books, 1994).

Vaishnavi: Women and the Worship of Krishna, ed., (Delhi: Motilal Banarsidass, 1996).

Sri Panca Tattva: the Five Features of God (New York: FOLKBooks, 1994).

Narasimha Avatar: The Half-Man/Half-Lion Incarnation (New York: FOLK Books, 1994).

In Defense of Reality -- Conversations Between Ray Cappo and Satyaraj Das (Hudson, NY: Equal Vision Records, 1993).

Passage From India: The Life and Times of His Divine Grace A. C. Bhaktivedanta Swami Prabhupada (Delhi: Munshiram Manoharlal, 1992).

Vedic Archeology and Assorted Essays (Borehamwood, Herts, England: Bhaktivedanta Book Trust, Ltd., 1991).

The Lives of the Vaishnava Saints: Shrinivas Acharya, Narottam Das Thakur, Shyamananda Pandit (New York: FOLK Books, 1991).

The Six Goswamis of Vrindavan (New York: FOLK Books, 1991).

Om Shalom: Judaism and Krishna Consciousness (New York: FOLK Books, 1990).

East-West Dialogues: Conversations Between The Reverend Alvin V. P. Hart and Satyaraja Dasa Adhikari [Steven J. Rosen] (New York: FOLK Books, 1989; reprinted by the Bombay Bhaktivedanta Book Trust).

Archeology and the Vaishnava Tradition: The Pre-Christian Roots of Krishna Worship (Calcutta: K.L.M. Firma, 1989).

India's Spiritual Renaissance: The Life and Times of Lord Chaitanya (New York: FOLK Books, 1988).

Lightning Source UK Ltd.
Milton Keynes UK
UKOW050243140612

194342UK00001B/11/P